restored
dreams

L.B. DUNBAR

www.lbdunbar.com

Restored Dreams
Copyright © 2018 Laura Dunbar
L.B. Dunbar Writes, Ltd.
https://www.lbdunbar.com/

This is a work of fiction. Names, characters, places, and incidents are the product of the author's imagination or are used fictitiously, and any resemblance to any actual persons, living or dead, events, or locales is entirely coincidental.

The author acknowledges the trademarked status and trademark owners of various products referenced in this work of fiction, which have been used without permission. The publication/use of these trademarks is not authorized, associated with, or sponsored by the trademark owner.

Cover Design: Shannon Passmore/Shanoff Formats
Cover Image: Adobe Stock Images
Edits: Jenny Sims/Editing4Indies
Proofread: Karen Fischer
2022 Reproof: Gemma Brocato

Other Books by L.B. Dunbar

Lakeside Cottage
Living at 40
Loving at 40
Learning at 40
Letting Go at 40

The Silver Foxes of Blue Ridge
Silver Brewer
Silver Player
Silver Mayor
Silver Biker

Silver Fox Former Rock Stars
After Care
Midlife Crisis
Restored Dreams
Second Chance
Wine&Dine

Collision novellas
Collide
Caught

Smartypants Romance (an imprint of Penny Reid)
Love in Due Time
Love in Deed
Love in a Pickle

The World of True North (an imprint of Sarina Bowen)
Cowboy
Studfinder

Rom-com for the over 40
The Sex Education of M.E.

The Heart Collection
Speak from the Heart
Read with your Heart
Look with your Heart

L.B. Dunbar

Fight from the Heart
View with your Heart

A Heart Collection Spin-off
The Heart Remembers

THE EARLY YEARS
The Legendary Rock Star Series
The Legend of Arturo King
The Story of Lansing Lotte
The Quest of Perkins Vale
The Truth of Tristan Lyons
The Trials of Guinevere DeGrance

Paradise Stories
Abel
Cain

The Island Duet
Redemption Island
Return to the Island

Modern Descendants – writing as elda lore
Hades
Solis
Heph

4

Dedication

For the readers who love seasoned romance for the over 40.
Thank you for giving me my dream.

L.B. Dunbar

1
Off-key Melody

[Lily]

"Are you sure I should go? You don't need me?"

My best friend for the past five years stares back at me with her chocolate eyes.

"If I say I will always need you, but you still have to go, will you finally leave?" She exaggerates as though I'm a pain in the ass, which I can be at times.

Esther Bankes came to work for me when I opened the bakery five years ago. Sassy mouthed with wild curls to match, my cappuccino-colored friend needed a job. I could only offer her part-time work, but she stuck with me and turned into a full-time employee. It's been a match made in heaven, or more so, through cupcakes. Because Cupcakes is more than my business—it's my baby. My you-can-do-anything-you-set-your-mind-to dream.

I take a deep breath of the sugary air around us and sigh. "If you insist," I tease.

"I do. I *do*. Now go." Esther pushes on my arm, forcing me to move my feet toward the back door of our industrial baking center behind the storefront. I love this room, but I admit I need a break from it. After five long years of working my ass off, I'm finally showing a profit. It seems frivolous to take a vacation, but Esther demands it.

"Celebrate your success," she encouraged.

I didn't feel comfortable taking the tropical paradise singles-only vacation she proposed, so I settled on something smaller, low-key, and a little closer to home. The beach. I can't wait to dip my toes in the sand and soak up a little sunshine. Obviously, I spend a ton of time indoors, but I like the outdoors. I balance life with yoga, preferably outside, but other than those sessions, it's been a while since I've spent quality time in fresh air. Esther jokes I'll turn into one of my cupcakes. Secretly, it's a fear, and I work hard at eating right and exercising regularly to ensure I don't become one of my tasty treats. I do love cupcakes, though.

Anyway, Esther further encouraged the vacation idea by roping in my new friend, Midge, to the encouragement team. Midge even went so far as to find me a reasonable house at Ocean Beach in San Diego. I've never actually been to the seaside town, but she assured me it was quiet and reserved and just what I would need. A mini-break from my mini-cakes.

Midge is a new friend and the wife of Hank Paige, the brother of an old friend. I cringe at the label. I've never known what to call Brut, other than ultimately a liar and a cheat. Twenty years later, I'm over the betrayal. I can forgive. Unfortunately, seeing Hank in my bakery a few months back brought an onslaught of forbidden memories. The old hurts still sting, but I push them away as I complete the drive down Highway 5.

You have reached your destination, the robotic voice on my phone's GPS warns. *Sigh.* Relief blankets me as I park before the two-story structure. Every place looks the same in this strip of narrow beachside homes. When I exit my Jeep, the sound of the ocean rushes through my ears, and my blood rolls in sync. This is what I need. A celebration of dreams come true.

Forget that I'm alone at the party. Esther pushed the singles-only resort so I wouldn't be, but I'd rather celebrate me by myself than try to hook up with a stranger. Not to mention, I'm not the hooking up type. I have trust issues that keep me alone, so I don't do random *anything*. I'm in a better place with my single status.

Party of one pleases me.

Entering the house, I spin, taking in the comfy couch, an oversized ottoman and easy chair, and the view.

Ocean.

Sand.

Sunshine.

Large glass doors lead to a partially covered deck. The layout is open concept complete with a wall of light wood cabinets, an island with a sink, and even an industrial stove. Standing in the kitchen area, I do a double take when I realize I can enjoy the view from there as well. I'm in heaven.

Racing up the stairs, I want to take a quick shower to wash off the drive through overheated LA and loosen my tense muscles after sitting in the car for three hours. Traffic prolonged the trip. The larger bedroom overlooks the ocean through French doors. Instead of your typical wood or iron railing, the balcony has glass panels, so nothing obstructs the breathtaking view. I open the doors wide to allow in the fresh air and sunshine heat. Heading for the bathroom, I find a deluxe, sort of hexagon-shaped shower stall in the corner with glass on three sides.

I undress hastily, thrilled the only attire I'll need for a week includes bathing suits and cover-ups. The rain-spray shower coats my body in luxurious warmth, and I purr as everything washes off me. No memories. No bakery. I'm singing one of my favorite songs about late love and promises when I think I hear a voice. I shake off the thought. A condition of being alone too often is an oversensitivity to sound.

Don't breathe. Listen. I blow out a breath knowing I'm being silly. I rinse the shampoo from my shoulder-length hair and sing again. I'm off-key, about to hit the harmony when I hear the soft click of the shower door open. Spinning, I find white hair on top of a toned male body and bright blue eyes roaming my figure.

And then I scream.

2

Life Break

[Brut]

As I drive south on Highway 5, the coast comes into view on my right, and the weight of Los Angeles, the shop, and Chopper, my grown-ass kid, slowly drifts away like the waves on the shore. Then again, the Pacific Ocean is a mild tempest and thoughts of those waves set my heart pattering in a way I hardly recognize. I'm excited and still a little surprised at how all this happened…

"You're sending me on a vacation?" I stare at my younger brother and co-owner of Restored Dreams. The auto repair and body shop has been my business for nearly twenty years, and I don't think I've ever had an official vacation.

"Yep. Give yourself some time off, Brut. I got this." With Midge, his new wife, standing behind him, her light brown eyes beaming at me, I know my brother means it. He can handle the shop alone for a week.

"I wouldn't know where to go. What to do." I don't know why I'm trying to talk myself out of this. I could use some time off. I'm tired. Plain and simple. I need a life break.

"Don't worry about it. I've taken care of *every*thing." The emphasis on the last word has me worried for the first time in this conversation. Midge steps forward, her excitement hardly contained as she hands me a padded manila envelope.

"We rented you a house at Ocean Beach. You can surf. Sleep. Anything. Just relax."

My head snaps up at the mention of surfing. It's been a rare treat over the years. The coast is so close but just far enough away from Pasadena that I couldn't overindulge. Not to mention, as a single father, I hardly had the freedom to head to the beach each day.

"I pulled your old board out of the garage. Sent it off to a shop to be cleaned and waxed." Hank really has thought of everything, and my heart skips at the possibility. *A vacation.*

I blink at Hank. He's always been a good brother—a bit wayward and reckless but good with me and my son. I know part of his attentiveness comes from guilt. He hasn't had an easy life, and I stood by him when the pieces crumbled. He thinks he owes me, but he doesn't. He's my kid brother, even at forty-three, and I love him. It's that simple.

I turn the envelope over in my hand. Inside is a lease agreement for a week and a set of keys.

"I don't know what to say." I swallow the lump in my throat. This is too generous, and I'm still a bit shocked at the idea of getting away from this place. The garage was never my ideal employment, but with my son, Chopper, and then the death of Pop, it fell into my lap. Restoring cars was something I could do but wasn't who I wanted to be.

"Just go. Have fun. Do you remember what that is?" Midge teases me.

I like my brother's woman. I might have joked I'd steal her from him if he didn't quit being an ass, but I knew from the moment I met her, she would only be Hank's. She looked at him the way I wanted someone to look at me. I had that once. I wish it had turned into something more, but it was so long ago it's a distant memory.

"Thanks, guys," I say, letting the memory fade and pulling back to my reality. My weak gratitude seems insufficient. "And yes, smartass, I think I remember what fun is." I laugh to cover the hesitancy.

Do I? Do I really remember what fun used to be?

It's been three days since Hank and Midge announced this gift, and a whirlwind of double-checking Hank's understanding of the schedule until Midge finally says, "I'm here. Don't worry."

Knowing that Midge was our former office manager sets me at ease. She was a quick study and went above and beyond what we needed to organize and clean up the shop. She set up things in an efficient and easy way for me to maintain if I dedicate an hour a day to the admin things. Thinking of Midge makes me smile. Again, she's been good for my brother, and I like her in a sister-in-law way. We'd been a clan of men

L.B. Dunbar

for too long. Midge joining the family brought three more boys—her sons. We need some sisters.

The thought reminds me of a pair of sisters I once knew. My mouth curls at the memory of the blonde hair, blue eyes of the younger one. She had the sweetest smile and amazing lips, especially when they were on me. My smile fades, remembering why I lost her.

I don't know why I did what I did to her.

Really? my heart teases.

It was because of me, my dick recalls. The snicker from the evil appendage gets choked off when my heart remembers it wasn't even a good lay that fucked my life. My stomach turns with the thought.

Exiting the highway, I let the memories fade. The roar of water crashing to the shore pulls me back to the present where it's safer to live. I park in the drive and stare at the narrow two-story house. My heart sprints. On the other side of this structure is the ocean, and I can already feel the excitement that something amazing is about to happen to me. After grabbing my bag, I circle the house, and my breath catches. The view is beautiful. Rolling waves, bright sunshine, and surfers on the sea. I can't wait.

Entering the house, the living area faces large glass doors that open to a partially covered porch and glorious view. A cozy open-concept kitchen falls directly behind the seating area. The stairs to the upper level are at the back, tucked behind the kitchen, and I climb the steps two at a time. I want my swimsuit and a beer. Then the surf.

As I reach the top step, I think I hear water running. I pause at the sound and decide it must be the ocean playing tricks on me. The house has air conditioning, but I want the windows open and the rhythmic crashing of the waves to fill my ears. I turn into the first bedroom, set my stuff down near a dresser, and hear water again, like a running shower. Taking a step toward the bathroom, singing filters toward me.

Lyrics of loving someone later, being better when she's older, being the greatest love of her life float through the air as I open the door to a steam-filled space and a female voice belting off-key.

Did Hank do this? Did he hire a girl for the night for me? For the week? He jokes I need to get laid. When he mentioned he thought of everything, is this what he meant? I pause a second, taking in the silhouette of a feminine body, twisting and turning behind the glass enclosure. The heat of the room is sweltering, and I whip off my shirt to wipe at my face. A spattering sound hits the tile floor of the shower, possibly shampoo rinsing out of her hair. Her voice continues to squeak out lyrics.

Strangely, the appendage that gets me in trouble begins to rise. I really do need to get laid, but can I do this? Can I fuck a hired female?

Another off-key lyric and I decide I can't. I step forward, preparing to tell the woman she'll need to leave. She doesn't hear me call out, "Hey," so I'm left with no choice but to open the stall door to get her attention. The first thing I notice is a large cupcake tattoo in hues of purple and pink on a smooth hip.

And then she screams.

3

Shower Fresh

[Lily]

"Brut?" I squeak.

He momentarily averts his eyes, but they quickly return to my exposed body. Suds slip over my breasts; my nipples erect from the sudden cool air on my warm skin. I'm too stunned to cover myself. His eyes flick away and then back a second time.

"Lily pad?" The old nickname snags my attention.

Standing in my vacation-house bathroom, staring at my wet, naked body is Brut Paige. The man I loved as a teen. The man who shattered my heart into smithereens.

"Get out," I shriek, arm extending for the edge of the shower door. When I lean forward, water drips off my body onto the tile floor, but Brut doesn't move.

His gaze is drawn to my breasts dangle as I bend, droplets falling to the ground with soft plops. He swallows. Licks his lips. And smiles. *Damn him.* I recognize the curl of his lip—like a frustrating flashback—and it infuriates me how my body responds to his perusal.

"Brut!" I snap again, tugging at the glass door, but he refuses to release it. Instead, he steps forward, and my breath catches. For half a second, I think he's going to join me. I envision him pressing me back until I collide with the cool tiles. His hands roam my body, frantically trying to touch everywhere. His mouth crushing mine in a fierce reunion kiss. Spreading my legs so he can lift me and enter my willing body. I pause in the fantasy to remind myself again—*this is Brut Paige*—a man of distant dreams.

He blinks, shakes his head, and mutters a quiet apology. He diverts his gaze from my body, and he steps back, leaving the glass door wide open. I'm left bare, chilled, and turned on by his approving gaze. And completely confused as to why he is in my bathroom.

I turn off the shower and wrap myself in a luxurious towel. I've already unpacked, placing my clothes in the bedroom dresser to make myself feel at home. I left the casual dress I intended to wear on the bed, though, and find Brut standing by the open French doors of my room with his back to the bathroom. When I cough for his attention, he spins around to face me.

Again, his eyes skim over me, and I watch his throat roll. My breasts are enhanced by the towel covering them, exposing a swell of cleavage, and I tug at the twist holding the material in place. The terrycloth is short, and I worry my backside isn't completely covered.

"I think there's been a mistake," I say, clutching the towel to my chest. Brut stares, unblinking, and suddenly, I imagine him stepping forward to tug the damp cover off me and throw me on the large bed in the center of the room.

Goodness, get a grip on the fantasies.

"Hank set this up for me. I have the lease papers with the address." His voice remains monotone, stunned even.

Instead of my daydream of being ravished by him, he goes for his bag on the floor by the bed. After removing a set of papers, he returns to me and I briefly glance down, the words blurring before me. His nearness distracts me. He smells fresh. Sunshine. Woodsy. Male.

Brut has this wild white hair, having gone prematurely gray. He's four years older than I am, making him forty-five. From the brief display of his abs—he wasn't wearing a shirt in the bathroom—he's built better than I remember. His abs stack like a pile of books, and I want to read every page. His eyes are still a playful blue, reminding me of our foolish summer days. We met when I was only nineteen, a girl on the eve of her sexuality. Now, I'm a woman of forty-one, and just looking at him revives the edgy sensation.

"Here's the address," he says, interrupting my wayward thoughts of rubbing against him. I read the line where his long finger points, and I worry for a moment I've made a mistake by entering the wrong house. This would be my luck.

L.B. Dunbar

But I had a key that worked in the front door of this house. Stepping to the dresser, I remove the contract I signed and find the matching address.

"I've rented the same place." I look at Brut, bewildered while my heart sinks.

"How could we be in the same place during the same week?" Brut asks. He looks as frustrated as I suddenly feel. This can't be happening. I can't be in the same house as Brut. It's bad enough we still live within proximity of one another. Every once in a while, I see him around Pasadena, where we both live, but it's been a long, long time since we've spoken, other than a rare smile or head nod of acknowledgment. Been even longer since anything else has happened between us.

"Midge found this place for me," I offer.

Brut chuckles, swiping a hand through his hair and making it lay back on his head. The white is a striking color, and with the matching stubble on his jaw, my mouth waters. He shakes his head, a teasing smile brightening his face, and I realize I'm missing something.

"Damn Hank and Midge," he mutters, slipping his hands into the pockets of his shorts. His shirt is covering his chest once again, and the blue material makes his eyes more intense. They drift to the bed, and he looks as though he wants to sit but thinks twice about it.

"I guess I could leave," I suggest although I really don't want to go. Something isn't adding up, but I need this vacation. I've earned it, and after weeks of planning, I have the mindset to be here. I don't want to go somewhere else, yet I can't stay here with Brut.

"Maybe I should go," he offers without enthusiasm, swiping awkwardly through his hair again. Little tunnels form in the white mane, making it stand up and look a little freshly rumpled as if he just rolled around in bed. *Damn, he's sexy.*

I've kept up on Brut. I know he owns his own business like me. If his work ethic matches mine, which I imagine it might, he hasn't had a vacation in years either and needs this time off like I do.

"I could see if something else is open along the beach."

I snort at his suggestion. It's an unattractive trait.

"What was that?" He chortles.

16

"What?" I say, dismissing the nasally noise.

"That sound?"

I ignore his teasing inquiry and wave a hand. The towel slips with my movement, and I instantly return my fingers to the wrap. "You'll never find another place here. It's the beach in August."

With his attention focused where my hand holds the wet terrycloth, I'm not certain he's heard me. Speaking of the towel, the damp material grows uncomfortable against my skin, and I grab the dress off the bed. His eyes shift left, and I take the moment to tug the dress over my head. In one swift move, I drag the dress down my body while removing the towel from under the new covering. *Deck change.* Swiping the towel forward, it waves like a flag between us. Brut's eyes widen at my skill, or maybe it's that my breasts stand more erect, nipples pressing at the stretchy bathing suit-like material. He swipes his hand through his hair again, and he turns his entire body away from me. The rejection stings.

"I guess we could both stay here," he offers weakly. "How difficult can it be?" He doesn't sound convincing. However, if I know one thing about Brut, it's that he isn't interested in me. When I think about it, there shouldn't be a problem with us remaining in the same place together. We could work around one another. Maybe set some rules...

"I mean, I'm sure we can work something out," he says as if reading my thoughts. "I plan to do a lot of surfing, so I won't really be in your way unless someone else is meeting you...." His voice fades, and he spins fully to face me again, resting his fists on his hips.

"Is someone meeting you here?" The sharp question snaps at me like a rolled-up wet towel. His eyes narrow, and his jaw clenches.

"No," I squeak. "No, I have no plans like that...I'm alone. I mean..." *Shut up.* My eyes close, and I take a deep breath. The exhale lowers my shoulders, and one strap of my dress slips to my upper arm. Suddenly, fingers brush the strap upward and linger at my collarbone. I flinch, and my lids snap open.

"Sorry," Brut mumbles, retracting his hand after straightening my dress. He nods, steps back, and reaches for his bag. "We'll figure this out," he states brusquely before stepping around me. When the soft click

L.B. Dunbar

of the door to the second bedroom echoes through the space, I realize I've been holding my breath. *Sigh.*

Of course, we can work this out. I'm an adult. I'm over him. Only my heart plays devil's advocate: *Yeah, right.*

4

Code 739

[Brut]

Lily fucking Warren. What are the odds? What is the chance? Then I realize, it's neither. It's all Hank. Damn him.

I hustle to the second bedroom, contemplating a call to my younger brother to rip him a new one. He set this up on purpose, and I have a few choice words for him. But the moment I press his number, I just as quickly end the call.

Would it really be so bad to share the house with Lily? It's only a week. We are adults. What happened between us seems like a lifetime ago. Water under the bridge and all that. But the drops of memory slowly filled a bucket lately as I kept hearing more and more about Lily. Ever since Hank told me he went to her cupcake place I haven't been able to stop thinking of her. However, I don't know what to say to her.

Hey Lil, I know it's been twenty years but...

Lily, we should talk sometime...

Lily pad, can you ever forgive me...

There was no easy way to start all the conversations we should have.

Add in the little fact of seeing her naked, and I probably should leave the house. But I don't want to. Not to mention, *holy shit*, aging has only enhanced Lily's beauty. At nineteen, she was a spitfire with long blonde hair and wild blue eyes. Ripe as a peach, she was ready to be tasted and savored for the first time. I was twenty-three back then and did the best I could to maintain her innocence, but she made it damn difficult to resist her.

With the memory of us then, I'm hard. Now, her toned body and subtle curves, along with the delicacy tattooed on her hip makes it impossible to settle my stiff dick. It's as if my body recognizes where it longs to go—a place it's never been—because I fucked that up.

Tossing my phone on the bed, I fall to my back. Both hands dig into my hair, tugging gently. Can I do this? Can I stay here? I chuckle without humor. *Karma, you fucking bitch.* This *would* be my luck. A week forcing me to finally face Lily and all I did to her, to us. I'd like to dismiss it as a long time ago—youth, alcohol, and other excuses—but the bottom line is I made a mistake. A big one with a capital B. That mistake cost me everything.

I sigh as I sit up, and my head tilts to take in the bright sunshine of late afternoon reflecting off the ocean. *Fuck it.* I'm not leaving, and neither is she.

I find Lily in the kitchen unpacking groceries, something I hadn't yet considered purchasing. Thinking I'd most likely eat out all week, I make a final decision in the moment.

"I called the rental agent." I'm lying, but I don't let guilt touch me on this one. "You're right. I won't find anything open this week along the beach." It's August, it's California, and it's a week before schools return to session. The beach is packed with visitors. "So maybe we can just work around this." I'd point between us, but she isn't looking at me.

"Sure," she agrees too eagerly. With her back to me, I focus on her body. She's wearing some kind of athletic dress—form fitting, brightly colored, the top-half shaped like a bathing suit bikini. Fuck me when she changed in front of me. Throwing caution to the wind, she almost found herself on the bed and me between her thighs, taking that dress back off her. Yet there's no chance in hell Lily would ever want me close to her again.

Don't touch me. The sound of her voice rings through my head from twenty plus years ago. It was a far cry from all her other requests. *Touch me, Brut. Taste me.*

I need to get out of here.

"I'm heading out for something to eat," I say although my feet stay planted and my hands come to rest on the kitchen island.

"Okay." Her answer comes too quick as if she wants me to leave, and I once again consider the possibility of someone meeting her here. She said no one was joining her, but that doesn't mean she won't set out to find someone to hook up with. The thought makes my stomach sick.

"Since we'll be roommates for the week, maybe we should work something out in regard to...umm...you know, if you want someone here." Scratching the back of my head, I'm unable to clearly put into words what I'm suggesting. *What the hell am I doing?* I don't want to give her an out. I don't want her to bring some random guy here. I don't want her to do *anything* with another guy.

She stops from her busy movements of opening cabinets and filling the refrigerator. Pausing with her eyes aimed at a cupboard, she speaks. "You mean you want a code in case *you* want to bring someone back here? Like a sock on the door or something?"

Her words tease, but her voice strains. *Did her eyes close with what she just suggested?* I lean to the side and tip my head, hoping to get a better look at her face.

"I don't need to bring anyone here," I offer. "I can always go..." *other places.* I swallow back the remainder of my suggestion. *What the fuck am I saying?* The words run together, like a freight train screeching in my head. Next, I'm thinking of Lily going other places, with other men, and doing other things with them. I'm not liking that image any better.

"I guess we could exchange phone numbers, and you could text me. Like a 411 or S-E-X, which would be 7..."

Did she just spell out sex?

"3..." Her finger dials in the air.

"9," she adds hesitantly. "I think."

What the hell?

"We could use that as a code." Bright blue eyes smack me in the cheek with the innocence of her suggestion. *Fuck no.*

"Yeah, umm, I think we'll be good. You can use the code with me if you need to, you know..." I don't know why I'm stammering or why I'm offering for her to use the 739-option. I don't need her texting me that she's having sex, or wanting sex, unless it's with me. *Never gonna happen, pal.*

"Oh." Her hands flutter in the air. "Oh, I'm all set." Her face pinks. "I mean, I have other methods..." The blossoming pink deepens to sunburn red as her breath hitches. "I just... I'm all good on my end." She

21

L.B. Dunbar

exhales sharply and returns to randomly opening and closing cabinets although she's no longer placing anything inside them.

"Okay, well. I'll see you later." I rap my knuckles on the island counter before I spin toward the side exit. "Don't wait up," I throw over my shoulder and then want to punch myself in the face for being such an idiot.

5

Seashells By The Seashore

[Brut]

The next day starts early although I purposely returned to the house late. There's no sign of Lily, and I panic for a moment, thinking she decided to leave after all. My heart drops with the possibility. I was such an ass yesterday.

Then I find small traces of her presence. An open book on the arm of the overstuffed chair. A glass in the sink. Leftovers in the fridge from the dinner she must have made the previous night. When I see her Jeep still parked next to my SUV in the drive, I exhale in relief. Removing my surfboard from the back, I remind myself I'm the reason for her vanishing act all those years ago, but she doesn't have an excuse to disappear from here. I promised her we'd work out this arrangement, and I mean it. The fact she even spoke to me is huge progress. Her smile gives me hope she's forgiven me.

Fat chance, pal. I'll never deserve her forgiveness.

As I stroll down the beach, carrying my board under my arm, Lily appears before me but doesn't notice me. She's walking funny, knees bent outward and open a bit too wide for a normal stance. She looks like she has crab legs. Her hips shimmy as if she's doing a convoluted dance. She's definitely quirky.

"What the hell?" I mutter with laughter, recalling the sound she made while standing in her bedroom yesterday. She snorted—nasally, cute, and eccentric. I hate that I don't recognize her noises. At one time, I knew all her nuances—her purrs, her moans, her sighs.

As we grow closer to one another, I notice her hands are curled in fists as if she's holding something in her palm. Her too-full fingers don't allow her to grab the shirt tied at her waist, so she's trying to use her elbows to hitch up the material. Slowly, I understand the shirt must be coming loose with her movements, and she's trying to catch it before it

23

falls to the sand. Her knees bend farther outward as if she can stop the slippage with her awkward crab-like walk.

"Can I help you?" My voice carries, and her head shoots up.

Her expression shows I startled her, and something falls from her occupied fingers. She reaches forward, attempting to catch it, but whatever it is drops at her feet. She bends to retrieve it despite her full hands, and the shirt at her waist loosens. She attempts to stand, and her hands go for the fallen clothing, catching it with her wrists at her knees while more items release from her palms. She looks awkwardly ridiculous and stunningly adorable. A soft, frustrated giggle escapes her.

"Here," I offer, stepping to her. I'm not quite fast enough to assist her, having to stake my board in the sand before reaching out for her. She blinks up at me, and I grab the arms of the shirt. She straightens, and I readjust the material, tightening the sleeves around her toned waist. She's wearing a body-hugging workout shirt which dips over her tits like a bikini. Tight triangular material barely contains the heavy globes, and my tongue thickens, wanting to lick the space between them. *Get a hold of yourself, man.* Khaki shorts, frayed at the hem, rest low on her waist. Her feet are bare, toes wiggling against the sand. I'm close—too close— and the fresh salty air mingles with the scent of her—sunshine, tropical fruit, and morning.

My hands pause on the tied shirt, and I look up to find her eyes watching me. Brilliant and blue like the heavens above us, the color hasn't changed one bit in twenty years. If only she still looked at me like she did twenty years ago, I might feel complete. Instead, I feel like a puzzle poured out of the box for the first time. Pieces scattering, nothing matching, waiting to be assembled.

"Thank you," she says, her voice hardly more than a whisper. She licks her lip before chewing a corner, and I swallow back the desire to lean forward and kiss her. I wonder if she tastes the same. A wayward hair blows across her face in the morning breeze, and she raises her wrist to swipe at the strands. Her hair is more a caramel color than the brilliant blonde from when she was a teen. Cut much shorter—just above her shoulders—she has it pulled back in two pigtails, one behind each ear.

"What's in your hands?" Seeing her struggle with the loose pieces from her pigtails, I chuckle. Without thinking, I reach out and sweep back the tendrils, tucking them behind her ear. They're too short, so they immediately blow loose again, and I repeat the motion, lingering at her ear a moment before my fingers skitter down the side of her neck and release her.

"Seashells." Her voice croaks. She coughs to clear it and holds up her full fists. Another shell falls free, and when I bend, I see several near her feet. As I pick them up, my eyes travel over her bare, tan toes wiggling in the sand. My gaze continues to climb up her shins, dripping with droplets of the sea spray. Her thighs clamp together as my view goes higher, and I take note of how short her shorts are on her toned legs. I stand slowly, remaining close to her. Holding out the three dropped shells, I notice she doesn't really have any more room in her small hands to carry them.

"What are you doing with all these?" I smile positioning the shells in my open palm.

"I don't really know yet, but they were too pretty to pass up."

Too pretty. The words catch in the wind and swirl around my chest. This is Lily. She's so beautiful, and I don't think I can pass her up again. Instead of returning the three shells to her, I slip them into my pocket for safe keeping.

"Is this where you were this morning?" I nod, implying the beach. The words release harsher than I intended, but the question mixes with my relief she didn't leave. Another thought strikes me. She could have met someone for coffee and enjoyed a little morning delight, and I hate that I'm guiltily projecting on her what I want to do *with* her.

"I was up early and went for a walk." Her eyes narrow in the blazing sun.

"I thought you left. Maybe reconsidered staying."

"Do you want me to go?" Her quick question comes out small and hesitant. She bites her lip again, and I tug at the tender flesh with my thumb, lingering on the plumpness of the bottom curve a second longer than necessary before releasing her.

25

L.B. Dunbar

No, absolutely not, I want to respond, but I hold back the truth. "No, we're good." I said we could work it out, and I plan to keep my promise. Maybe she'll at least have dinner with me and let me explain myself from years ago.

Not gonna happen, buddy.

Then I see her gaze roam my body, taking in my naked chest. I take a deep breath and watch her eyes expand as my pecs heave. *Is she checking me out?* A flicker of hope sparks within me, and my lip curls. It's a nice feeling to have someone scan my skin like she is.

Another hair blows across her face, sticking to her lips, and I can't resist. I swipe my fingertip over her cheek, drawing the hair behind her ear and hold it in place. My fingers linger.

"I must look a mess." Her face pinks, and I want to trace the dawning color on her skin.

"You look beautiful, Lily pad." The honest truth escapes me.

She looks incredible. She chews at her lip as her cheeks flush and her eyes shift to the side.

Please let me kiss you.

"Well, enjoy the surf," she mutters, tugging her head free from my fingers and tipping it toward my board. She ignores my compliment.

"Thanks." My chest pinches at her rejection. She brushes past me, continuing in the direction of the house, and I'm torn between following her like my heart begs or running for the rolling waves. The ocean seems like a safer choice. If I follow Lily, I can't be held responsible for the things I want to do. A cool rush of Pacific water should deflate the hard-on in my shorts and restore my thoughts to reality.

Lily Warren will never want me again.

6

You're Hot

[Lily]

I can't seem to get away from him fast enough. He has no idea what he's done to me. His tender fingers curling around my ear, tickling the side of my neck. His touch exploding everywhere across my skin. Thank goodness for the bright sunshine and the possibility of rosy cheeks from the heat to cover up the blush creeping over my face.

Scampering up the beach, I refuse to look back at him. I recall our conversation before he went out last night. Could I be any more awkward, giving him a texting code and a free pass to bring some skank back to the house? If I had to listen to Brut grunting and groaning with someone else in the next room, I'd die. *Don't wait up*, he'd announced.

Around ten, I gave up on what I was doing—waiting for him. I wanted to kick myself because I should have known better. Who am I kidding? Brut wouldn't need to bring someone here. He probably picked up some chick at the local bar and went back to her place. How cliché. Yet why wouldn't he? Better yet, who wouldn't be attracted to him? Breathtaking to view, flirting like a master, and with steady employment to boot—he's a trifecta for the win.

My feet can't move fast enough over the sand as I replay each word of our recent exchange. I'm not certain I liked his tone when he asked me where I was this morning. An innocent walk to clear my mind after a restless night of sleep is none of his business. Still…

"I thought you left. Maybe reconsidered staying." The comment surprised me.

"Do you want me to leave?" I hate that I asked, sounding so desperate for him to say *no*. I don't know why he'd want me to stay. I don't know why *I* decided to stay other than convincing myself I deserved this vacation as much as he did and determining I could handle sharing the house. Still, there was an urgency in his voice. What did he

27

L.B. Dunbar

think I'd been doing? I fought a smile by biting my lip. His eyes had followed the motion before his thumb pressed at my skin to release it.

"No, we're good."

So good, I thought as my eyes wandered over Brut's physique. The stacked-book abs. A smattering of white hair on his chest to match that on his head. Not a drop of ink on him. Bright orange board shorts with a blue floral design hung low on his hips. A darker trail of hair led lower, hinting at what lay beneath his dipped waistband. My eyes snapped upward, as I recalled what rests below, and the smirk on his face let me know I'd been caught.

Yummy. My libido drooled, but I quickly dapped up the spittle. My heart is the problem, and that beating organ has gotten me in trouble before with this man. I promised myself never again with Brut Paige. Been there, done that. *Only I didn't ever do him.* Someone else did him before he would give himself to me.

My shoulders sag with the sudden memory, and I squint out at the rolling waves. The ebb and flow are a metaphor for my wavering emotions.

"You look beautiful, Lily pad." Did he want to kiss me? What a foolish thought. His words made me melt a little, but then a look of uncomfortable uncertainty crossed his face. They were only words, not a compliment. I had to put some distance between us. He stood just a little too close.

The idea he'd want to kiss me, after all these years, is simply stupid. There's no way Brut would be attracted to me after all these years, if for no other reason than Chopper. I've met his nearly twenty-two-year-old son. He's the perfect reminder of Brut's indiscretion—a constant reflection of him and *her*.

The memories wrestled sleep from me last night, but I refuse to allow them to be my nightmare again. Awake and restless early this morning, I'd decided to get out of bed at the break of dawn and take advantage of every second of my vacation—Brut or no Brut. Except now, exhaustion taps on my shoulder, and I sense a nap is in order even though it is only midmorning. After rinsing my shells in the kitchen sink,

I change into my bathing suit and return to the beach for a little sunshine snoozing.

+ + +

"You're hot." The words startle me awake although I instantly recognize the rugged male voice. He's been haunting my daydreams since the moment we parted this morning. The high afternoon sun illuminates the outline of a masculine form. I don't need to see him directly to know it's Brut. Slowly, he crouches beside me as I lie on a lounger.

When I returned to the beach earlier, I searched for Brut on the waves, but he wasn't recognizable from this distance. I cursed myself for seeking him out, but he'd gotten under my skin with his soft touches and sweet words. Not to mention his nearness. Him invading my space messed with my head, and I tried to rid my thoughts of him. Instead, I focused on the multitude of people bobbing on boards, lulled by the roll of the ocean before occasionally standing and riding the waves. Surfers make surfing look effortless and graceful, and I wonder if I could learn. I never want to use my age as an excuse for not trying new things.

"You're turning pink," Brut clarifies. "Like that cupcake." He gestures toward my tattoo, a giant pink and purple frosted delicacy covering most of my right hip. The ink permanently marks me as a reminder that I did it—I opened the bakery I promised myself I would have one day.

With the way Brut looks at me, I become hyperaware of the bikini I'm wearing and how much of my skin is exposed. His eyes roam over my hip as if he's licking up the inked icing, ready to take a bite of the maraschino cherry topping the masterpiece. His appraisal is refreshing but also unnerving. I take care of myself, but I'm still self-conscious enough to be uncertain about wearing two pieces of skimpy material. I bought the baby blue bikini, assuming a vacation where I had my own section of beach would be private enough for me to wear something risqué.

My arms curl over my waist as Brut's eyes travel up to my shoulders.

29

"Here, allow me." At some point, Brut has picked up my bottle of sunscreen, and he slathers his hands with the creamy white lotion. He hitches his leg behind me, slipping his body snuggly behind mine. I tense at the unexpected intimacy and scoot forward enough for his legs to straddle the outer sides of my thighs. We're tight—my back sensitive to his strong chest. The heat between us is more than just the sunshine above. My skin prickles. Brut is so *close* to me.

Warm liquid hits my shoulders along with firm fingers, and he rubs the contours of my upper back. Thick thumbs join the massage, caressing up the nape of my neck. My head lolls forward. Fingers stroke the sides of my neck and lower to press at my shoulder blades. Brut works in soothing circles, increasing the pressure until he comes to the band of my bikini crossing the middle of my back. His thumbs dip in equal measure under the tie and gently swipe away from my spine to my sides. His touch leads to the edge of each breast, and I stiffen, warring with myself not to get too comfortable with the pleasure of his hands. I shouldn't turn this into some fantasy, but my brain can't stop the thought of him untying the bikini strings, slipping those firm hands forward, and forcefully cupping each of my heavy breasts. I'm a hormonal mess near this man, and the sensation of his palms against my skin feels so amazing. His nearness feels *too* good, and I mentally moan.

Brut freezes, and I realize the sound escaped. He pauses as if reality hits him, and he has realized too late what he's actually doing—he's touching me. His hands still on my skin.

"I really wish I knew your sounds." His breath tickles the back of my neck, and I shiver as he speaks into the hollow dip at the base of my skull. A thick knuckle brushes at the wisps of hair loose from my pigtails along my nape, and then he blows at the fluttery strands. I tremble again.

Is he flirting with me or is he teasing me?

"I think I'm good," I lie, wiping away my daydream and ignoring his comment. My sounds, as he calls them, are embarrassing. And while I don't want his fingers to rest, he needs to stop massaging me because a problem develops lower on my body. My core pulses, and I sense the wetness. *Hot mess from application of sunscreen.* I'm ridiculous. Even worse is the second fantasy I conjure up where he slips his fingers down

30

low, dipping into the bottom piece of my suit to relieve the rapidly growing ache. I close my eyes as if this will shut off my imagination, which has leaped into overdrive.

The tension returns, and despite Brut's closeness, distance slowly wedges between us.

"I think I'll shower," Brut says, his voice another tickle to my sensitive skin, and I nod without vocally responding. He shifts and removes his body from behind me. With the ache growing out of control between my legs, and the knowledge Brut is who I want to relieve it, I hate the loss of him.

My body shifts as I prepare to watch him walk away. I can almost feel my core cry out to him. *Don't go.* Don't leave me to another night of wonder—if you'll meet someone, if you'll touch her like I want you to touch me, if you miss me.

My eyes fall to his chest where sea salt has dried on his skin, circling his nipples, and mixing with his chest hair. My mouth waters. Images of warm water and suds sliding down his naked body fill my mind, and I blink. He catches me staring, and his lips crook in a knowing grin, lighting up his tan face. He's caught me again. He hesitates a moment, his eyes twinkling, and the motion pulls forward an ancient memory. He used to look at me this way. Then he surprises me.

"I'm going out for dinner again. Want to join me?"

My heart skips a double beat, pattering like a two-step line dance. I swipe my forehead, brushing back loose tendrils of hair. I've never officially been on a date with Brut—an out to dinner kind of date. I so badly want to say yes, but for some reason, I don't.

"I brought groceries but thank you."

His smirky expression dissolves. The smile brightening the edge of his jaw turns to clouds. He nods, his grin weakening.

"I understand," he says as his form blocks the sun, casting him in a shadow, and I can't help but consider the irony. Once upon a time, Brut had been sunshine for me, but something—no, *someone*—got in the way.

7

A Bottle of Truth Serum

[Brut]

"I understand."

I do. Asking her out to dinner is a stupid move. She isn't interested, and I know all the reasons why. Unfortunately, my mouth got ahead of my thoughts and blurted out the invitation. I've thought of nothing else but her all day. I spent most of the morning surfing, and then the afternoon avoiding, but my mind circled through a loop of positions—namely pleasure-fulfilling ones—that I shouldn't have imagined with Lily. Her revealing shirt this morning riddled my brain, along with images of her nakedness from the shower. My eyes wandered the beach, hoping to spot her throughout the day, but the distance was too great.

Then I see her in this tiny two-piece, accentuating her athletic form, perky breasts, and that damn tempting tattoo.

I'm a mess around this woman, especially with all the skin she keeps exposing to me.

I need to leave before I beg her to go to dinner. I eat alone often enough, so the loneliness isn't an anomaly, but I was hoping for a little company, especially with her. Last night, I left as soon as I could after the whole sex-text code fiasco. But when someone approached me at the bar, I didn't even think twice. The answer was immediate—no thank you; I'm taken. The lie had come easy enough because my heart held the truth. I was taken by Lily, once again.

Another bar. Another night alone. I order a burger, but I can hardly eat. With all the energy I expounded during the day, I should be starving, and I am, for a certain someone. Twisting my cool beer between warm fingers, I drown under the too loud noise around me. The sun lowers in the sky but hasn't set, and I realize I'd rather be on the quiet of the beach than wallowing here under the pretense of waiting for someone. I've waited long enough. With that, I slap two twenties on the wooden bar top and head back to the house.

"What is that smell?" I blurt as I walk through the side entrance. Fragrant spices assault my nose, and my mouth instantly waters.

"Just a little something I whipped up," Lily says, smiling sheepishly. She's sitting on a stool by the kitchen island with a book in one hand and a fork in the other. She looks relaxed and in her element as she props her elbow against the counter. The tension in her face from earlier appears washed clean. A vision flashes of her sitting in my kitchen but knowing how run-down it is compared to this place, I scribble away the idea.

"Of course, you did. You cook for a living. It smells amazing." Whatever she made looks heavenly and too healthy with lots of vegetables. Her smile lowers a little, and I sense I've said something wrong.

"Actually, I bake."

I'm about to say, *same thing*, when I notice her head lower. *What did I say?* I don't move, and the tension trickles between us. She pushes her dinner around with her fork.

"Would you like some?" Her head lifts, and her eyes soften as she asks, but I can't read her.

Damn it. Is she only being polite, or does she want me to stay? I rub my stomach, exaggerating the lie I'm about to spew. "Thanks, but I'm full. I think I'll head outside for a bit."

She smiles weakly in response, and I take a deep breath as I cross the living room, rushing for the glass doors leading to the deck. I can't escape fast enough. I kick off my flip-flops as I hit the wooden planks, and trudge through the cool evening sand until I reach midway between the back steps and the foamy white edge of the shore. Plopping into the sand, I cross my ankles, lift my knees, and rest my arms loosely around them. I stare at the waves softly lapping at the wet sand. A lick and a retreat. The imagery brings me comfort and agitation. Energy ripples under my skin. I'd like to think I don't recognize it, but I do.

When I first met Lily, I felt this way. Funny how time passes, yet you can be projected backward in an instant. A look. A glance. A scent.

L.B. Dunbar

Something triggers you, and you fly into the past, dusting off a memory suddenly so crystal clear it overwhelms you.

Lily shouldn't have been in our shop way back when. I don't even remember why she was there. She didn't own a car that needed repairs, but there she was with miles of hair, a long, loose skirt, and a revealing tank top. She was too young for me, but my heart skipped a beat when she looked up at me all innocent and sultry. A subtle curve to her rosy lips and a shy dip of her lids. My dick jolts with the recalled vision, just as it did all those years ago.

"May I join you?" The softness of her voice invades the memory, and for a moment, I think I've projected the sound into my thoughts. Then I look over my shoulder to find her staring down at me with a beer and a hard lemonade pinched within her fingers. My breath hitches just as it did with the first sighting. *My God, she's even more beautiful with age.* She's lost a little of the roundness she had as a teenager. Not that she was ever flabby, but she's just more fit now.

"Of course." Letting my legs fall, I slide them forward in the sand and cross them again at my ankles. Lily hands me a beer.

"Heineken?" I hadn't stocked the fridge. In fact, I still hadn't even thought of groceries or pleasantries, like beer. A protein bar I found in my bag was the breakfast of champions this morning.

"I remember." The quiet in those words hits me in the chest as she folds herself down to the sand. She's wearing another athletic-style dress with a bright pattern. The top is cut like a bikini again. Damn if I don't want to rub my nose through the crease between her breasts and then bite the peak of her nipple through the stretchy fabric. *Down boy.*

"You remember my favorite beer?" The thought startles me. She simply nods, not looking at me as she takes a sip of her hard lemonade. I watch the roll of her throat as she swallows, and I swallow involuntarily, my mouth filling with moisture as I long to lean over and kiss under her jaw.

"Thanks," I choke, finally recalling some manners. "It's been a long time."

"Almost twenty-two years actually," she responds instantly, her voice somber. The words sound hollow like when she spoke in the kitchen. As though I'm an idiot and I'm missing something.

And I am. Her timing is accurate, however. Chopper is almost twenty-two, and his birth coincides with our distance.

"That's a long time," I repeat, keeping my eyes on the side of her face as she stares out at the darkening sky over the lulling waves.

"A long time," she parrots with another one of her snorts, this one gentle and dismissive, and it's my turn to take a heavy pull from my drink.

Damn, this tastes good. As good as sitting next to her even if I don't know her sounds or their meanings. Quickly, I amend the thought. Sitting this close to her tops any taste, any flavor, any anything.

"So, besides Because Cupcakes, what else have you been up to?" My eyes close the second I ask, wincing as I feel the weight of weakness in the question. I open my lids to find her looking at me, her brows pinching in question. "I know about the bake—"

She cuts me off. "Are we really going to do this?"

"Sure, why not?" I shrug. *See? Idiot.* Her head twists away, and I decide now is the time, like it or not, to spill my long overdue apology.

"I'm sorry."

Her head pivots back in my direction, and her eyes open wide. "What are you sorry for?"

"Everything." There's no denying what I mean. I don't think I need to lay out all the details, and an unspoken name falls between us like a cement wall. The air shifts from summer breeze to winter blizzard. She nods a few times, turning her head away from me again, and my gut twists. "I never meant to—"

"You didn't do anything," she interjects again.

"The fuck I didn't." I snort, sharp and disgruntled. I did everything to ruin our relationship without ever intending to kill it.

"Fuck is what you did." The statement knocks the wind out of me until she giggles, and I chuckle with mild relief. We shouldn't be laughing, but the weight on my shoulders gets a chip lighter.

"I never meant to," I say again, and I didn't.

35

L.B. Dunbar

One night.

A few too many drinks.

And the wrong sister.

It was the biggest mistake of my life. Epic. Colossal. Unthinkable. I've hated myself ever since, but eventually, I had to forgive myself because that error gave me Chopper. Adding insult to injury, the result of my misguided indiscretion gave me a child. I couldn't—*wouldn't*—trade him. I just wish I could forget the circumstances of his conception.

"I never blamed you, not directly at least, but I won't lie and say it didn't break my heart." She shrugs as if it was no big deal, as if hurting her didn't kill me inside.

Our relationship was…complicated. We were only fooling around. I guess you could say she was a booty call before those were a thing, but that belittles how I truly felt about Lily. We snuck around because I didn't want to get caught with her, or rather, I didn't want her to get caught with me. Garage mechanic. Struggling student. Dad a known alcoholic. Those were good enough reasons. Plus, at nineteen, Lily was still a kid in my head. I couldn't even take her to a bar. We didn't go out on dates. We were each other's dirty little secret.

I didn't want to be the one to steal her innocence—well, not all of it at least—but my feelings for her were strong, stronger than I wanted to admit at twenty-three. My life was in chaos then. Pop. The shop. Classes. Lily was fun for me in a world lacking anything remotely funny. Still, I could have had her virginity. Another man eventually took her, I suspect, and I cringe at the thought. I could have had everything from her, and I threw it away.

Guilt wracked me for weeks after what happened with Lauren. Being old enough myself to know right from wrong, I chose *stupid* instead, *so* stupid, and then kept the truth from Lily until I had no choice. Fuzzy memories swirl at the edges of my brain. I'll never have back all the facts of that night, but I know the timing coincided with my life falling apart. Lost my scholarship. Pop too sick to work. Debt for the garage.

"Remember Rick Begerton?" Lily blurts, interrupting my memories. Rick Begerton was a guy from my class in high school. He was trouble—car racing, drugs, minor thievery. "Lauren was in love with him. Well, as much as you can be in love with someone at eighteen." Lauren is two years older than Lily, which means when said love happened, Lily was sixteen. Rick would have been twenty.

Lily swallows, gaze staring out at the rolling ocean. She's lost in her head for a moment, and my fingers itch to touch her and pull her back from the memory. My skin tingles like an insect with ten thousand legs crawling over my bare feet. Something bad is coming with the mention of Rick.

"He was into me, instead," she clarifies. If she said she killed someone, I wouldn't have felt as sick as I suddenly do.

"I don't understand." Although I do in some strange way. Who wouldn't be into Lily? But Rick? "Son of a bitch. Did he touch you? Did he hurt you?" I shiver as I recall Rick was eventually arrested for domestic abuse.

"No." She shakes her head. "But he was persistent, and it drove Lauren mad. She was willing to be with him, and I wanted nothing to do with him. Anyway, Lauren was jealous because she wasn't the one Rick wanted, and I was." She pauses, her eyes drifting to the bottle in her hand. "She was convinced I encouraged him. Said I led him on, and I was a tease. But I would have never done that to her." Sadness fills Lily's voice.

We didn't discuss her family much when we were younger. Her home life wasn't good, despite her living in a nicer part of Pasadena at the time. I thought the reason she didn't want her family to know about us was because of me, who I was. Slowly, hindsight sees there might have been more to her keeping me a secret.

Her older sister's voice haunts me. *So the little tease got to you, too?* Jet black hair and heavy makeup hinted at her sinister, reckless side. Lauren Warren was a known flirt, a vicious tease, and an easy lay by the time I met her. She was twenty-one, new to the bar scene, and knew how to make a scene. Somehow, I think that's how I ended up in the corner with her. It also might have been how her eyes matched her sister's. Those damn blue eyes got me in trouble.

I can prove I'm better than her.

I shiver in disgust at myself. I want to kill someone as the truth hits harder.

"Lauren found out about you. She knew how I felt. And she went after you because of me."

How did Lily feel about me? I want to ask, but I don't. The revelation weighs between us. There isn't forgiveness of her sister but an understanding of motive. Lauren's jealousy was so malicious it destroyed her younger sister and me.

What was my excuse?

Lily exhales deeply, and my throat clogs like the murky seaweed spit out of the ocean. My stomach feels nauseous, and my beer suddenly tastes sour although I take another sip for something to do. My arms tremble with the need to wrap them around Lily and hold her to me.

How did I fall into Lauren's trap?

Oh, right. My dick. My head. And too much alcohol.

"I mention all this as a way to explain why Lauren did what she did. Not defend it but understand it," Lily clarifies, pausing as she wipes sand off her toes by rubbing each foot with the other.

Two things strike me. One, Lily is too good. She isn't forgiving her sister, but she understands her, and that's more than her sister deserves. It's more than I deserve because I don't even understand why I did what I did. Why I didn't go to Lily with my problems.

The second thing I question is this: *She knew how I felt about you.* We never shared emotions. No declarations of love. Maybe an occasional 'I love when you touch me like this', but nothing deeper. We were having fun, but my heart knows I'm lying to myself. Did she feel something more for me?

"When I was young, I was looking for love, and marriage, and a baby in a baby carriage. Any means to escape my family. Make a better family. I wanted someone who would dance with me in the rain, build dreams of *what-if* someday, and make love to me under the moonlight." She scoffs a dismissive laugh, and I add it to my catalog of her noises. "Romantic dreams, I guess." She brushes sand off her shins, and the movement distracts me for a moment.

Does she still want these things?

"Anyway, after you, I lived with the next guy. We were together for five years until I realized it was never going to happen. Not marriage, not babies. We were playing house, and I was holding out for something that would never be. He's the one who hurt me."

My head rattles with all I'm learning. I'm about to ask if she still wants all those things when something else hits me.

She speaks before me. "Annnnnd I have no idea why I told you this."

"Hold on. What do you mean *he's the one who hurt you*?" My heart rate skyrockets in my chest. Lily doesn't look at me, keeping her eyes trained on the ocean. I have my answer, but I still want to hear it from her.

"Lily?" I question.

She huffs, an anxious dismissal of things as she lifts her hard lemonade bottle and drinks heartily. Again, I watch the roll of her throat as she momentarily drowns herself in the drink.

"It wasn't that bad," she says, her voice quieting. "A little grabbing and a few slaps. A fist was the final straw."

"Don't excuse him," I snap. "Don't excuse any man for laying a hand on you." My voice rises, my anger matching it. I'm ready to punch something myself, but it sure as fuck wouldn't ever be a woman. And I'm pissed as hell that someone touched her like that—in anger, with his fists.

"I'm glad you told me, though," I add, after a moment of seething rage and feeling helpless for a number of reasons. "I never knew." Not about Rick. Not Lauren's motives. Not Lily's romantic dreams. Certainly not some asshole's abuse.

Her shoulder lifts, and her head tilts. Finally looking at me, she smiles weakly. "How would you?"

My chest pinches, heart aching for Lily—the one I didn't know at sixteen, whose sister's vengeance held until she was three years older. For nineteen-year-old Lily, who I lost because I was stupid. I should have taken better care in how I handled her then. Should have slowed her down when she wound me up. It's almost laughable in hindsight how slow we went, and I'd chuckle if the sourness of what she just revealed

L.B. Dunbar

wasn't so unsettling. Because I also ache for the twenty-something Lily, who struggled to find dreams of happiness in an unhappy situation. It wasn't fair, and it was all my fault.

"Anywho," she exaggerates, trying to sound more cheerful. "You have Chopper, and he grew into a great kid, right?"

I'm startled at her mention of my son. He wasn't born with that name. I had it legally changed once his mother abandoned him to me. I suppose Lily and I know circles that circle each other, but I still find it strange she knows his name.

"He has. He's full of trouble like his old man." I chuckle with a hint of pride, still troubled by what I've just learned but letting it pass for the moment. "Not certain what he wants to do with his life, though." The irony strikes me. Chopper grows closer and closer to the age when I fucked up. I've pressed the issue of higher education, and his concession was community college. He says he wants something in the music industry, but he isn't musically inclined like his uncle Hank. Me, I don't hold a musical note in my body.

"He'll figure it out," she assures me. "You did." Her added smile is meant to comfort, but she's wrong.

"Did I? I held Pop's shop together by a thread for a long while after he drank and gambled away the profits. I did it out of necessity, but I never became who I wanted to be." My words are harsh, bitter even. The road to keep the shop afloat was long and rough until recent years.

"But I thought…" Her voice drifts.

When we met, I worked for my dad, restoring cars, but it wasn't my first love. I wanted to be a teacher, and I was taking classes to be one. I liked history; only I'm better at making it repeat itself. I got the wrong girl pregnant, just like my old man, and raised my son as a single father, just like Pop. Only Pop had two boys. The comparison brings me little solace.

"It doesn't really matter now," I say, shrugging like her, dismissing my past and finishing my beer.

The sun sets slowly, but the sky has turned cloudy off in the distance, so the night is not as stunning as I would have hoped. The light filters around the hazy clouds, but the golden globe hides behind gray darkness. Lily remains silent as we stare forward, each lost in our own thoughts. Mine are a jumble crashing into each other like the growing irritation of the ocean before us.

"Want another?" she asks, and I peer down at the empty green bottle.

"Sure. I'll get 'em. I owe you." My knees creak as I stand. After brushing the sand from my shorts, I reach for her empty.

"Brut." She voices my name with a serious edge. "You don't owe me anything."

8

Frolic In The Sand

[Lily]

I don't know why I went all serious on him or spewed the history of my life. *Good Lawd, Lily, way to strike up a conversation.* Maybe it was his abrupt apology. Maybe I wanted him to know I was a messed-up kid with crazy, romantic dreams. I can't say I understand why he did what he did with my sister, but I get it. I mean, I don't really, but I also kind of do. We were so young and foolish—stupid even. Well, maybe he was more stupid than I was, but then again, he probably didn't want the things I did when I was nineteen and he was twenty-three. Maybe that's why he went for Lauren one night.

Brut returns with another round. He seemed rather surprised about the Heineken, his face morphing to pleasure when I said I remembered. Funny how your memory tricks you and takes you on a damn roller coaster ride. One minute, I'm reminiscing about drinking his favorite beer in the office of his dad's garage, and the next, I'm prattling about Brad. I shiver with the memory, but I'm also good at repressing it, and as soon as I released the information to Brut, I was ready to block it once again.

"Here," he offers, holding out another hard lemonade for me and squatting before he sits in the sand. He opened the bottle inside, so I don't have any hassle with the cap. I watch his face as he takes a long pull from his beer—the hard line of his jaw sprinkled with white, the crow's feet by his eyes, the curve of his nose. He's so handsome he redefines the word.

My heart flutters as I stare, and I shift to better memories. Kissing Brut. Straddling his lap. Moving against him like a dance. A pulse races between my thighs, and I close my eyes at the growing ache.

"You okay?"

"Mmm…" Meant more as affirmation, it sounds like a moan.

Brut chuckles. "Heavy stuff you just told me."

I nod as I open my eyes. "Would you mind if we let it go?" I really don't want to keep talking about all these things from the past. It's out there. I've shared one of my deepest, darkest secrets, and it's up to him how he interprets it. I, on the other hand, don't want to rehash more.

"Sure." The pause after that word feels heavy, but I'm sensing something heavier coming. "But I'd like to know more about the man. The one who didn't marry you or give you babies." He swallows. "The one who hurt you."

And there it is. I laugh without humor. "You mean Brad?"

"Brad. As in the name of a car in those insurance commercials? That Brad? Sounds like a pussy name," Brut mocks. "Give it to me, *Brad*," he exaggerates as he throws his voice to sound feminine. "Nope, doesn't work for me."

"I didn't sound like that," I snap, my voice rising an octave, filling with honest laughter, and almost matching the whiny noise he made.

"Right there, *Brad. Harder, Brad.*" Brut continues in mocking disbelief.

"I didn't say those things." I chuckle.

His head swings in my direction. "You didn't?" His eyes widen.

I'm wagging my head, laughter filling my cheeks. I'm not discussing my sexual history with him, and I see what he's doing. He's making fun of Brad to lighten the heaviness of discussing him. He continues.

"Fuck me...*Brad.*"

"Okay, now you've gone too far!" I bellow, but I'm giggling like a teen.

"You're kidding, right?" His eyes widen farther, the blue sparking to midnight. I don't know what he thinks my sex life has been like, but I'm not interested in correcting him with details. Despite Brad or anyone else, I haven't had the kind of sex which has me begging for *harder, deeper, faster*, even if I've wanted it.

"You know you share the same beginning sound in your names," I clarify. "As if, fuck me, *Brut* sounds so much better."

His breath hitches, and I swallow what I've said, nearly choking on the fierceness in my tone. *Fuck me*, Brut, my brain repeats.

"Lily pad." My nickname lingers on his lips. He's the only one to ever call me that. The wind kicks up, and my hair blows in front of my face. Just as he did earlier in the day, he brushes back the strands, his fingers holding them in place behind my ear. "Actually, that does sound better."

He's right, and in one swift move, I'm on my back, Brut's hand cupping my head, so I don't hit the sand. His upper body presses over mine. He licks his lips and bites the plump curve of the lower one, peering down at me like he's ready to attack.

"Say you forgive me, Lil."

"I forgive you."

His eyes search my face, reading me. I speak in earnest. The past was a long time ago and holding a grudge takes too much negative energy. Lauren is a perfect testament to such negativity.

"Lil," he says, his voice barely a whisper, his dusky blue eyes softening. His gaze grow more intense as he stares down at me, stroking my hair around my ear. I've seen this look on him. The one that says he wants me, but he doesn't want to give in. We already lived this struggle when I was nineteen. I can't go through this again. Not with this man. "I'm sorry anyone ever hurt you, especially me."

"It's okay," I say from habit but not from truth. It's not okay, and we both know it. What he did to me, to us, and all the rest of my history is not acceptable. Good thing we are adults now and can accept the past.

"It's never going to be okay," he says, still holding himself off my upper body, but my lower portion beats in rapid succession underneath him—a rhythm ripe for friction. My core rests under the heat of his abs, which I know are hard, but not quite the part of him that can soothe the pulsing ache.

"It already is okay," I offer because it is. Life moved on. Brut got Chopper. I have my bakery. Brad is gone. Lauren too.

"Really? Are you really all good, Lily?"

I want to say I am, but the truth is, I could be better. I'm perfectly happy with Because Cupcakes, and I'm living a dream with my small business. Life *is* good, but it isn't perfect. I'm still missing what I yearned for at nineteen. Love. Marriage. A baby.

"Lily pad." His voice is so low it blends with the breeze, begging me for something I can't read. He leans forward.

"Don't kiss me," I blurt, sucking back a breath as I curse myself. Why would I say that? *As if he wants to.* The truth is I don't trust myself. If his lips touch mine, I'll take too much from a man never willing to give in to me.

His body shifts, and of their own volition, my knees spread, opening my thighs for him to slip between them. He's balancing on his elbows, still sweeping back my hair with each toss of the evening air.

"I can't," I say although I don't know what I'm denying. I only know if he kisses me, I'll combust. He nods once and presses up on his hands like he's doing a push-up over me. He's prepping to stand only the motion shifts his lower half forward and something hard, long, and firm thrusts at my center.

I moan, my head tipping back, sand mixing in my hair as the tip of him taps at the beat strumming my core.

"Lil?" he questions.

I'm too mortified to speak. He knows where we connect. He knows what he's done to me. So, he repeats the motion.

My hands dig in the sand as my knees fall farther open. As my eyes close, I'm willing him to get off me and begging him to stay in the same breath. His hips roll, and he spears me again. Clothing protects us from going any further, but I'm flung back in time to grinding on Brut on the leather couch in the office of his garage. The memory mixes with a fantasy of him taking me on this sand, and before I know it, I'm pressing back at him, hands on his quivering biceps, nails digging into skin.

Holy shit.

The world dissolves into a million grains of pebbly stone. I'm one with the sand underneath me, sifting, shifting, drifting.

Slumping back into the grainy ground, I feel my heart race as I take a jagged breath. My head lolls to the side. I can't face him. I can't believe what I've done. Fully clothed, I might add. Within record time.

"Lily pad?" The question in my name along with the hint of smug pride nearly brings me to tears. My eyes prickle, and my head swings back to face him. I don't even fully form the words *get up* before he kneels back. My legs are still spread on either side of him, and I awkwardly sit up, my knees trembling as I try to bring them together.

Brut towers upward and reaches for my hands. I want to tell him not to touch me. I need him to step back because his presence overwhelms me. His aura. His scent. Not to mention, I'm so thoroughly embarrassed. The way my legs rattle, though, I can't stand on my own. Begrudgingly, I accept his warm fingers. Once upright, he continues to hold my hands, rubbing his thumbs over my knuckles.

"Brut, I—" I begin, tugging back as he holds firm.

"Lil…" he starts, but I free one hand and raise a palm to him.

"Just-just stay right there." He releases my other hand, and I back up slowly, speaking to him like a rabid animal about to attack. *Good boy, stay.* Please, don't come near me. I want a sinkhole to open and just suck me in. My undies are soaked, and I don't allow myself to look down at his zipper region, afraid to see he's still hard, afraid to see he didn't come. My lids lazily blink, and I take another hesitant, humiliated step backward.

"I'm sorry," I mutter.

Brut steps forward, his mouth opening to speak, and that's my cue. I turn on shaky feet and sprint for the house, relieved when he doesn't follow me.

9

Buckets Collect Rare Things

[Lily]

The next morning, I find a child's yellow plastic pail on the counter with a Post-it note attached: *Fill me.* Inside are the shells Brut put in his pocket yesterday. I cover my lips with my fingers as I grin, fighting back memories of the night before. I came so hard I saw stars, and he gives me a bucket.

Brut bought me a bucket to collect seashells. I squeal inside, warming at the sweet gesture. Picking up the pail, I cross the living room and exit the double doors for the fresh air of a new day. I'm hoping not to see Brut because I'm still too embarrassed over what happened and how I reacted to him. I'm almost to the foamy sea on the sand when I catch something out of the corner of my eye. Brut is running toward me, bare chested. His shirt dangles from his shorts as he slows to a jog when he nears me.

"Seashell collecting?" He stops short before me, his lips curving into a full smile. I'm blinded for a moment. The white scruff, the whiter teeth, and the sheen of sweat on his brow. He's too sexy for his own good.

I hold up the bucket in response. "Thank you. This was very sweet." My eyes meet his but quickly divert to his feet. The moment is more than awkward, and a restless quiver ripples up my skin. Only too bad, the trembling stops between my thighs, recalling the sensation of last night. My eyes shift up to the center of his jogging shorts and away. I'm caught in the moment of look-don't-look and eventually close my eyes to recover before I state the obvious.

"Morning wood?" *What the?!* "Morning jog, I mean. Morning jog!"

Brut's mouth lazily crooks, and I'm silently praying for the sea to swallow me. *Good Lawd, Lily.* He watches me as he scrubs at the back of his neck.

L.B. Dunbar

"Couldn't sleep. Had a few things on my mind." His smile grows, and there's a hint he's been wrestling with the same thing as me—about last night. "Mind if I join you?"

His question startles me, and before I can think, I'm shaking my head at his offering. "I'd like that."

Brut kicks off his shoes, and with a strong toss, he chucks them toward the deck stairs. We fall in step next to one another without speaking. Beach sounds surround us—the breeze, the squawk of seagulls, the ocean lapping at the shore. The noise is strangely peaceful and it's surprising, not awkward, to stroll without words between us. I stop occasionally when I find a perfect shell. Eventually, Brut peers into my bucket after I do this a few times, and asks, "Why are you only picking up those?"

I peer into the bucket to see each shell is complete: no cracks, no chips. Also, most of them are white or speckled with lighter colors.

"I want them to be perfect," I say, proud of my discoveries and envisioning them in a jar in my bakery. I'm testing out some summer flavors, and it might be fun if I can replicate a seashell candy as a garnish. I've been working with salty caramel and chocolate lately. My latest concoction is titled Salty Summer Nights.

Brut bends at the waist and lifts a shell between two fingers. "But the imperfect ones tell a better story." He holds a broken piece in his hand, gray and tattered. I'm stumped by his comment, contemplating what he means—*does he think I'm imperfect or is he referring to himself*—and then I notice something about the shell. I take the piece from his fingers and force his hand to open, palm upward. Then I lay the chip on his skin.

"It's a hidden heart." My head snaps up to his eyes, but he's looking at what he holds in his hand. His brow pinches in question. "A hidden heart is when you find something in nature shaped like a heart. A rock, a formation in the sidewalk, the curve of bark on a tree."

Brut looks up at me. His lip curls.

"A heart-shaped shell is a rare find." I speak as if he's just made the greatest discovery known to mankind.

"Does this mean I hold your heart in the palm of my hand?" He's humoring me, his eyes twinkling.

"Not *my* heart. A hidden heart," I mock.

"Rare find? Same thing," he mutters, closing his fingers around the shell and slipping it in his pocket. "I think I'll keep this one. Don't want to mess up your perfect collection."

"Suit yourself," I tease, but something in my stomach flutters.

We continue walking, and two men pass who simultaneously mutter, "Good morning."

We greet them as well.

"You can stop drooling," Brut snarks, a teasing lilt to his voice but also a hint of something deeper. He swipes at the corner of his mouth in mockery.

"I wasn't drooling," I defend, but it was hard to miss the toned bodies of either male specimen—lean and smooth, tanned and grooved in all the right places.

"They're gay anyway," Brut adds, and I twist to look over my shoulder. The move is more a double take at their physique than a perusal of their sexuality. However, when I glance back, one walks backward, smiling at me. He winks and tips up his chin.

"They are not," I refute. Feeling the man's eyes on my backside, I fight a grin, knowing I'm being watched. "At least one of them likes women. He's checking me out."

Brut stumbles in the sand and spins to look back at the two men.

"Don't look," I admonish, and he twists back in my direction.

"How do you know he wasn't checking me out?" Brut nods, his head bobbing as though he's proud to one-up me. I stop and slip the bucket handle over my wrist.

"How would that work with three men?" I'm making a circle with the fingers of my right hand and aiming my left index for the hole while my middle finger sticks out…

"Stop." Brut laughs, reaching for my hands and dragging one away from the other. He's bent over chuckling at the serious expression on my face as I try to decipher the mechanics. "Just no. No threesome."

"Not your thing?" I tease, and Brut straightens, his hands still holding mine.

"Never into sharing." The declaration spirals around us, and my mind immediately races to Lauren. We shared Brut although I didn't do it willingly.

"Lily pad." As if reading my mind, Brut draws me back. He strokes firm thumbs over my knuckles, restoring me to the present. Dropping one hand, he begins walking, and I follow his lead as he entwines his fingers with mine. His fingers are warm, and I like the comfort they give me after my thoughts of Lauren. After only a minute or two of connection, Brut looks down at our joined hands and releases me as though my touch burns. The release is somehow a reminder of how I felt all those years ago. I wasn't the one he wanted most.

10
Surfer Girl

[Brut]

Dammit. I lost her. Something in what I said pulled her away from me for a moment, her cheerful expression pinching in pain. Saying her name, I hoped to draw her back to me. The breeze blows, and as her hair slips loose, she twists her head to free it from her face. When turns back in my direction, she grins.

We walk forward a step or two, and then I notice I'm still holding her hand. Her fingers are delicate yet warm, and I like the way they curl with mine. We fit, Lily and I, and I've missed her. The thought reminds me I'm moving too fast. The orgasm last night. Holding hands now. I don't want to let go, but it seems like too much, so I drop her hand.

"So, about las—"

"Was a mistake," she interjects, cutting off my start.

I stop walking. "I wouldn't say that," I suggest, scratching at the back of my neck. My face pinches at the directness of her rejection.

Was I startled by what happened? Absolutely.

Was I surprised she got off so fast? Definitely.

Would I take it back? Not a fucking chance in hell.

"I don't know what happened." She lowers her head, aiming her gaze at her feet. I glance down to see her toes digging in the wet sand. Cupping her chin, I force her face upward. I don't like her looking away from me

"I do," I say, my grin growing, hoping to tease the tension away. Lily closes her eyes, again trying to cut herself off from me. I gently tighten my grip on her chin. "I liked it, Lily pad."

The comment reminds me of one of our firsts together. Her mouth on me, sucking me dry despite her inexperience. Presently, her face a shade of pink not warranted by the sunshine heat on her skin.

"I'm so embarrassed," she offers, eyes still shut, her voice soft. I don't want her to be, and I'm about to say as much when her eyes snap open. "It won't happen again." Determination and finality fill her tone and a head nod adds emphasis. My mouth falls open, ready to tell her how much I want it to happen again *and again* when she tosses out, "I think I'd like to learn to surf."

Any man knows a change of subject from a woman means the conversation is dead, and most men might see this is as a godsend, but I don't want Lily thinking our moment on the sand was a mistake. I refuse to see it as anything other than a sign she is still attracted to me in some way, and God knows I'm attracted to her. But I won't force the issue.

I tell myself to stop touching her, only I cannot seem to pull back my hand. I'm no longer cupping her chin but stroking the side of her face. My fingers feel a magnetic pull to her, always reaching for her and wanting to connect skin to skin in some manner. Her skin is so soft, and she smells so good. Tropical. Fruity. New. I want more of her. I want her under me again.

I want a second chance.

There's a million reasons why I can't have one. Why I shouldn't even consider asking for one. Forefront in my mind has been that asshole Brad guy and all she laid on me last night. I'd like to bury him alive for what he did to her, and without wanting graphic details, I need to know she's really healed from all that happened to her. Thoughts of Brad remind me I will not force her to do anything she doesn't want to do. Being with me again is obviously something she sees as *not* happening.

"You want to surf?" I swallow down the rejection I feel and the questions I long to ask and allow her this moment to distract us.

"I'd like to learn, yes." Her lips twist as she squints in the direction of the surfers bouncing on the waves.

"I guess we could find you an instructor…" I hesitate. "Or I could teach you?" The offer simply spills forth, and for a slim moment, I think this is a great idea. Then I pause. *This is a horrible idea.* This means more of Lily on display. I'm already having a hard enough time keeping my hands off her. Speaking of hard, her bikini from yesterday nearly killed me on the beach. All that exposed skin. A news report would read:

"Death by heart attack from the sight of a beautiful woman skimpily clad." I don't trust myself.

"You would do that?" Her question laced with eager hope catches me off guard. *I'd do anything for you, Lily pad,* I want to reply but instead, clench my teeth to hold back the confession.

"Of course." The terse answer sounds strained, and she flinches, but I haven't removed my hand from her face. A fingertip strokes down her cheek to her lips, tracing over the curve of the bottom one. "I'd like to teach you things."

"I'm ready to learn," she replies, her voice lowering, adding fuel to the heat already burning inside me.

When I first met Lily, she was so innocent. She was sultry, sexy, and completely unaware of the temptation of her body. She sauntered into our garage one day, and I was a goner. Instant attraction combined with her enthusiasm, and that was it for me. Close the book.

"Then I'll instruct." My voice croaks, rusty, and rough.

There is so much I'd love to teach her now and so much I'd like to learn from her. Her playful grin reminds me surfing is on the docket— not the sexual fantasies building in my mind. Though surfing with Lily is going to add to the bank of self-pleasuring images.

+ + +

"Fuck," I groan. I've shown Lily how to paddle out on the board and then rest until the timing feels right. We are in a little inlet, a bay of sorts, where the waves aren't as rugged as the open ocean but perfect for learning to surf. With Lily's athletic build, she's agile, just as I sensed she would be. She hops up easily. Knees bent. Body shifted forward. Arms outstretched. She surfs.

She's a natural, and I love the sound of her squeals as she becomes more confident with each attempt.

Until she falls off.

She's under for a moment too long, and I flip from my board, searching the sea for her. I find her legs under the water, treading the waves. Her hands cup under her armpits, arms crossed over her chest.

She should be using her arms to support her, and I curse with fear. She must be hurt. Popping out of the water mere inches in front of her, she screams at the surprise. The next thing I know, she's against my chest and her legs have locked around my hips. I struggle at first because the added weight throws me off balance, but my hand comes to her lower back.

"Are you hurt? Did you hit your head?"

She shakes her head in the crook of my neck, muttering something I can't distinguish. Her lips tickle my skin, and I shiver despite her heat. I'm trying to paddle us forward, boards drifting off beside us as they are tethered to each of our ankles.

"Lily, tell me what happened." I'm still panicking that she hit something although we are deep enough for the water to break her fall.

"I lost my top." The comment halts my one-armed swim, and I slip my other hand upward to find her back is bare…of everything. I can't help the chuckle as I warned her surfing in a bikini was risky. She didn't own a wet suit and refused to let me buy her one at the board rental shop. I told her she should at least get a sun-resistant T-shirt, but she didn't listen to me.

The seriousness of the situation slowly dawns on me.

She's bare on top and pressing into me.

Suddenly, I'm hyperaware of the sharp peaks of her nipples poking my chest. I stop dragging us forward when my feet can touch the sandy bottom, keeping us covered by water up to my shoulders. My eyes drift, trying to catch a glimpse of the swells teasing me. Lily didn't heed my warning, but I realize Karma is fucking with *me*.

"Where did it go?" I ask, my voice raspy from the knowledge she's mostly naked. And against me. *And naked.* In my arms.

"I don't know," she says, pulling back only slightly. Her arms loosen from my neck, slipping open so her hands rest on my shoulders. Her legs are loosening as well until I grip under one thigh, holding her in place at my waist. "I was trying to find it the second after I fell."

My eyes scan the water, looking for a scrap of light blue material possibly floating on the surface. The search is futile, and my gaze returns to the hint of her breasts, barely hidden by the roll of water between us.

Her fingers come to my temple, and she brushes back my hair, which I can only imagine looks wild from the tumble in the water. The touch feels hesitant but gentle, loving even, and my body trembles for a new reason. I like her touching me. Her hand cups the back of my neck, and I lick my lips, wanting to kiss her. My eyes catch on hers, noticing her watching my mouth.

"Lily pad," I whisper, leaning for her.

"Don't kiss me," she whispers once again, and I bite my tongue hard enough to draw blood.

Why? I want to scream, but I know why. *I wasn't going to,* Sarcasm suggests I mock her, tell her I wasn't going to do any such thing, but my heart knows the truth.

I nod once, slowly, exaggerating my understanding. She releases her hold on my neck, but both my hands cup the back of her thighs, tugging her against me. I shift my hips, rocking upward to show her what she's once again done to me. I'm solid stone beneath the tepid water because of her. Her heat envelops me, and I feel nothing below my waist but her core at the tip of my length. I drag her downward and feel her buoy back up. Her hands return to my shoulders for leverage.

"Lil, I want you." The truth is painful, as painful as the pressure building at the base of my spine. I want this woman. Her sounds. Her movements. I want inside her in a way I've never been. She smiles in response, a teasing curl to her lips. She knows what she's doing to me. "You temptress."

She chuckles as she drags herself down my length and pulls herself upward with the help of my shoulders. My fingers dig into the underside of her thighs, forcing her to grind harder and dig deeper against me. My eyes watch her mouth, open and wavering, sucking in breaths with each press against me. I'm on the verge of taking that mouth and dipping into her core when an annoying beep bubbles up from under water.

"Damn it." The timer on my waterproof watch warns me the hour rental of her board is almost up. In fact, we only have five more minutes, and it isn't enough time to complete what I need to finish with her.

"We should go," she says although she doesn't move from my grasp.

"It's time to leave," I reiterate but thrust against her once more. Her nails scratch on my shoulders, and I relish the sharp sting. My fingers press firmer at her cool skin underwater, holding her in place. My hips roll, and I imagine filling her in one hefty thrust. The release would be so sweet, but I can't do this here. My dick weeps, but my heart cries out—*you need to do this right*.

My forehead lowers to her shoulder.

"Brut," she whispers at my ear, and I shiver from my name in her sultry tone. Another sound I'll add to my list. "Thank you."

My head springs up, and I stare at her, my expression asking the question: *What for?* But she simply shakes her head, a pleasing grin illuminating her features. A glow of something I can't read graces her cheeks. She presses back from me, and without a word, she treads away.

11

More Warning Bells

[Brut]

She pauses as she nears the shallow depths, and I hesitate, wondering what she'll do next. The upper half of her suit is gone forever, and as much as I want to see her parade up the beach only partially clad, the image sparks me to swim faster. I don't want anyone else looking at her.

"Lil," I call out, and she stills, hesitating as I approach. "Here." I peel off my surf shirt and hold it out to her. The material is sticky and drippy because it's soaking wet. She hovers in the shallows, turning her back to the shore so others won't see but I get a damn peep show.

I turn away out of respect but, fuck, if I don't want to tackle her in shallow waters and finish what we started, completing our sexy act by satisfying her. We haven't even kissed, I realize. We haven't had physical skin contact either. The thought makes me chuckle; it's so reminiscent of our experiences when we were younger. Lily on my lap, her skirt hiked up, grinding against me. Lily on her back, my legs between her thighs, dry humping her. Clothing was a dreaded barrier. But back then, she let me kiss her. Kiss the fuck out of her.

She's struggling with the wet material but finally wrestles it to her waist. She stands to her full height.

"Well, how do I look?"

Like a fucking wet dream. She's wet, and I'm dreaming of rubbing my dick between the seam of her breasts now plastered under the material of my shirt. She's a wet T-shirt fantasy I can live with for years. The vision will include the fact she's wearing my clothing.

"Beautiful," I choke out because I can't find a stronger voice. She looks ethereal with water dotting her skin and the sunshine enhancing her tan. She takes my breath away, and when she slicks back her short, waterlogged hair with both hands, I'm a goner. My obituary would state: "Man drowns from wet dream vision."

I stand as well, tugging at the hem of my shorts which can't hide the wood that won't subside. Lily breaks the meter stick of my threshold. I've accepted I'll be perpetually hard around her.

We've had a great day. Once we hand in her board and return to the house, I ask her to dinner.

And she refuses me again.

What the fuck?

"I think I'll take a warm shower. My muscles are starting to feel the ache of surfing," she offers by way of excuse.

Let me relieve those muscles. However, the sting of her rejection leads to other emotions. Irritation.

A great day and no dinner.

An orgasm and no lip action.

I'm beginning to waver in my patience.

$$+ + +$$

I shouldn't have gone out alone. I should have demanded she go with me, or better yet, I should have stayed in. Only, when she thanked me for the surfing lesson and excused herself for the shower, I was pissed. I showered quickly myself and then left the house. My body hums. My limbs limber with pent-up energy, and my heart races with desire, because I don't understand what happened.

I replay the day as I pull into the lot of a famous seafood bar and stare at the restaurant sign. I don't want to be here alone. I don't want to eat out anymore. I want company, and I want Lily. I reverse my SUV but chicken out on returning immediately to the house. I opt for a long drive instead.

One of my favorite parts of restoring cars includes the test drive. The purr of a project finalized is a sweet melody. I love to wind up the hills around LA and wander down to the coast, listening to the hum of a well-tuned engine in a classic ride brought back to life. This is what Lily is doing to me. She's revving me up, only she's not letting me drive.

Highway 5 curves in front of me, and I take in the dimming light of another day. People seem to stop along the southern coastline and breathe a moment, as if inhaling some unknown fragrance from the dipping sun.

Somewhere along the way, I've lost sight of how much I enjoy California living. Maybe I don't always recognize the easy pace because LA is so fast, but down here, life moves a little slower. As I pull into a parking lot along the public beach, I consider exiting my SUV, but a peek at the lowering light, closing out the day hits me in the chest—I'm missing out on another evening with her. We only have the week, and I can't keep running away. And I'm not letting her run away either.

A slower pace. Lily and I aren't in a race, even if I want to speed things up. But we've already missed out on twenty-two years. It's been my fault, and I admit as much, but I'm not making any more excuses. I want Lily back.

I peel out of the lot and head to the house. Opening the door, another heavenly fragrance assaults my nose. This smell is rich and sweet, causing me to salivate.

"What is that?" Whatever it is, I want to frost her in it and then devour every inch afterward. Her back is to me. Her hips wiggling as she pours something in a rhythm. *Plop. Plop. Plop.* Then squeaky lyrics echo in the kitchen, and I realize she has earbuds in. I step up behind her, finding a cupcake pan filled with gooey batter waiting to be baked. Another tray bakes in the oven. Vanilla, cinnamon, and something I can't distinguish waft around the room. My mouth waters.

Lily turns with a sharp twist, her eyes widening at my close proximity. I'm swiped across the chest with a spatula, coating me in batter. The offending utensil remains in her hand as she pulls back, and her eyes widen even more.

"Oh, my gosh. I'm so sorry." She tugs at the wire leading to the buds in her ears. "I didn't hear you come in." A playful expression dances in her blue eyes, doing nothing to lower the beat of my heart. Her gaze falls to my chest, which lifts and lowers as if I've just run a mile. She bites her lip, holding back laughter as she waves her free hand at me. "I didn't mean to get your shirt."

The batter mixture soaks through my linen button-down, and I reach for the buttons, unlooping one at a time.

L.B. Dunbar

"I guess I should take it off." The blue of her eyes dials up to a deeper shade. I'm enjoying the heat on her face as I slowly unwrap myself, exposing my chest to her. Her lids lower as she follows the trail of my unveiling, and her breath hitches when I tug the halves open, forcing the material loose from my shorts. I stand a moment, allowing her to drink in my skin on display for only her, dripping with cupcake batter.

"Although I think all is only fair..." My voice fades as I tap her wrist, forcing the spatula to tip toward her and hit her in the chest just above the edge of the tank top covering her breasts. Still holding her wrist, I drag the utensil downward, painting her exposed skin and the front of her shirt with the sticky mix. Her breasts rise and fall, matching the pace of mine. Still holding her wrist with the spatula in hand, I drag her arm forcing her to paint over one breast. The wet mixture catches lightly on her firm nipple. She's definitely turned on.

"Why are you baking?" My voice remains deep and low as I ask.

"I bake when I'm wound up."

My brow twitches upward. "What's got you wound up, Lily pad?"

"You." The whispered response is all I need to hear. She will not escape me again.

My mouth crashes against hers. Fingers find her cheeks but quickly delve into her hair as her mouth opens to match mine. I breathe her in like I haven't breathed in years, gulping at the air only she can provide. The spatula falls to the floor with a clatter before her hands slip to my waist, sliding inside my shirt and wrapping around my lower back. I lean forward, pressing her into the counter behind her as I grind against her, and all the while, my mouth does not leave hers. I won't be close enough until I enter her, but for now, I want her lips. Tender yet fierce. Demanding yet taken. I savor each pass of our mouths, the curl of tongues, the linger of lips. My hips roll forward, but still, my mouth takes more. She's the meal I've hungered for, and a starving man is...well, starving.

Slowly, I'm lowering us, tugging her down by the force of my fingers still wrapped in her hair. Her body folds against mine as we near the hard wood, and I rotate us so I'm over her. Our position is reminiscent

60

of last night on the beach, only our mouths are joined tonight, and I want everything.

I drag my mouth down her jaw, lick at her neck, and release her hair to reach for a breast. My palm settles over one firm globe and massages the weight. I groan, returning to her hungry mouth. She seems to suddenly be famished for me in return, and I relish her eagerness. My fingers continue to knead her breast until I find the hard nub of her nipple. I pinch, and she squeaks.

"I love all your sounds," I mutter, breaking the kiss for only a second.

Her thighs have opened, and I lay my length at her hot center. Clothes are not going to be the barrier anymore. I need her skin. Fingers deftly find the hem of her shirt and press upward, finding her braless.

"Fuck, Lily," I moan, massaging her ripe breast in earnest. She's built for her frame. Firm. Stacked. Perfect. My palm covers all of her, and I squeeze, eliciting a deep purr from her that rumbles down to my dick. My fingers release, pleased with the sound but needing more contact. I tickle down her tight stomach, reaching the waist of her jean shorts.

Beep. Beep. Beep.

My head pops up at the alarm from the oven.

"Cupcakes," she explains. I ignore the annoying trill and return to her shorts. Popping the button, I find her hands eagerly pressing back at my shirt. The material slips over my shoulders and down my back. My bare chest rubs against the batter covering her. Her fingers spread within the mixture, and her nails scrape over my nipples.

"Fuck," I breathe against her neck. I continue working at her zipper while she forces my shirt off. Our hands become frantic, each searching, seeking. I'm inside her shorts, cupping between her legs when...

Beep. Beep. Beep.

"Tug at the handle," she demands. *Is this some strange euphemism?* But I quickly realize she means the oven door as she's peering in that direction. I reach to my side, not releasing her wet panties, and yank at the oven catch. Heat releases from the inside, and I return instantly to the

L.B. Dunbar

heat at my fingertips. I scoop aside the band of her underwear and meet tender folds.

"Brut," she chokes, a plea in her voice, and I remember the first time I touched her. Her willingness. Her eagerness. Her sound as she came around my fingers. I'm so hard, I'm ready to burst at the reunion of my touch on her sweet center.

"Lily. Sugar," I whisper as a second finger slips forward, and together they dive into her. Her hips roll. Her channel clenches. She's sucking my fingers into her, and I want to give her everything.

Until we hear a banging on the door.

"Fire department."

I look up to find the kitchen filled with smoke. I release Lily too quickly, instantly missing the warmth of her against my fingers, but the heat in the kitchen is overwhelming. Incessant rapping continues on the side door. I kneel up to find a fireman has already entered through the open back screen door.

"Hey," I snap, annoyed at the intrusion and concerned for the compromising position of Lily on the kitchen floor. She tugs down her top which is now coated in cupcake batter. Her nipples both stand at attention, and her eyes close at the unsatisfactory position I've just left her in. She was so close.

"Sir, we got a call when a beach walker saw the smoke."

I stand, holding up a finger for Lily to stay hidden behind the island. I reach over for the stove and turn off the oven. The timer stopped with the open oven door. A charred cupcake smell slowly hits me.

"Burnt cupcakes?" The teasing lilt of an officer comes from behind me, and I turn to see a second fireman has entered through the side door. He takes in my shirtless attire and the position of Lily, who slowly rises to sit on the floor. She covers her chest in a giant X as her hands slip up to her shoulders. He addresses her. "Ma'am?"

I reach out my hand, and Lily stares up at me, her face pink with embarrassment.

"What's going on?" the first officer asks, and I twist to find his eyes leering over the island counter down at Lily who still hasn't grabbed my hand.

62

"Burnt cupcakes," the second officer teases. "Me and the missus have been in the same situation. Might want to keep the windows open to air out the place and call the owner who might think you're burning the house down." The officer's eyes shift to Lily and back to me. "Although by the look in both your eyes, cupcakes had nothing to do with the heat."

Even though a good-natured chuckle follows his comment, I don't appreciate the humor at Lily's expense. I'm about to say as much when I gaze down at her.

Her blue eyes twinkle. *Is that yearning I see?* A hint of days long ago hovers at the edge of my mind. The glow of her face familiar. Something about those eyes. Her throat pinkens, and she quickly turns away. I lose the vague memory and glance over at the officer. He winks at me, keeping his eyes respectfully off Lily.

"Thank you, sir. I'll call the rental management," I offer, dismissing both men with a nod. They exit together out the back door. When I turn back for Lily, I find her body curled around the stairwell entrance behind the wall of kitchen cabinets.

"I think I'll go clean up." A question lingers in her tone but then her expression shifts. A weak smile graces her face, signaling the moment between us has passed. She disappears behind the wall, and my shoulders fall. I've lost her again.

12
Finally

[Brut]

I hear the shower run, and then I wait. She doesn't return downstairs, and I don't know what to do with her supplies. Stacking the unused trays on the counter, I place the remaining batter in the refrigerator. I call the rental management office to explain what happened—with the cupcakes, not with Lily—then I toss the burnt cupcakes into the trash and take the bin out to the dumpster.

When I return, Lily still hasn't come downstairs, and I decide to shower. But I don't touch myself. Willing down the hard-on, I'm holding out for bedtime fantasies instead of a quick jerk in the bathroom. Thoughts of Lily have me taking myself in hand more often than normal lately, and I'm finding the release isn't enough. After the tease of last evening on the sand and the romp in the ocean earlier, not to mention the kitchen floor, Lily is what I need.

I pull on a pair of basketball shorts, commando, and decide to head back down the stairs. As I pass Lily's closed door, I hear a subtle moan and stop, cataloging it as another sound of hers. Tilting my head, I listen, anticipating more.

I shouldn't do it, I warn myself as my hand reaches for her bedroom door. I knock lightly. I almost think I don't want her to hear me, but then a soft moan greets me again, and instantly, I'm hard. I turn the knob and enter without permission.

Stepping forward, I find her room dark. Evening fell quickly after our tryst on the kitchen floor. Lily lies wrapped around a pillow, her back to the door. What she's wearing has stopped me in my tracks. A deep purple colored scrap of lace covers a sliver of her backside. A matching camisole partially covers her back.

"Lily?" I question, keeping my tone low while my excitement rises. "You okay?"

She rolls to face me and then quickly turns away. She tugs the pillow closer to her chest and her leg hitches upward, her knee lifting over the edge of the pillow. The cupcake at her hip is on full display, and I swallow hard. Stepping forward, I stare down at her perfect form. Her firm ass. Her toned legs. Her eyes remain closed, but her knee shifts, dragging higher on the pillow.

"Lily pad," My voice remains quiet as if I might disturb her. Instead, I reach for her ankle as I want her attention. We need to talk. Her skin is warm, still damp from the shower and mixing with the heat of the night. The French doors are open, and a salty breeze enters. Lightning crackles somewhere out over the ocean.

She hasn't kicked off my touch, so I risk moving my hand up the back of her calf. Her leg stiffens a moment before she relaxes. My eyes jump up to find her still not looking at me, but she's letting me explore. I stretch forward, pressing gently at the firm muscle under my palm, and Lily purrs. Traveling higher, I cover the back of her knee and kneel on the edge of the bed. I whisper her name, and she moans quietly in response. My hand crawls higher, kneading the back of her thigh. Getting a closer look, I see the lace falls between the seam of her ass cheeks and cuts high over her hip. A piece of it brushes over the tip of her cupcake tattoo—which is a maraschino cherry.

"Lily," I groan, allowing my hand to cover the firmness of one ass cheek. My gaze doesn't leave the cherry as I squeeze. Her hips roll, and I lower my head. A sweet sexy scent captures my nose.

"Sugar, were you touching yourself?" My head shoots up, anticipating I've walked in on her getting herself off. The thought excites me, and while I couldn't get any harder, my dick jolts.

"No," she whispers, her head shaking slightly for emphasis.

"Were you waiting for me?" I tease. She doesn't answer, but her lip curves. *Fuck me.* I straddle her one leg, then move my hand to her other ass cheek. With a growl I say, "I want to take a bite out of that cupcake."

Her hips flex against the pillow, and I can't hold back. I lower to suck at the inked skin, lapping at it as though I can literally taste the pink icing—sugary sweet just as I imagine her pussy tasting. With the thought, I take a sharp nip of the purple wrapper. Then I drag the tip of my tongue up the center of the design, stopping at the bright cherry to scrape my teeth over the red ink as if I could take an actual bite. Then I swirl my tongue around the shape and suck harder on her flesh to leave a mark.

"So delicious, Lily. Sweet like sugar, just like I thought you'd be. I wonder how the rest of you tastes." The comment elicits a deep purr from her as she hugs the pillow to her middle. I push up the back of her cami and return my mouth to her skin. Nipping. Sucking. Licking. I draw designs with my tongue along her spine.

"I always loved this dip." I pull back to run a finger over the tiny valley of her lower back. Then I flatten my hand to press the remaining material upward.

"Lift," I command, and Lily does as I request, pressing up enough to allow me to remove the cami over her head. I toss the silky fabric to the floor while she lies back down on her side. The curve of her breast is exposed as her arm returns to the coveted pillow. Her knee remains raised, and I like her position. I kneel up to rub two hands down her back, returning to cup both the globes of her ass. I push them apart as I massage, then drag a finger under the lace that falls between them.

"Anyone been here?" I ask, holding my breath for her answer.

"No," she whispers.

A smile creases my lips, and I continue my exploration of her body, moving to another place of pleasure. She's wet and ready, and I slip a finger inside her easily. The angle is different, and her ass lifts a little to allow me deeper. I quickly add a second finger and watch as I slide in and out of her heat.

"You've been waiting for me, haven't you?" I groan

"Yes," she whimpers, and I remember the unsatisfactory position I left her in earlier. I wasn't nearly satisfied myself.

"I promise not to leave you hanging like that ever again, Lily pad." I take the oath seriously. I will not leave her wanting for anything from me *ever again*. "Feels so good, sugar."

Her hips rock back, sucking me in as she had earlier but with the new position and easier access, the pace quickens. She's clenching around my fingers, drawing me into her and taking what she needs. Her knee presses upward as she pushes her bottom backward. Her back curls and holds as she falls apart under my touch.

"That's it, baby." I kiss up her spine. She squirms under the attention of my lips and the fullness of my fingers. "You want more, sugar?"

Her head nods, her cheek rustling the pillow underneath. I remove my soaked fingers, lowering to grind my covered dick between the seam of her fine globes. She reacts to my thrust and presses back at me. The cotton of my shorts and the thinness of her lace doesn't distract anything between us.

"No more barriers, Lily pad," I warn as I rock forward, and she rolls back to counter me. Our bodies dance a moment, the movements sultry and seductive. When I can't take it anymore, I push down the waist of my shorts, lowering them to my knees before crawling out of them. My dick is hot, hard, and ready, and when I place it between her ass, she squeezes.

"Brut," she hesitates.

"This is our first time, Lily pad. I won't be going anywhere you aren't ready." I'm not interested in that adventure tonight either. I want inside her conventionally even if our position isn't missionary. "But I'm going in, Lily. I'm going in so deep." I hook a finger through her lacy undies and tug until they spring free. She pushes the pillow from her chest, but her knee remains upward near her waist, keeping herself open to me in this position. I hold myself, dragging the throbbing tip between her wetness, coating my hot skin with her slick moisture.

"No barriers, Lil. I don't have a condom, but I can go get one in the other room if you'd like. It's been six months since I've been with someone." I rush the last words because I hate bringing up these things. "But I've never been with the woman of my dreams, the woman I wanted to be with most."

"No barriers," she mutters, pushing back at me. Although I should ask, I don't bother with questions about the pill or any other precautions on her end. It would be the responsible thing, but as she sucks my tip into her warmth, taking me inside her channel, I lose all senses other than the fact I'm sliding within her.

L.B. Dunbar

"Fucking finally," I groan, pressing to the hilt, disappearing into her as far as I can, and then I pause. Drinking in the moment, the heat of her wrapped around me, raw and bare and just everything. I bite her shoulder tenderly, then suck at the skin to soothe the sting.

"Again," she whispers, and I repeat the motion on her other shoulder. Then I'm pulling out of her, until her hand reaches back to my hip, tugging at me to reenter. And I do. I fill her while my teeth nip, and my lips soothe until I can't keep up the multiple motions. My focus all goes to the pleasure of sliding in and out of her. Deep. Wet. Willing. My position matches hers as I rest on one elbow. One leg extended between hers; the other bent at the knee behind hers. My hand cups her breast as my chest presses to her back. Her spread angle allows me to delve deep, and I blanket her as I plunge forward, increasing the pace.

"So fucking good, sugar," I groan against her skin, growing wild and needy. I'm so close, all the blood rushing to one place. "So deep."

I want to live inside her. I want to do this every day of my life. I want to never separate from her again. And my body says all those things as I plunge within her, setting a steady beat until I feel her squeeze.

"Lily pad?" I question but know the answer. She's coming undone—on me, around me, over me—and I implode. Shooting off, I don't let one drop escape. I jet forward, holding a hand at her hip to steady her while I release like I never have before and know I never will again. *Only with her.* I'm in my place. I'm where I always should have been. Inside only Lily.

13
Breakfast Proposal

[Lily]

As I sit on the couch the following morning, I stare out the sliding back door at the gray day. It's raining—sheets of rain—and I sit in the quiet peace of a gloomy day. Both my hands cup my tea mug, and I blow softly at the steam, waiting for the liquid to cool before I take the first sip. My lips curl of their own accord as I remember last night.

Brut entering my room just before I was ready to touch myself. He'd wound me up all day—first surfing, then while making cupcakes—and I needed a release like I've never needed anything before. I wasn't typically a fan of doggy-style sex, but I'd take sex any way I could with Brut. I was ready to beg.

My smile grows as I realize I didn't need to take such desperate measures. Brut took me willingly, and I loved every second of it. I always imagined sex with him would be heavenly, and he did not disappoint. Actually, he destroyed me for all other men. No man would stand a chance compared to how I felt after last night. Warm. Tingly. Pleased.

I sense his presence before he touches me. Hands cover my shoulders, and two thumbs dig deep up the back of my neck. My head lolls forward at the welcome touch. Brut's fingers are amazing.

"You weren't in bed." It's a question, and the heat of his voice tickles below my ear. He's kneeling behind the couch as he massages me.

"I couldn't sleep." Not because of nightmares or worries, but more from waking next to Brut and wanting to repeat everything we'd done again. And once more. And a third time. Last night, he pulled out of me and disappeared for a moment. My breath held, thinking he'd leave me, but he returned to clean me off and then curled up behind me, looping his arm over my waist and snuggling into my back. He kissed my shoulder, keeping his lips on my skin as we drifted to sleep.

69

"I—" His hands still, and I close my eyes. I don't want any regrets from last night, and I bite my lip, hoping he isn't about to say such a thing. *It was a mistake* are words that would crush me. "I'd like to make a proposal."

My heart shouldn't skip a beat at the *p*-word, but it does. I lift my head and twist at the neck but can't see him directly behind me. His hesitation concerns me.

"We're both here on vacation, right? Taking a break from life, and I don't want any regrets, so I'd like to suggest we live in the moment." He exhales. "No talk of the past. No concerns for the future. Just right now. Let's take this time for what it is."

My lips twist, and I bite the corner, holding back a giant *whoopee!* for what I think this means, but I still need clarification. "And what is it?"

"I don't know. But I'm happy to explore." Before I can speak, his voice lowers. "For the rest of the week, forget everything else."

I know what he means, *who* he means. I hesitate for only a moment, uncertain if it's possible despite my forgiveness. The old wound went deep. *We were so young*, I remind myself. *It was a long time ago.* Can we rekindle what we had? Do we even need to? Sort of friends with benefits on vacation? One week to just pretend? My silence triggers him to clear his throat, signaling a redirection in the conversation.

"Did you enjoy last night?" For a confident man, the question seems strange. As if, he's worried he might not please me, when he's been the man of my dreams for years.

"Very much." I swallow back the bubbling giggle threatening to burst like some schoolgirl, but I feel giddy.

"So, let's do this? Let's just *be* for the rest of the week."

The rest of the week with Brut all mine? "Okay," I reply sheepishly. The acceptance chokes out because I'm not sure what exactly I'm agreeing to, but as long as it involves a repeat of last night, I'll do anything he asks.

To my surprise, Brut releases me and hops over the back of the couch. His white hair is rumpled from sleep, and my fingers twitch to comb through the spiked tendrils. He removes the mug from my hands and places it on a tray on the extra-large ottoman. Then he cups my face as he straddles my legs, careful not to place all his weight on me.

"You agree?" His face glows with excitement, but his eyes seem wary.

"Yes." A smile breaks free from me, and his eyes soften.

"First rule, then. No sneaking out of bed." He doesn't wait for my response before he kisses me—hard and firm—while he gently holds my face. My body melts under him, and if he greets me each morning like this, I'll never leave the bed. He sucks at my lower lip before releasing me, and his bright eyes twinkle as he looks down at me. "Good morning."

How is it possible to make those two words sound so sexy?

"Are you hungry?" he asks. "Breakfast is my specialty."

I chuckle. His morning cheer is too much. "I bet you say that to all the ladies." As soon as the words leave my mouth, his eyes narrow and his expression grows serious.

"No ladies, Lily pad. None." There's no way he's been a monk for twenty-plus years, but his point is made with his sharp tone. "I'm a single father. Breakfast foods are fast and cheap."

"Okay." My soft smile proves I accept his statement. I nod brushing off my mistake of teasing him about other women.

"And another rule would be no 739 code. You are all mine for the rest of the week, and if you need 739-ing, you text me."

Laughter erupts from me, and Brut gives me a second kiss to enforce his new declaration.

"I have a rule for today, too, then."

His head tilts as his hands remain on my cheeks. My fingers find the silky basketball shorts he wore last night and tug on the material. "As it's supposed to rain all day, I propose we have a pajama day."

"Pajama day?" His lips breaking into a grin. "What's that?"

"You're kidding, right? You're a dad. You have to know it's a day when you stay in your pajamas all day."

"Oh," he exaggerates. "Those are only on special days?" He winks to let me know he's teasing, and I push at his chest. With his hands still on my cheeks, he doesn't fall back but tugs at me and returns his lips to mine, dragging out another deep kiss. My fingers brush under the T-shirt

L.B. Dunbar

he wears, needing to feel his skin. I roam upward over the patch of hair between his pecs. He pulls back too quickly and stares down at me. "First, we eat."

I pout, and he chuckles at my expression as he stands. Then he holds out his hands for mine. Pulling me up from the couch, he watches as the light blanket covering my legs falls free to expose short shorts and a fresh cami.

Brut blinks. "Are these your pajamas?" His eyes scan down my body, and my nipples peak at the appraising look. I nod.

"Damn, I like this kind of day." He swings out an arm and smacks my backside when I pass him. The crack hits right where my ass meets the back of my thigh. The echo of the slap on my skin and the sting stops me. My lower belly flutters to life. I shouldn't have liked his teasing spank, but I did.

"Fuck," Brut groans as he moves behind me, wrapping arms around my waist and pressing his lips to my neck. "Waffles first," he growls in teasing warning, and I wonder if he's worked up like me. When I push back with my backside, the stiff length I encounter answers me. He growls. "Be good, Lily pad."

"Was I good last night?" I flirt.

He groans at my ear. "Too good."

My body heats all over, and I don't care about food. I only want Brut, but he guides us forward, walking at an odd angle as his feet straddle mine. He keeps his arms around my waist until we reach the kitchen island a few feet behind the couch.

"Sit," he commands. I want him to enforce his demand with another smack to my ass, but if he touches me again, we won't get to breakfast. I sit, and Brut rounds the island. He looks good in the kitchen, removing eggs from the fridge and taking flour from the cabinet. "I owe you some groceries."

"Brut," I warn and stop when his returning glare warns me not to say anything.

"So, tell me about your breakfast skills, oh master of the waffle iron," I joke, and Brut commences with stories of teaching Chopper about measurements through cooking. I'm listening to him speak, but

I'm also envisioning this hot man coaching his young son. The image does all kinds of funny things to my insides. I always wanted children, but it didn't seem to be in the cards. I could have adopted on my own, but then the bakery happened, and it became my baby instead. It doesn't mean I don't look at young mothers without longing, though. Or single fathers, for that matter.

Brut serves me the first batch, which is more food than I can possibly eat. He asks me to explain where I learned to bake, and it's suddenly my turn to speak despite the breakfast before me.

"The neighbor." The truth is a reminder that it wasn't some sweet granny or my mother like people want to believe, but the neighbor lady who took care of Lauren and me after school. She made all kinds of baked goods, but the first time we made cupcakes, I was hooked. Brut holds my gaze. He knows my family situation wasn't the greatest when I was younger, and he nods, chewing at his lip. My family situation now is nonexistent.

"What were you making last night?"

My face heats at the memory of two firemen walking in on us. "I was experimenting with a fall recipe."

"It smelled delicious. Like vanilla and cinnamon and something sweet."

"Apples," I explain. "Apple cupcakes."

Brut smacks his lips as if he can taste the treat.

"You'll need to visit the bakery in September when it's the house specialty." I spoke without thinking. We just promised no future plans, and Brut looks over the island at me, his eyes growing a deeper blue.

"I'd like that, Lily pad. I'd like that a lot."

Me too. Living only in the week is going to be harder than I thought.

14

Rainy Day Games

[Lily]

After breakfast, I clean up, and Brut sits on the couch. He wanted to help, but I told him, "The cook never cleans."

He's reading when I join him, and that's when I notice his glasses. Dark rimmed and resting on his nose, Brut takes on a studious look. Hot, naughty professor, I decide, and I want to raise my hand to volunteer to learn something. Instead, I take a deep breath and reach for my book on the tray near my forgotten mug of tea. Although I open the pages, I'm staring at the words, imagining myself straddling Brut's lap while he's wearing only his specs.

Yes, professor, I say as I ride him. *Is this how I earn an A?*

When Brut's hand lands on my thigh, as if he's read my thoughts, I haven't read a single word on the page before me. His fingers lightly stroke over my skin, and my flesh pebbles at the tender touch.

"Cold?" he whispers, and I huff. He shakes his head without looking up at me. "I really wish I knew your sounds."

I chuckle as I continue to stare at the words blurring on the page, not able to read a single letter while his palm squeezes my thigh. We last all of a few minutes before he tosses his book on the tray.

"Let's play a game." Under the window to the side of the sliding door, behind the overstuffed chair, is a low shelf with board games. Brut stands and returns with Scrabble. "Up for a word challenge?"

I smile at the possibility. I'd rather play other things, but an official game might cool the jets of my oversensitive imagination. I love word games, and this one is my favorite. Brut removes the tray covering the ottoman and lays out the board. He peers at the inside cover of the box lid before tossing it to the side.

"I suggest we make up our own rules. Dirty word Scrabble."

My head shoots up to look at him as he settles himself on the floor. With one knee raised and bent, his arm perching over it, he's the epitome of casual with his suggestion. I, on the other hand, want to skip the mind challenge and do something physical...and dirty. Instead, I swallow, ignoring the deep flutter in my lower abdomen. *Hold it together, Lily.*

"So, what are the rules?" I ask, spreading the wooden tiles within the bottom of the box, then flipping them so the letters are hidden.

"It's going to be *hard*," he exaggerates. "But *come* up with words related to *sex*. We each take ten or twelve tiles at a time and see what we can spell from them. Squares on the board remain the same for points. Person with the highest score wins."

I swallow again as his eyes narrow in a teasing squint.

"And what do we have for the winner, Brut?" I throw my voice like a cheesy game show host, and Brut bursts into laughter, deep and rich.

"Don't quit your day job, sugar." The endearment warms my insides, and the fluttering turns to flight. A pulse beats between my thighs at the carefree laughter of this man, and I want to tackle him to the floor, sucking in his sound as he's always referencing mine. "But actually, let's wager..." He taps his chin. "Sexual favors."

Forget the flock of flapping birds or the thumping beat. I may have just had a mini-orgasm at the suggestion combined with the hot stare he's giving me.

"Winner takes all," I suggest, trying to keep my voice steady. I don't think there's going to be a loser in this game.

"Winner's choice," Brut clarifies. "I'll go first."

+ + +

The game ends when Brut places the last tiles on the board. M-E.

"How is that a dirty word?" I laugh. Brut has clearly won the game. He's quick to connect tiles while I've been struggling the entire time to come up with combinations, especially as each word he places on the board has me distracted with other thoughts.

"Me. I'm dirty because of all the things I plan to do to you." His rugged, raspy tone pushes me over the edge. If he doesn't kiss me, or touch me, or something, I'm going to combust.

"You're the winner," I say without needing to tally the score. "What would you like to win?" I don't recognize my own voice as it drops.

Brut stands slowly and steps to the couch where I sit. His eyes dance as he peers down at me.

"You're my prize, Lily pad. Lie back." I do as he says, swallowing the dryness in my throat. I'm already so wound up, and his low commanding tone has me on the dangerous edge of imploding before he even touches me. I wiggle to settle on the cushions, and Brut watches me a minute before he tugs the cushions from the back of the couch and tosses them behind it. He climbs between my legs, forcing me to spread for him. His gaze lingers on my body, and I feel self-conscious, but I also feel alive in a way I've never felt before. He wants me—*really wants me*—and I want to please him.

His fingers reach for the hem of my cami, and he briskly pushes the material upward, exposing my breasts. Both his hands cover the roundness, palming the heaviness. He pinches my nipples at the same time, and moisture pools between my thighs. I'm going to have a problem too quickly if he does *that* again.

"You have great tits, sugar." His eyes admire them as he tugs the cami the remainder of the way up my body and over my head. He lays it on the back of the couch and returns his attention to my exposed body. My hips roll upward with ambition of their own. My core wants at the length straining behind the flimsy material of his shorts. He tsks me. "Patience, Lily pad."

I receive my own strip tease as he tugs his tee by the hem and takes his time to drag the worn cotton up his body. With arms stretched over his head, I take in the full view of each book-stacked ab, his lightly salted chest, and the muscular biceps straining to remove his shirt. He catches me watching him and smiles a crooked grin.

His fingers move to the waistband of my shorts, and he takes his sweet time removing them, letting the fabric caress my skin as he shimmies them down my legs. His brow hitches when he notices I'm not wearing any underwear. The slow tease continues, heightening my arousal, which can hardly be contained. Sexy scents waft between us, and Brut lowers his head. He inhales near the apex of my legs.

"You smell delicious." He adds to the torture of his flirty words when he swipes his thumb through my wet folds, pleased with his discovery. "And you're fucking soaked."

Spread-eagle in broad daylight, I should be covering myself from his appraising stare, but I don't feel one bit of hesitation. Desire burns in his bright eyes, and I etch the expression on his face into my memory.

"Here's how we're going to play, Lily." He quickly removes his thumb and reaches with his other hand for tiles on the board game. Six cool, wooden squares hit my stomach. I stretch to read the word, and they slip.

"Uh-uh-uh…no moving. That's the challenge for you or else you don't win."

"I already lost," I snark, my voice sharp as I grow frustrated. *Where's his thumb?*

He replaces the tiles against my belly as he speaks. "Let's see if you still think you lost when I'm done." The tease in his statement forces me to stare up at the ceiling. Taking a slow breath to calm myself, I will myself not to move. The challenge is real because I want to rub against him.

"What does it say?" My voice croaks as I ask.

"Sample." We argued over the word as we played. He said it wasn't sexy, but when I rolled the word over my tongue in a sentence—*I want to sample you*—his pupils dilated. He understood *sample* could be very seductive.

His finger outlines the cupcake at my hip, and I shiver, then hold my breath, hoping not to dislodge the tiles on my belly. As I'm thinking about the possibility of his fingers, his thumb brushes over my clit again. I clench, willing myself not to chase that thick pad, and realize holding still heightens the sensation. Damn it, if I get any higher, I'm going to float away.

"Let's see how sexy the word really is."

77

I don't dare move my head for fear the wooden chips will shift. His firm hands spread my thighs, and then warmth hits my center. I don't flinch as his tongue laps over my clit, but it takes all my strength to remain still.

"Brut," I warn already. "I'm so close."

He smiles against that tight nub before his tongue hits me again, spreading through sensitive folds. He swirls and sucks, and I struggle not to move. My fingers curl into fists, holding back from reaching for his head. He bobs and sways, plunging into me with that strong muscle, and I explode, screaming his name. The tiles slip, but I slap a hand over them, holding them against my belly so he won't stop.

"Don't stop. Please." My back itches to curl, and my thighs quiver to close around his head, but I follow his demand and stay as still as I can. I'm coming so hard stars dance across the ceiling. He doesn't stop his ministrations, and I feel myself building again.

"Brut, I—" Letters won't join to form words. The only joining I want is him and me.

He must sense where I'm going because he removes his mouth too quickly. He leans to his left, and I roll my head to find his forearm swiping the game board to the floor, scattering the tiles in all directions. Brut wraps his arms under my back and hoists me upward. My hands find his shoulders for stability. The concentration on Brut's face remains intense as he removes me from the couch and tosses a blanket on the floor near the ottoman.

"Say yes, Lily pad," he pleads, and I hum my approval although I have no idea what I'm agreeing to. He twists me away from him and gently folds me to my knees, pressing between my shoulder blades so I lay on my front over the ottoman. My breasts hit the cool fabric and pebble harder, if that's even possible. The sharp scrape of the material reminds me how turned on I am. I hold still a second, hearing Brut shuffle with his shorts behind me. Then he slaps my ass and rams into me.

"Brut," I scream as I come the second he enters me. I reach forward for the edge of the ottoman cushion as he grips my hips and fills me repeatedly. Back and forth, he races as my channel clenches at him, fighting the challenge to keep him contained as I release a second time more intensely than the first. I'm lightheaded, but his hammering continues, and I curl back, encouraging him to take what he needs from me.

"Give it to me," I taunt, and he jets off inside me. His fingers dig into my hips as his seed pumps into me, filling me. Pure, unadulterated pleasure courses through my body, flooding my system. I collapse on the ottoman and Brut falls over me.

"Lily, I—" His breath catches, and I'm left to fill in the blanks and form my own words to follow his lead.

I never want to live without you.

I only ever want it to be you.

I've always loved you.

I'm projecting my own thoughts as he takes deep breaths behind me. Exhausted from the exertion, he rests a few minutes, still inside me, and I find I'm up for the challenge he presented earlier. I never want to move from this position.

15

Fun And Games And Dancing In The Rain

[Brut]

I slip out of her and use the blanket to wipe up the mess. I came more than I ever have before, and combined with her soaked pussy, we're sticky and slick.

"Don't move," I say, and she whimpers as if moving is the last thing she wants to do. I worry I've hurt her with my roughness, but the smile on her face alleviates my concern. Kissing her cheek, I rise and reach for another blanket on the arm of the overstuffed chair. Returning, I scoop her up and drag her to the couch, laying us both on our sides to spoon under the light cover. We remain naked, and while I'm spent, my body enjoys the heat of her skin.

"Sleepy?" I ask, but I know she is. However, I'm wound up. The orgasm should have taken everything out of me, but my body won't settle. I wrap my arms around Lily and hold her tightly against me. Words form phrases, and I will her to read my thoughts, like osmosis, as I press my forehead to the back of her head.

I never want to let you go.

Promise you won't leave me.

I love you, Lily. Always have.

"I can hear you thinking," she teases, and I start at the possibility. When I chuckle, she adds, "I like your laugh."

The compliment warms my cheeks. I'm not used to receiving them, and I press a kiss to her nape in response. Her fingers tickle up and down my forearm, and I find the touch soothing, relaxing even.

"My mother used to do this when I couldn't sleep," she says quietly. It takes me a second to process she means the light touch.

"You haven't mentioned your parents. How are they?" I ask. I remember her not having a great relationship with them, and I'm surprised at this seemingly pleasant memory.

"I don't have much to say." Her voice remains soft. "They moved to Texas. We don't talk. We weren't really your typical family."

"Whose family is?" I chuckle lightly. "I had Pop, Hank, and Chopper. A clan of men, one more stubborn than the next."

"I heard about your dad. I'm sorry." Pop died when Chopper was eleven, leaving me under mid-thirty, a single father, and a businessowner. I wasn't any more ahead at forty-five than I'd been at twenty-four when Chopper arrived. I exhale with the thought.

"I really wish I knew your sounds," Lily mocks, and I nip at her neck. She squeaks. "What was that for?"

"Being a smartass."

"I think you like my ass." Her playful voice makes me grin. To emphasize her point, she presses said ass back at me.

"I do like it, especially when it's aimed at me. But behave."

"You're no fun," she jokes, but the comment strikes a chord.

"Am I...no fun?"

Lily twists at the seriousness in my question. I don't let her fully spin, so she looks at me over her shoulder. "You're kidding, right?"

"No. Hank and Midge sent me on this vacation to have fun, and Midge asked me if I remembered how to have it...as if I didn't have fun anymore."

"Do you?" Lily asks, pausing a beat. "What do you do that makes *you* happy?"

I have to think about it and find no immediate answers. I work. For years, I looked after Pop, the business, Hank, and Chopper. With Pop gone, Hank solidly on his own feet, and Chopper itching to leave the house, the business is the only thing left for me. The garage isn't fun.

"I don't know." And that's the truth. I don't know what would make me happy, or be exciting, or even just pleasant for a day.

"What about surfing?" Lily asks as if reading my mind again.

"Okay, there's that, but I hardly get to do it."

"What about spending time with Chopper?" Something in her voice hesitates, and I shake my head behind her.

"He's getting too old to be with his old man." The thought makes me sad. I don't often consider how much I enjoy my son until he isn't

L.B. Dunbar

present, and lately, he's been very absent, taking classes and trying to find his way in the world.

"What about…?" When the pause lasts too long, I sense she's changed her mind about asking what's next on her list.

"Ask," I tease.

"What about dirty Scrabble?"

I only take a second to consider it before a smile breaks on my face. "Yeah, Lily. That was fun."

Her shoulders relax, and I press a quick kiss there. I recall teaching her how to surf, swiping batter on her chest, and the sex we've had. "I think being here with you has been the most fun I've had in years. Possibly ever." I hold my breath after I speak, afraid I've revealed too much.

"Me too," she whispers, raising my hand to her lips and kissing my knuckles. I snuggle into her, knowing I'll never get her close enough. "Maybe we can play again."

The suggestion makes me chuckle. "I'd love to play with you anytime, Lily."

And I would. Surf boards. Board games. Sex games. I'm willing to participate in anything with her as long as I feel like I do at this moment.

Being with Lily is…fun.

+ + +

We sleep with the sound of rain peppering the back deck. The gray day keeps the room dim as we cuddle on the couch. We remain naked, and when I wake, I run my hand over the outline of her body. She isn't overly curvy as much as her body is firm. She takes care of herself, and I appreciate the work she's done to stay fit. Her breasts are large for her size and fill my hands, which means they're plenty big. My mouth waters to be filled with them.

But there's more than just her body.

I've heard my brother say "I more you" to his wife. It's a secret code between them, yet I suddenly understand what it means. I want more of Lily. Her body. Her heart. Her soul.

She shivers under my stroking. "That tickles," she says in a groggy voice. Another sound I want to hear every day.

"I didn't mean to wake you."

"It's okay. I need to pee." She groans as she stretches upward. "That might have been too much information."

"Maybe." I laugh as I move the arm she slept on and squeeze my fist to get the blood flowing again. I watch Lily's backside as she stands and then she reaches for my T-shirt on the floor. Covering herself in my clothing, I stare as she rakes her fingers through her chin-length hair.

"You're so beautiful, Lily." The words tumble out, and I like the crook of her lips as she looks back at me.

"So are you." Her smile widens, before she steps out of my view for the bathroom. When she returns, she sits on the ottoman facing me. The blanket rests low on my hips but doesn't contain the stiffy growing the longer she looks at me like she is. *This.* This is the look I want.

Longing. Yearning.

Possibly loving?

"What's on your bucket list, Brut?"

"My bucket list?" I scoff.

"You know, your list of things you want to accomplish in life. More than a list of fun activities, but things you want to achieve. Maybe things that would be *fun* to achieve."

"I guess I haven't thought about it." I rub a hand over my hair as I lie on my back. I'm sure the locks are standing up, but I don't care. I feel Lily watching me as I stare up at the ceiling. "I wanted to be a teacher."

Her voice softens. "History, right?"

I twist to look at her. Her memory is impeccable, and something pinches in my chest. *Before*, she knew I was taking classes part time but talking about my studies was the last thing on my mind when Lily was near me. Going to school fell to shit around the time we broke apart.

"Tell me more. Which history?"

"American, I guess. I like the progress we've made, but we have so much more to learn."

"Yes, we do," she teases. "What about fatherhood? Was that on your list?"

L.B. Dunbar

I close my eyes, not really wanting to discuss Chopper with her. Fatherhood wasn't ever officially on or off a list. It certainly wasn't something I thought would happen in the manner in which it did. I can't explain to her how I don't regret him. I regret *that* night. The one when my son was conceived. Stupid, weak, drunken decision.

"I always knew I'd be a father, but I hadn't given it much thought. I knew I'd want kids, but…" My voice drifts. *But not in the way I did.* I roll my head to look at her, expecting to lose her in the memory, but her expression says she isn't judging me. She's smiling weakly, looking down at me with something else in her eyes. Another form of longing. She doesn't have any children.

"He's a great kid." Even when he's a pain in the ass. This conversation makes me nervous, though, so I switch the tide. "What about you? What was on your bucket list?"

She waves dismissively. "Oh, my list is fulfilled. The bakery was the only thing on it."

I raise a brow in question. *That's it?* She mentioned love, marriage and babies. But I think better of digging deeper into why she doesn't have those things. I also hate how I notice I'm not on her list. Then again, why would I be a number in her life plan? I scratched myself off it.

The more I think about this, the more I don't like the cop-out I'm giving myself.

Fucking win her back, my heart knocks on my ribs.

I notice the rain is a soft drizzle outside behind her. The sky lightens, and the sun breaks for a moment. I sit upright, startling her when I reach for my shorts, slipping them up my legs. I stand quickly and hold out a hand for her.

"Trust me," I say.

Her blue eyes peer up at me, and a small grin curls her lips. Her hand slips into mine, and I tug her upward, then lead her outside.

"What are you doing?" She lightly laughs as our bare feet hit the damp wooden planks. A soft rain kisses our skin as the sun seems to hover over only our section of the beach. A sun shower of sorts.

"I'm dancing in the rain with you." I wrap an arm around her lower back and link my other hand with hers. Holding our joined fingers pressed between our chests, I sway at the hips, encouraging her to follow my lead.

"Dancing in the rain." Her voice lowers as she parrots me, but her face fills with sunshine. She tips her head back, letting the feathery drops caress her cheeks. Then her head rights, and her eyes widen as she repeats on a whisper, "Dancing in the rain."

Check one of the things she thought she'd do with another man. Sorry, *Brad*. He didn't deserve her, and I'm glad it never happened with him. I want to be her first at something.

In my head, I make my first bucket list.

She's the only item on it.

16

Dining In

[Brut]

After three rounds of dancing, the sky darkens and opens up again. Lily squeals as we take the few steps back into the house. She's drenched, and my wet T-shirt serves as a second skin. *Damn*, I like her in my clothes.

"I think I need a shower," Lily says, and my lips curl.

"I'll join you."

Our time spent under warmer water is another game of discovery. We don't have sex again, but we touch, caress, and massage, and when I can't take it anymore, we simultaneously give each other hand jobs. Other than the handiwork I give myself, I haven't had one like this since Lily gave them to me when she was nineteen. Just thinking of her eager fingers back then—hastily unbuckling my belt and slipping her hand into my pants—makes me shake my head. Why did I ever hold her off?

I didn't want to ruin her.

Not only was she younger than me, but I always felt as if I would never get where I wanted. I worked hard, but I didn't want to make any commitments until I had a clear path. The shop. School. I wanted more from life, but life asked more of me. When I made one terrible mistake, I threw myself off course, and I always look back on *that* night as a sign—Lily was not meant to be mine.

However, she's with me now.

Patting dry, she says, "I'll meet you downstairs." We showered in my room, which is nearly identical to hers, but her clothes remain in her bedroom. When she walks away, I have the strangest sense of loss. *You're being ridiculous, man.* It will only be ten minutes. Fifteen tops.

Downstairs, I flip on the television while I wait for her on the couch. The Dodgers are playing, and I'm a huge fan. Wonder if Lily would like to attend a game with me? *That's making plans*, I remind myself, and we aren't allowed to go there, but watching the game makes me think of Tommy Carrigan's new wife, Edie. I met her at a small dinner to celebrate Hank and Midge's wedding. She told me her son plays in the minor leagues in the Midwest, and he's hoping to be called up someday. Lily already knows Midge from various occasions, including the cupcakes served at the dinner. Midge told Lily about this place. Does Lily also know Edie? Are they all friends? Could we all hang out together as couples when Lily and I return? All these questions lead to thoughts of the future, and suddenly, the self-imposed time limit on our sexcation makes me a little nauseous. I don't want us to end.

My ankle rests over a knee, and my foot shakes with anticipation. *What's taking so long?* Then, I hear her behind me in the kitchen. Twisting on the couch, I watch her. My breath hitches for the millionth time at her beauty. A smattering of freckles covers her cheeks from her fresh suntan. Her semi-wet hair kinks and curls. Her eyes shift up from whatever she's doing, and she catches me observing her. I'm disappointed she hasn't walked over to join me on the couch.

"I've missed you." My voice is quiet, but the words carry to her, and her blue eyes sparkle with my comment.

"It's only been twelve minutes," she teases, evidently misunderstanding me.

"No, Lil. I've *missed* you," I repeat, willing her to interpret my meaning. It's not the twelve minutes, though I appreciate her exactness. It's the years we've been separated. It's the time between then and now.

She doesn't speak, her lip twitching at the corner as though she's forcing the smile to remain in place. My heart drops as I realize I've said too much. *Don't push*, I remind myself, wanting to kick myself because it's clear she doesn't feel the same way. Why would she have missed me? I made it impossible for that to happen.

"Anyway…are you hungry?" I ask when she still doesn't respond, continuing to stare back at me from too far away. "I could order something for us?"

"Don't worry about it. I'll make us something." Her eyes drift down to her hands on the island. Something's up, but I can't put my finger on what it could be. We had a great afternoon, but her sudden quiet unsettles me.

"Want help?" I offer. I'm practically sending telepathy for her to invite me to the kitchen.

"Can you cook dinner, too?" One eyebrow arches as she jests, the edge to her forced smile softening.

"Single father, remember?"

"Yes, but I thought breakfast was your specialty." Another huff of air mixes with the humor, and I think we've returned to normal. My concerns at her standoffishness are nothing, I tell myself. "Why don't you just sit there a minute? Watch the game."

Sit still? Relax? I've found over the years that no sooner do I sit to watch a baseball game then someone needs me. Pop, my son, Hank. For me to just sit is a foreign concept, and I ask for confirmation, "Are you sure?"

Lily nods with a more reassuring smile and I turn back to the television.

Even though my eyes focus on the game, I'm listening to her behind me instead. Metal clangs against metal as she removes pans from a drawer. Cabinets open and close. The fridge does the same. Water is poured into a pot, and something grainy follows. Next comes a sizzle in a pan. I listen with intent. *Is this what it would sound like if she were in my home?* My gut twists at all I've missed and all I don't have.

When I hear a mixer whirl to life, I spin to watch her instead of baseball. Lily is a natural in the kitchen. The look on her face says she's in her element. It's like me working on cars. I concentrate. I'm producing something.

The mixer wheezes to a stop, and she catches me observing her again.

"I promised I wouldn't do it, but I checked in with Esther. She works for me." Something in her voice causes my worry from moments ago to return.

"I know," I admit.

Lily blinks. "You do?" Her response seems to derail her from her initial intention.

"I came into the bakery about a month ago. You weren't there."

Obviously.

"What were you doing there?"

Suddenly, I'm nervous to admit I went to her shop in hopes to see her. "Buying cupcakes, duh."

Her responding snort along with a tilt of her head wordlessly questions me.

"Hank told me all about your place. When Chopper admitted he'd been there, too, I guess I was curious. Esther introduced herself, and when I told her to tell you Brut said hello, she looked like she wanted to stab me with a cake knife."

Lily laughs. "That sounds like Esther."

"So she's heard of me, perhaps?"

Lily's face pinkens, and she swipes her hair back, tucking it behind one ear. "Maybe."

I stand, circle the couch, and stop opposite her at the island. "What did you tell her?"

Lily shrugs as she chews the corner of her lip. My shoulders fall. Whatever she shared, it wasn't good.

"So, what did Esther say? How's business?"

Something in the way Lily's lips twist tells me business might not be what they discussed. I was the topic of their conversation, and it wasn't good again.

"It's fine." Her tone solidifies my fear. Nope. *Not good.* At. All.

Switching subjects becomes imperative. "Whatcha making?" I don't want anything to spoil how great this day has been for me, so I'll play the ignorant card and let things slide for the moment.

The combination of grains and vegetables in the pan reminds me of the dish she enjoyed two nights ago when I came in from the bar. "You're a pretty healthy eater," I comment, not scoffing at the food, but I typically need a bit more protein than what she's making. "Are you a vegetarian?"

"No. I just watch what I eat. I bake cupcakes for a living, so if I don't eat right, I'll weigh three hundred pounds."

I can't even imagine Lily on the heavy side, but I do envision a bump on her belly. She'd be beautiful pregnant.

L.B. Dunbar

"You're making cupcakes again?" My question expresses my concern as my eyes drift to the hand mixer. She told me she bakes when she's anxious. Did something make her nervous? Her discussion with Esther perhaps?

"I don't typically bake day-old batter, preferring to make everything fresh and from scratch the day of baking, but sometimes, we have too much. I bake the extra and give it to a homeless shelter."

The comment reminds me her bakery isn't in the best neighborhood. On top of that, I don't even know where she lives. Hopefully not near her shop.

"You're a good person, Lily." Her face lights up as a flush slowly climbs her cheeks. "But your shop isn't in the safest neighborhood."

Lily turns her back to pop the cupcakes in the oven. She's multitasking, and once again, I see how the kitchen is her happy place. There's a rhythm to how she moves.

"It's all I could afford. Besides, the kitchen was more important than the location. I just needed a place to bake other than my original tiny apartment."

"Where do you live, Lil?" When she turns back to face me, her lips twist, locked tight. "You don't have to say if you don't want to." Admittedly, I'm crushed.

"It's not that. It's just…I thought you didn't want any future stuff, so you probably shouldn't know where I live."

My head flinches back, startled by her comment. "Is that what you want? To keep it a secret?"

We agreed not to talk of the future, but knowing her address isn't a commitment. Chewing on her lip, she avoids my eyes as she thinks.

"I already know where you work," I remind her.

She nods slowly, working the corner of her mouth before she speaks. "I live above the bakery."

"*What?*" Maybe this is why she didn't want to tell me where she lives. She knew how I'd react. "Lily, that can't be safe."

"It's fine."

"Why the hell do you live there?"

"Because the apartment came with the shop."

90

"Are you struggling? Can't you afford to live somewhere else?" Her business isn't my business, but I don't like her arrangement. Her cupcakes are delicious, and when I visited the bakery, the place was busy for an evening. Esther was explaining to another customer about some big order she was working on in the back. Because Cupcakes has to be financially sound.

Lily's hands pause from stirring vegetables. "No, Brut. I'm just frugal."

Her sharp tone startles me while making me chuckle. I walk around the island and pin her from behind, stretching out my arms to cage her in. "Okay, Lily pad." I soften my tone. "What did I say?"

She ignores me at first but finally speaks. "I've been taking care of myself for a long time, Brut."

"I know that. I'm not suggesting you aren't competent. It's just…I worry about your safety." I press a kiss to her shoulder to emphasize my concern.

"Why?" Her mouth remains open a second before she clamps her lips closed and shifts directions. "I can handle myself."

"I'm sure you can."

I don't doubt she can take care of herself, but I'm worried about her. *I* want to take care of her. She doesn't seem appeased by my words, though, so I dismiss the conversation. I don't want to fight with her, and whatever has her on edge, I'm ignoring the tension in the room as well. I want us back to where we were an hour ago.

My chin rests on her shoulder, and I peer down at the counter to find a mixing bowl filled with a creamy substance.

"This place is so well stocked."

"Oh, most of these ingredients I bought. I always travel with cupcake tins," she says, flipping the veggies into the air and catching them back in the pan.

"Why?"

"Because I never know when inspiration will strike, or stress needs to be relieved." Her voice teases.

"Are you stressed out?" I mumble the question into her neck, my heart rate slowly rising.

L.B. Dunbar

"I don't know what to think." Her tone remains low, hesitant, as if something weighs on her mind.

"Don't think." I press into her skin. "Not yet." *Please*, I beg. *Not yet.*

She nods, and I wrap an arm around her waist while she finishes cooking our dinner. Holding her against me, I'm afraid to let go. Afraid of ever letting her go again.

17

Close Call

[Lily]

I shouldn't have called Esther. For the first time ever, I didn't want to check on my business. I just wanted to be, like Brut said. However, my head overruled my heart, and doubt bombarded me the second I went to my room alone to dress. Pajama day was obviously over, so I pulled on jean shorts, a tank, and a plaid shirt sleeves rolled to my elbows. I wasn't going to go for my phone, but the next thing I knew, I had it in my hand.

"How's the vacay, boss lady?" Esther had asked without a formal greeting.

"Good. It's really a great house. Nice setup."

"What's wrong?" she'd asked, an instant shift from pleasantry to mother bear.

"Nothing." My voice squeaked, and I scrubbed my head. I didn't know what to say next. Esther waited me out, knowing I couldn't take the silence. "Something's happened."

"What?" Her voice returned to playful inquiry, as if hoping for juicy gossip. Oh, what I had to tell her was juicy all right.

"So, it turns out Brut Paige is here."

"What? In the area? What are the odds?"

"Umm...no. As in literally staying at this house. The same house as me."

"What?" Esther had bellowed. "How did that happen?"

I scratched my forehead, a nervous giggle on the edge of my lips. "You know, I'm not exactly certain."

"Huh," Esther huffed.

"Yep."

"So..."

"So?"

L.B. Dunbar

The conversation wasn't going anywhere, and I should have hung up. Instead, I hung on.

"Okay, Lily. What the hell is going on down there?"

"I don't know." I fell back on the bed, staring up at the ceiling. What were we doing? *That was the question I'd intermittently been asking myself.*

"Oh my God. Did you sleep with him?" Esther has an uncanny way of reading people, and she's pretty direct.

I closed my eyes even though she couldn't see me. My silence answered her question.

"Brut, huh? How do you feel about this? I mean, I bet it felt good, but I mean how do you feel-*feel?"*

"Yeah, Brut," I answered dreamily in monosyllables because I couldn't form coherent answers.

"That good, huh?"

"So good." I exhaled.

I haven't felt this physically alive in a long time. My skin practically tingled from his touch. My body hummed. But my heart? My heart knocked inside my chest, asking: what are you doing? This is the man who broke your heart. He slept with your sister. He had a baby with her. He never looked at you again.

Just what. Are. You. Doing?

Fulfilling a fantasy, I want to answer. Completing my bucket list.

What's something you wish you could accomplish? I'd asked Brut earlier. Having his love would have been on my list.

"Lily." My name sharply spoken had snapped me from my thoughts. *"So why did you call?"*

"Talk some sense into me."

"Oh no, girlfriend. Sense walked out the door as soon as you let him crawl between your legs."

"Esther," I'd squeaked, hoping Brut had already gone downstairs, but then I remembered he couldn't hear Esther anyway.

"Look. The first question you ask yourself is do you regret what happened?"

"*No.*" I didn't even hesitate. I didn't regret it, and I didn't consider it a mistake. I just didn't know what to consider it.

"*Okay, definitely between-the-thighs talking. Next question is do you want it to happen again?*"

"*Yes.*" Another answer without hesitation.

"*More vagina-speak.*" Esther had tsked. "*I say, just go with it. You aren't committing to anything. You're on vacation. Enjoy yourself.*"

"*That's what he said.*"

"*Am I supposed to bah-dum-dum here?*"

"*No, just he set some rules. Like one week. No past. No future. Just be.*"

"*Sounds like you've already broken a few rules, like the 'I will never be with Brut Paige again' rule.*" A heavy *mmm-hmm* followed Esther's reminder. "*But as the saying goes, rules are meant to be broken.*"

I wanted to smile in triumph, but something still weighed heavily on me. I'd always lusted after Brut, but I swore I'd never be with him again. I said I forgave him, and I did.

Then why did I feel so guilty?

+ + +

Brut and I eat dinner at the kitchen island while the baseball game plays in the background. I'm curious if the hum of the sporting event is a typical sound in his house. He turns occasionally at a cheer of the crowd or groan from the announcer, but for the most part, he's attentive to our conversation, which steers suspiciously clear of our past.

I've missed you.

I didn't know what to say. *I've longed for you. Why did you do it?*

The two thoughts run together in my head. All those years ago, I had some answers, but over time, my perspective changed. My opinion of Brut as a liar and a cheater matured into acceptance that he wasn't fully to blame. He was young, vibrant, and horny. Keeping me at arm's length made me wonder, though. Maybe it was me. He liked to play with me but didn't want to finish the game. *With me.*

He's into finishing *in the past twenty-four hours,* I remind myself.

95

I don't think I've had as many orgasms in the past year as I've had with him in the past day. This worries me. Maybe Esther's right. Maybe it's a different body part thinking for me. I can't get reattached.

I worry about you.

Why now? I wanted to ask. Why does he suddenly care?

"Let me help you frost." I'm standing opposite him at the counter when he asks and I notice he's waiting for an answer.

"I got it." My tone is off. My brain working too much as the evening transitions to night. "Besides, they need to cool."

"Hmm," he moans as he rounds the island and stands behind me, caging me in like he did earlier. "So do you."

What does that mean? What is *wrong with me?*

Brut reaches around me and swipes a finger through the homemade frosting. At room temperature, the mixture is easier to spread. With this thought in mind, I feel frosting coat the side of my neck. Instantly, Brut's mouth follows, sucking up the sugary topping, and I melt a little at the contact.

"Brut," I mumble as another swish of icing hits the other side of my neck. I spin to face him, and he lowers without a word, lapping at a second helping on my skin.

"You seem off, Lily pad. What's going on?" Slowly, he unbuttons my shirt. My hands grip the counter behind me, willing them not to touch him. I don't know what's wrong. It's like a switch flipped, and I can't stop wondering what we are doing.

But then he touches me like this, and I can't think anymore.

When he finishes opening my shirt, he pushes the material off my shoulders. I'm wearing another cotton tank without a bra. He angles around me again, covering the spreading knife with frosting while his other hand lifts the top of my tank.

"You aren't coming anywhere near me with that knife," I choke out with a laugh, the tension slowly leaving me at the teasing expression on his face.

He sets the knife back in the bowl and hooks another finger in the creamy mixture instead. Lowering the front of my tank top, he trusses up my breasts and tweaks one nipple with a coating of frosting. Leaning

96

forward, he covers the globe with his mouth and sucks at the dollop covering me.

"You're better than a cupcake, Lily pad." He reaches for another helping of frosting, but his hand freezes. I twist to look over my shoulder, following the direction of his eyes.

"What's this?" He lifts the bottle and holds it between us.

Caramel.

I planned to decoratively garnish the apple-vanilla cupcakes I'm experimenting with. My breath hitches, my chest rising and falling with anticipation of what he might do next. With firm fingers on my sternum, he presses me back a little and drizzles the gooey liquid over one breast. Sticky and thick, the gel slowly rolls down the slope, and Brut watches before diving forward to follow the trail with his tongue.

"Delicious," he mutters as he chases the drip.

I'm lost once again to the way he devours me. His tongue working over the sensitive tips of my nipples. His hands grip my waist before his fingers deftly travel to my shorts. The button on my cutoff jeans unsnaps, and then…his phone rings.

"Ignore it," he mutters, but the vibration of the mechanism on the counter can't be dismissed nor can the gritty rap music with the name *Chopper* in it. Brut lifts his head and peers over my shoulder.

"Damn it, Chopper," he mumbles.

"You should take it." I don't want him to ignore his son. In fact, the trill of his son's name draws me back to reality.

Brut reaches around me, picking up his phone with one hand but stilling me from moving with the other on my breast. He squeezes as he answers with a choked greeting and a teasing glint in his eyes. He watches his fingers tweak me while he nods in response to something his son has said.

Two can play this game. Swiftly, I tug down his basketball shorts. He's wearing a pair similar to what he wore earlier in the day. To my surprise, he's commando, and I drag myself downward between the counter and his thighs. He pulls back, surmising my intention, but I grip his shaft before he can step away from me.

My eyes narrow up at him as my tongue slips forward and licks across the swollen tip. He chokes again into the phone while his other hand falls behind me, bracing himself on the counter near my head. He's shaking his head at me, warning me, knowing he's in a precarious position. With the hold I have on him, I can't pull back, and something in the way he stands says he doesn't want to.

"Chopper, can I call you back?" With the question on his tongue, I draw him into my mouth and suck him deep. My tongue twirls around the thick length. A soft *fuck* purrs above me as his hand covers my hair. Hollowing my cheeks, I drag back to the tip before filling my mouth with him once again. He tenderly cups my chin.

"Sheila? What did *she* want?"

Something in his voice instantly stops me. The way he said the other woman's name along with the bitterness of his question prevents me from continuing. I release him, embarrassed by what I'm doing. I'm sucking his dick while he asks about another woman.

Brut has other women in his life, despite what he said earlier in the day. The past crashes into me fiercer than the wave that took me off the surfboard yesterday.

I stand slowly, using the cabinet at my back to guide me upward on shaky legs. Once fully upright, Brut pins me to the counter with his hips, but my hands come to his shoulders, pressing him away from me. I can't look at him.

"Chopper, I gotta call you back."

"No," I say, too loud, too close to the phone. I glare up at him, and then I hear his son's voice.

"Who's that?"

Brut's wide eyes weigh on my face as I try to press more firmly at his shoulders.

Let me go.

"That? No one. Television is too loud."

I stop shoving at him, my body going lax at his words. His eyes hold mine for a moment.

I'm his dirty little secret once again.

When his body relaxes against mine, I use the moment to push him again. The force breaks me free of his cage, and I race for the stairs.

I can't believe I fell for him…a second time.

18

Making Plans After All

[Brut]

I climb the stairs with heavy feet and an even heavier heart. I admit I panicked. And the look of horror on Lily's face will be forever burned in my brain next to the expression she wore when I finally told her the truth all those years ago.

I slept with someone else.

I pause for a moment outside Lily's door, uncertain how to proceed. I raise my knuckles to knock, but I freeze once again. What do I say to her?

The truth. Always go with the truth.

I decide not to knock. Instead, I turn the knob and let myself into her room. "Lily," I call out softly.

"Please leave me alone." Her words are choppy and short. She lies on her side with her back to the door like last night. She's hurt. I saw it written in her face downstairs. And she's crying. Shit. Shit. *Shit.*

"Don't cry, Lily pad," I coax, crossing to the bed in two quick steps. She rolls to face me, tracking my movements.

"I'm not crying," she snaps. "I'm pissed."

"Why are you mad?" Taken aback by the sharpness of her voice, I round the corner of the bed to stand next to it.

"I'm mad at myself."

"Why?"

"I can't believe I'm doing it again."

My throat tightens at her words. I don't like where I think this is going. "Doing what?"

"This morning, you said there wasn't anyone else." Her voice sounds petulant, riddled with jealous anger. I shouldn't like it, but I do.

I also notice she hasn't answered my question. "There isn't."

"Then who's Sheila?"

My head flinches back at the mention of the woman who comes into the shop a little too often for my liking.

"She's no one."

"I thought I was *no one*," she bites.

"Lily," I admonish softly, reaching out for her hip as I sit on the edge of the mattress next to her. "You aren't no one. I didn't know what to say. Did you want me to tell my son I was here with you?" *I would tell the world if you wanted me to.*

Her eyes close, and she shakes her head. A subtle tension trickles between us.

"Right," she mumbles. "One week."

As much as I wish to discuss our calendar, I need to tackle one issue at a time. "Sheila's married."

Lily's mouth falls open, and her shock says she's ready to rip into me.

I hold up a hand to stop her. "She's an unhappy woman who comes into the shop looking for something more than I'm willing to give her."

"Have you given her something that she'd want more of?" Lily chokes.

"No. I don't do married women."

"Why would she want something from you?" The hesitation in Lily's voice brings back a wave of unwanted memory.

"Because she assumes that, as a single man, I'm desperate to get under her hood. Which I'm not."

Her bright blue eyes narrow as she glares at me. "Did you just try to be funny? Was that a car joke in the middle of...of our fight?"

For some reason, this makes me chuckle. I shift to crawl over her and reach for her wrists, pinning her to the bed as I straddle her hips. I want her full attention, and I lower my head bringing our noses close.

"Are we fighting?"

"Yes." The singular word cracks like a whip. Her hips buck under me, and my response forces me to firmly press her into the mattress with a thrust of my own.

L.B. Dunbar

"What are we fighting about?" Because there's nothing to argue over. Sheila is a dead issue. I'm not interested in married women—or any woman—other than Lily.

"You were thinking about another woman when…"

"When what, Lily pad?" My voice lowers as does my nose to hers, rubbing along the tip. "When you had my dick in your mouth?"

Lily gasps, and her hips shoot upward once again. If she hopes to force me off her, she's sadly mistaken. I'm not getting off, except *with her.*

"Speaking of that…" I lean forward and nip at her neck. Her head dips as her shoulder lifts at the sudden sting. "That was rather naughty of you when I was on the phone."

Her mouth pops open again, but before she can speak, I bring my lips within a millimeter of hers.

"And for the record, I was *not* thinking of another woman when my dick was deep down your throat. But I like that you're jealous."

"I wasn't jealous," she snipes, still feisty beneath me. "Besides I have *nothing* to be jealous of, right?"

For a second, I hear the nineteen-year-old Lily with a whine in her voice. The one who used to beg me to take her, plead with me to have sex with her. *Don't you want me, Brut?* She had no idea then, just as she has no idea now. I want her with every part of me. Dick. Heart. Soul.

My mouth hovers over hers, breathing into her. I need what I say next to sink inside her somehow.

"Lily pad," I begin, her name rough on my tongue. "You are not, nor have you ever been, no one to me. I wanted you more than I was willing to admit back then, but I want you more than anything else now. I'm the one who's jealous. Jealous of any other man who's had a taste of you. Jealous of fucking cupcakes, for that matter, and the attention you give them. I want you all to myself. I want your everything and beyond, just for me."

My lips cover hers, not allowing her to argue back or bite me again. *Kiss me, Lily,* I silently plea as I hungrily devour her tender skin, which slowly melts beneath mine. My hands still hold her wrists hostage, but she relaxes underneath me. My palms flatten, coasting down her inner

102

arms to her elbows before reaching for her face. Cupping her cheeks, I deepen our kiss.

I want you, Lily. Then and now.

Frantically, she reaches for me, tugging at my shorts. Her feet come to my sides, and she uses her toes to press my shorts farther down my thighs.

"Uh-uh-uh," I mutter against her. "Paybacks are a bitch." My fingers fumble with her jean shorts. "You left me hanging down there. No pun intended."

Her fingers reach between us, encircling me and stroking. "Let me finish, then." A hitch in her voice—desperate, panicked, hesitant as if she wants to prove something to me—forces my rebuff.

"I *should* make you finish," I warn, hastily removing her jean shorts. "But I think I'm going to enjoy torturing you instead."

I lower between her thighs, and my tongue splits her open. Her knees spread wide, and her fingers fist in my hair as I take my time to devour her.

"Right there," she purrs, but then I move. Tender fingers nudge me to return where she wants, but I don't readily comply. I take my time, dragging my tongue lazily around where she wishes.

"So close," she whimpers as she tenses. Moving to kiss her inner thighs, I drag my tongue along her skin, trailing away from where she wants me.

"Brut." She grunt-groans, and I add the frustrated noise to my list of her sounds.

I want all her sounds. *All of her.*

"Don't ever do that again, Lily pad." I nip her inner thigh, then shift and blow a warm breath into her center. Next, I circle my nose close to her core, still refusing contact where she needs.

"I won't," she whines in promise. Her head rolling back and forth on the pillow. "Just finish me." Her voice squeaks as her legs squirm, eager for the friction from my tongue.

"Say it. You won't ever leave me." I know what I'm asking, but does she? Does she catch my double meaning? I don't want her walking away from me again.

103

L.B. Dunbar

Euphoric and edgy, her fingers tighten around my head. "I won't ever leave—"

The rest of her promise is cut off when I return my tongue to her wet heat and finish her as she asked.

+ + +

I wake to an empty bed. Again.

Goddammit.

Rolling to my back, I stare up at the ceiling. A quiet laugh and small smile grace my lips, recalling the past twenty-four hours. My dick currently stands at attention with the reminders of all we've done. We didn't have sex last night, but the oral discoveries were enough. I haven't felt this alive in years.

Is it just the sex?

I roll my head to her empty pillow and then twist my body to caress the cool covering. I have my answer instantly.

No. No, this is not only sex for me.

I wake missing her. I smell her scent on my skin and in the sheets, and I ache for her. It's not just my lower appendage's longing, either.

One week, she muttered last night. Does she think that's all I want? Does she not see that, in the course of one day, I want all things with her? Everything and beyond.

I spin lazily from the bed, stretching before reaching for my shorts on the floor. Another chuckle escapes as I recall her wild maneuvers to remove them. Her feet are wicked talented. Crossing to the double doors leading to the balcony, I see another glorious day of sunshine. The brightness is a welcome reprieve from yesterday's rain. Don't get me wrong, I enjoyed every second of yesterday, but I feel itchy to get outside and do something. Lily and I need some time beyond our bubble. I need to prove we are more than the space inside this house.

As I stand at the door, gaze roving over the sand, I catch on Lily stretching and twisting in rhythmic movements. Arms extended, she turns her head slowly to one side. Her moves are graceful and purposeful, methodical even. Is she doing yoga? The movements and thoughtfully timed pauses hint she might be.

I return to my room to retrieve a T-shirt and head to the first floor. Coffee awaits me in the machine, and I help myself to a cup, sipping slowly as I walk across the deck. *Dang, even her coffee is delicious.* After another sip, I set my mug on the railing and cross the sand to her setup.

"You weren't in bed this morning." The words burst forth sharply because a strange hum under my skin builds from her absence. I don't like waking to find her gone.

"Good morning," she says, not breaking her pose. "I didn't want to wake you."

"I didn't want to wake alone." I cross my arms, emphasizing I'm upset.

Her head snaps in my direction, and her brows pinch. "I couldn't sleep."

Suddenly, I'm concerned because I suffer from lack of sleep at times. My mind races with all the things I need to do, all the things I didn't complete, and all the things I should have done.

"Just woke early," she amends, shrugging as she shifts to a new pose. "It happens. Insomnia, I guess."

With all the sexual exertion yesterday, I was exhausted by the time we went to bed. With Lily curled into me, her head on my chest for a while, I'd fallen into a deep sleep. I've slept alone for a long time. I don't know that I could sleep with someone on me, but once Lily moved away from me in the night, I missed her touch. I followed the curl of her body and wrapped an arm over her back as she moved to her stomach. She must have sensed my need for closeness because her foot hooked over my ankle as if she sought me in her sleep. At least, that's what I told myself when it happened.

"Whatcha thinking about?" I assume her insomnia comes from racing thoughts, like mine. The past popped up last night. Was she thinking of unspoken things?

"I just find the older I get, the less I sleep. If I have six hours, I count it as a good night. Maybe it's the bakery. I'm used to waking early." She elongates her arm, curves her hand upward, and straightens her body.

L.B. Dunbar

Her blue eyes hit mine, and I want to crumple to the sand from the intensity. I reach out for a loose hair of hers and curl it over her ear.

"I'm sorry I snapped," I mutter, feeling repentant for more than just my tone. Not willing to get any heavier with my emotions, though, I amend myself. "Good morning."

Then I kiss her.

A silent prayer escapes me.

Lord, let me wake every day to this woman, and I promise to kiss her like this in greeting without question.

Lily pulls back first, slowly, lingering. Her soft smile grows to a sheepish grin. She's so fucking pretty.

"Let's do something today," I blurt. "Go out for a bit."

"Really?" She beams like sunshine, and I'll do anything as long as she keeps looking at me like she is. Excited. Eager. Energized.

"Sure. What did you want to do besides hang at the beach? Was there somewhere you wanted to go in the area? Someplace you wanted to see?" We aren't far from San Diego. "There's plenty of shopping, more surfing, hiking, sightseeing, cave kayaking—"

"We could go to the zoo?"

Say what?

Admittedly, I've never been to the zoo, which probably tosses me into the bad parent category. Never took Chopper. Never signed up to chaperone when the school went on an educational visit. For some reason, the concept of caged animals reminds me of myself. Trapped. Confined. Enclosed in a space I didn't want to be. The garage is my exhibit.

"Orrrrr not." Lily's excitement falters as her brows pinch. Her hands have found their way to my chest, smoothing over my T-shirt in her enthusiasm, but her palms stop stroking. I reach for her wrists, encircling them and lifting one palm to my lips.

"The zoo sounds great."

"We can do something else," she begins. "Something you want to do instead—"

My finger on her lip stops her from speaking. "Going to the zoo with you is what I want to do."

And I find I mean it. I want to spend the day with her in any capacity. So, the zoo it is.

19

Caged Animal

[Lily]

Brut seems hesitant about the zoo, but I drop my cautious questioning when he swears he wants to go. Twenty minutes after leaving the house, we park at one of the most famous zoos in the world. I haven't been to one since I was a kid. Considering I thought I'd be a mother one day, I'd believed visits to the zoo would be a staple in my life. The thought hits me hard for a moment—because I'm not a mother.

"Did you take Chopper to the zoo often when he was a child?" I ask Brut as we cross the parking lot for the ticket booth.

"I didn't actually." He's quiet for a second. "I did what I could, but I didn't have much extra cash when Chopper was little. Pop had all the funds tied up in the shop or gambled away."

We step up to the counter, and Brut pulls out his wallet.

"I got it," I offer.

But he levels me with a glare when he says, "This is my date. I pay."

I'm a modern woman who can cover her own expenses, but I appreciate his gentlemanly command that he is responsible for our day. We receive the admission tickets and cross into the official park.

"Your date, huh?" I huff teasingly, looping my arm through his.

"Our first ever." He kisses me briefly before flipping open the extensive map, and I stare at him.

He's right. This is our first date. When I was younger, I'd often sneak into the garage after hours. We didn't go anywhere. We stayed in the office. We made out on the leather couch. Sometimes, we'd go for long drives in a car he'd finished, but we never went on dates. Once we went to a concert, but it was a disaster. We also never had sex.

"Lily?" Brut's cautious voice interrupts my thoughts.

Asking him why we never went out is on the tip of my tongue, but I bite back the question. *No thoughts of the past.*

"Nothing," I say as if answering an unspoken question and tighten my arm on his.

Observing the map, we realize there is no way to see everything in one day, so we narrow it down by selecting two general exhibits apiece. I choose the pandas first, and Brut wants the big cats next. With a plan mapped out, we begin our date.

Standing in front of the panda bears, Brut stares at one gnawing on bamboo.

"You know, I've never lived anywhere other than my dad's house."

The out-of-the-blue comment surprises me. If he still lives in the same house he grew up in, he hasn't had the adventure of packing boxes, physically moving, or living anywhere different.

"Why didn't you move out?"

Brut leans his forearms on the railing and his hands clasp together as he watches the bears.

"I guess it just seemed easier to stay." His tone is somber as his brows pinch. He's quiet for another second. "When Chopper arrived, I needed help because I didn't know what I was doing. I didn't know how to be a parent. Not that Pop was a great role model, but he didn't kick me out. When he died, I inherited the house." He nods to the black and white novelty before us. "I'm like him. Trapped in captivity. In the same place where I started."

"You don't like working in the garage, do you?"

"It's not that." He turns his head to me. "I'm just stuck. I've grown complacent with the garage. I mean, I own it. It's mine in name although I try to be fair to Hank."

Brut's younger brother was once a famous musician. Hank doesn't need the money the garage provides, but Brut has always been a good older brother. I remember reading things about Hank in the news. Life couldn't have been easy with a wayward superstar as Brut's sibling.

"What about teaching? Why not go back to school?"

"You sound like Hank." He chuckles. "But I'm too old."

"I don't believe that," I say quickly. "You're forty-five, Brut. If you've only lived half your life, what will you do with the other half, especially if you aren't happy?"

His eyes scan my face before he turns back to observe the pandas.

"I'm not unhappy. I'm just…" The words fall away as he twists his lips.

"Incomplete?" I ask softly. I might know how he feels if he agrees with me.

"Maybe." He scoffs lightly.

"What about moving? If you feel you've been in one place too long, then move."

"It's not that simple," he says.

"You're making it too easy to stay." I laugh with a wink, but there's a serious edge to my tone. I've moved more times than I can remember. Left home as soon as I could at twenty to move in with Brad. Slept on a friend's couch for a summer after him. Lived in a commune-style home for a while. Got my first studio apartment in my thirties. Then opened the bakery.

"It's not that. I'd need to renovate to sell, and I just haven't had the motivation to do it. With Hank moving out, it's been strange. Chopper will leave soon, too, I suppose. It's weird to think I'll finally have the place to myself." Brut's tone suggests while he has reasons to go, he isn't convinced he should leave.

"Update it then. It sounds like the perfect time if everyone else is moving out. Make it what you want, if it's finally yours alone. I could help." I bite my lip the second I offer. *One week.* My suggestion implies more time, and I don't want to insinuate we could be more. I don't even want to hint at the possibility. Thinking ahead would only bring heartache. Who am I kidding, though? When this week ends, I won't be able to walk away as easily as I think.

"Really?" Brut interjects. "Would you help me?" His eyes scan my body. "Know how to use a hammer?"

"Nah, but I could make some decent cupcakes to inspire you," I tease, hoping to lighten the conversation. I don't want the day to turn serious, so I reach for his hand. This draws his attention to our linked fingers, and then his gaze jumps to mine.

"You could be very inspirational for me, Lily pad."

I have no idea what he means, but he smiles before lifting our joined fingers and kissing my knuckles. Then he tugs me forward, and we continue our day at the zoo.

+ + +

On our way back to the beach house, Brut stops at a seafood shack, swearing they have the freshest fish. I love the atmosphere of the little dive diner with its red-checkered oilcloth table coverings and deep wooden benches for seats. I order a margarita while Brut orders a beer.

"Tell me your favorite thing about the day."

"You," Brut says without hesitation. He doesn't even look up from the menu to respond.

"I'm serious," I tease. "What was your favorite part?"

"Spending time with you."

"Brut," I admonish with a giggle. "At the zoo. Your favorite thing you saw."

He glances up at me. "The expression on your face. You're like a kid each time you saw something new. Your face would light up, and your smile would beam. It was fascinating."

My shoulders fall. Not in defeat but in awe. "Brut, that's...that's incredibly sweet."

"I had fun." His shrug dismisses what he said.

"See, you do know how to have fun." I emphasize my words with a clap of my hands. When he asked me yesterday about fun, I didn't know how to respond. Despite my past, I've lived a good life. Not every moment has been perfect, but my life has been decent, fulfilling in many ways. Brut doesn't seem so confident to say the same even though he has Chopper and his shop. Not to mention, his brother is his best friend. I don't have anything like that with family, but I do have Esther.

"You bring it out of me." Brut taps the edge of my glass with the neck of his beer bottle before taking a swig.

I can't help the heat on my cheeks. He really is sweet.

111

When dinner ends, we drive back to the house, and Brut rounds the car to open my door. Taking my hand, he walks me to the side entrance and then pulls me to a stop.

"Would you kiss on a first date?" he asks sheepishly, lifting our joined fingers to his lips.

"It depends." I tilt my head, wondering where he's going with his question.

"I don't date, Lil. I don't know how these things work." He shrugs.

I can't imagine Brut not dating. There's no way he's been a monk all these years, but then again, you don't need to go on dates in order to have sex.

"I want to end our first date the right way."

Oh Brut. "As it's our first date, and because it's you, I would definitely kiss on the first date."

"Why because it's me?"

I could reply with—because we've already had sex, so we are past the first kiss—but I somehow sense what Brut wants in this moment.

"Because I've been waiting a long time for a first date with you, Brut Paige. I don't think I'd want to wait any longer for a first kiss."

"I'm sorry, Lily," he says, his voice softening. He strokes my hair behind my ear.

"Kiss me, Brut," I quietly command. To my surprise, the kiss is light and tender. Brut keeps it chaste and delicate, just as a first kiss might be. One hand cups my cheek, and he takes it no further. Pulling back after a few minutes, he presses his forehead to mine.

"Thank you for that," he says, rubbing his nose against mine.

"I'll be your first kiss anytime, honey."

20

Bump. Set. Spike.

[Brut]

I'm still on the high of our day, the kiss at the door, and her calling me *honey*, so while I want to do it right, I don't want to spend another night without her.

"Okay, enough first date stuff," I say, letting myself into her room and crawling into her bed. I spoon behind her, and her body jiggles with her chuckle. After I drape my arm over her waist, her fingers come to my forearm and gently stroke. She's right; it is a soothing sensation.

"Would you have sex on the first date?" I ask, nuzzling my nose into her nape while holding my breath for her answer.

"I don't think so."

"Not even with me?" I nibble at her neck, sucking her warm skin.

"Especially not you." There's a jesting note in her tone.

"Why not?" I kiss the hollow spot at the base of her skull as my hand skims over her hip.

"I don't want you to think I'm easy." Her tone turns serious, but then she giggles.

"Nothing with you was ever easy, Lily. You were so hard to resist."

"You did a good job back then." We've subtly hinted at the past here and there with casual references. As much as I don't want us to go backward, I'm afraid the past will always be there between us. Still on the upswing of our date, though, I'm not looking behind me tonight.

"Lily," I warn.

"Okay." She sighs. "If you want to do it right, it shouldn't be until date three for sex."

"It sounds like you know a bit about this?" I realize I haven't asked her if she's dating anyone, but I don't think I want to know the answer. I don't even want to consider her cheating on someone, but that would be the pot calling the kettle black.

"Not really. I read a lot of romance, though."

"Romance, huh?" I nip at her again where her shoulder meets her neck. "Okay, so sex on the third date? Shit, I messed this up." I wouldn't trade the sex we've had, though, and I'm running out of days. It's already Wednesday night. I only have two evenings left before we leave.

Lily squirms, causing her ass to rub against the front of my shorts.

"Maybe it's the third time you have sex should be on the night of the first date?" she suggests, hesitantly, however, as she curls into my hard-on, a soft purr from her tells me she has no question as to what she wants.

"I like that rule better," I say, gripping her hip tighter, holding her firmly against me as I deepen the bites on her skin before attending to the rest of her body.

+ + +

I wake alone again.

"I give up," I huff aloud. I don't understand this woman. She's an early riser, for one thing. I envision her jumping out of bed ready to start the day at a sprint instead of a jog, but I wish she'd linger next to me. To my surprise, I find her downstairs curled up in the oversized chair in the living room, wearing one of my T-shirts. She's staring out the window even though a book rests on her lap.

"Mornin', Lily pad," I say, crossing the room and kneeling before her.

"Hey," she says quietly. I slip my arms around her legs, and she rakes her fingers through my hair. A soft grin that doesn't reach her eyes greets me.

"How long have you been awake?"

"Just a little while," she offers without more explanation.

"You're breaking the rules," I tease, hoping to lighten whatever is on her mind. "You keep leaving the bed when the rule is not to let me wake alone."

Her smile deepens only a little.

"What's in that pretty head of yours, sugar?" I ask, lifting a finger to brush back her hair. She lowers her gaze, but I'm not letting this question slide, no matter how good she is at deflecting. To my surprise, she answers with something I didn't expect.

"It just seems like too much. If I stay, it makes it seem so...so official." Her eyes squint at me before looking away. "That's not the right word. I don't know how to explain it. It just seems lingering in bed makes a statement, and you said—"

My thumb has been stroking her cheek, but I move it to her lips to stop her.

"Forget what I said. I don't want to request anything that makes you uncomfortable."

"It's not uncomfortable," she says, chewing at her lips as her lids lower and her gaze return to her lap. "It's *too* comfortable."

"Lil?" Is she saying what I think? Does she feel the same way as I do? I find it comforting to be in bed with her, too. It feels right. I don't know how things will be in a few days when we return north, but I know I don't think I can sleep without her ever again.

She doesn't respond to the question in her name. Instead, she leans forward to kiss me. At first, her hands cover my jaw, fingertips rubbing at the scruff while she deepens the kiss.

"I think you want me in bed in the mornings because you have an issue." Before I can respond, she's gone into distraction tactics, and her feet come to my waist, pressing down my shorts with those powerful toes. The length of me, stiff and hard, is quickly on display. We need to talk, but something in her eyes tells me not to speak. She scoots to the edge of the chair, her legs on either side of my hips, and suddenly, the center of her meets the heat of my dick. Bare. Raw. Ready.

Lily's hand comes between us, and she positions my tip at her core.

"Lily?" I question again, but she simply shakes her head, then slides forward, drawing me into her depths. Her mouth comes to mine, ravenous and demanding, and my libido kicks in despite the unspoken weight between us. I scoop my forearms under her knees, lifting her lower legs to my shoulders. She grunts as her body curls, and I use the arms on the chair to leverage upward. I'm in a near plank position as I

115

piston into her, thrusting in rapid, short jabs. Lily has slipped to her back, her ankles by my ears. Her eyes focus on mine, but the intensity is too much. I turn to kiss her calf as my hammering deepens.

Let me in, I demand with each movement forward. *I want back into your heart.*

There's a hesitation between us, a line. I put that line there, but her body...her body doesn't hold back. She's meeting me pulse for pulse, groaning my name as her hands come to the arms of the chair. Lily has strength, and she uses the solid armrests to roll upward. Within seconds, she screams my name, milking me so hard I see stars. I explode inside her. I can't seem to stop. I'm coming and coming and coming...

Take me back, I beg.

Finally, I still, but our chests drag and drop. Ragged breaths fill the silence between us. I hover over her although one of her legs has slipped down my arm. My arms shake, and I collapse to my elbows, unwilling to pull out of her, unable to move.

"What was that?" I chuckle softly, feeling myself jolting within her.

"Good morning," she whispers, leaning up to kiss me too quickly.

It certainly is a good way to start the morning, but she's telling me something else. Something I'm certain I won't like.

+ + +

Lily says she's going to read for a bit after we clean up. I'm too antsy to sit still and decide to go surfing. Unfortunately, I'm on edge and can't find my groove, so I fall one too many times. It's not my balance but my concentration. Our rapid morning sex felt more like a desperate goodbye than a morning greeting.

Eventually, I give up on the waves and rest on the edge of the shore.

"Hey, old man, come play." A guy bouncing a volleyball with his fists calls out to me. A few of the younger set have teased me about my skill on the board—despite my age—but it's all in jest. I stand slowly, wiping sand from my quick-dry swim shorts. I should head back to the house, but I'm not ready to face Lily. I don't know what we're doing.

Something lingers between us like a fine mist, though I'm pretty certain I know what it is.

The past.

I can't take any of it back, and I'm sensing Lily can't let it go even though she said she forgives me.

"Sure, I'll play," I decide, knowing full well I'm using the game as a stall tactic. I can't face her saying goodbye to me too soon. We still have three more days.

The game is rough at first. I haven't played beach volleyball in years, but slowly, a rhythm comes back to me.

Bump. Set. Spike.

We play four on four, and I enjoy the competition as we razz one another within our team. It's been a long time since I've hung with guys of any age. I don't have many friends outside Hank and the mechanics who work at the garage. Our game isn't a scene from *Top Gun*, but healthy male bodies on the beach can't be dismissed, and it doesn't take long for a crowd to start building around us. I've gone up for a block when I hear my name.

"Nice save, Brut." Her sweet cheer turns my head. How long has Lily been standing there?

I stop paying attention to the game, too busy taking in her pink Because Cupcakes baseball cap and the skirt like material at her waist accentuating her bikini body, when I'm knocked in the head with the ball.

"Come on, old man. Keep your head in the game."

I wink at Lily and turn back as a man around my age on the other team comments. "I'd be distracted by that, too." His rough voice and deep laugh sets me off. The next ball that comes to me gets spiked right at him. The crowd goes crazy as my teammates hiss and clap with a resounding, "Oh," and, "Take that."

"You got this, boys," filters to me again from Lily, but I keep my focus. We need one last point.

It's my serve. I haven't jump served in years, but wanting to show off a little, I attempt it. Two steps, a short leap, and a hard smack, and the ball goes to the back, left corner of the makeshift court. Game point.

L.B. Dunbar

The crowd goes wild again, and my teammates rush me with claps on the back and high fives. A few well-wishers watching also step onto the court and pat me, but I'm distracted, searching for Lily.

Finding her in the crowd, I jog up to her. Adrenaline still courses through my body because of the win, but my heart bumps with excitement that she watched me play.

"Did you see that?" I clench my fists and tug my arms to my waist with excitement.

"I saw it," she says, laughing at my antics. "You were amazing." She chews her lip as her loose hair blows in the breeze despite her ball cap. She looks adorable.

"What are you doing here?"

"When you didn't come back, I thought I'd come down here to find you." There's more to her statement. Was she waiting on me? I'm covered in sweat and sand from the game, but I want to hug her. My eyes roam over her pink cap and the light material draped at her waist.

"Can that get wet?" I ask.

Her eyes narrow, and her head tilts. "Yes, but—"

"Got a cell phone on you?"

Her eyes pinch deeper, and her mouth curls. "Yes." She's lying, though.

There's no place to tuck a phone in her bikini or short skirt. I bend and wrap my arms around her thighs, hiking her up and over my shoulder.

"Brut," she screams, laughing as her hands lightly smack my back. "You wouldn't."

My response is to race to the water's edge. Knees high, I traipse into the ocean until we are deep enough. She bellows my name one more time as I call out, "Hold on." And under we go. A wave crashes over us, refreshing my skin.

I stand, righting Lily before another wave knocks her over. Her cap comes loose, and while still holding her hand, I reach out for it before it drifts away. Lifting the sodden hat, I flip it backward and place it on my head.

118

Lily's breath catches as she looks at me. Her hands come to my cheeks, and she rises on tiptoes in the water.

"You are so hot, Brut." Her mouth crashes into mine, nearly knocking us back into the waves. I chuckle under her attack, and when she pulls back, a large smile graces her face. "But that was so mean."

She's still smiling, so I know she's not really upset. Scooping up water, I rinse the wet sand off my shoulders and my chest. As Lily watches me, my heart races again. I like how she's looking at me as though she wants to do naughty things under the surface. I reach out for her waist and drag her to me for another kiss.

"I'm glad you walked down here," I say once I draw away from her mouth. If we stand here any longer, under the sea, things are going to be happening. Instead, I take her hand and lead us to the shore. We head for my board.

"I feel kind of bad about yesterday."

My head snaps in her direction as I lift the board from its perch in the sand. "What? Why?"

"The zoo. I feel like I bamboozled you into going. I wanted to make it up to you."

"Lily pad, you didn't make me do anything I didn't want to do. It was the best first date ever. But I'm curious how you want to make it up to me." My brow raises as we begin walking. I'm still wearing her cap backward on my head.

"I found a kayak cave tour. I thought…maybe…you'd like the adventure."

"Hell, yes." I chuckle, reaching out for her nape and drawing her to me for a quick kiss. "That sounds awesome. When?"

"In about an hour."

"Oh my." I laugh heartily, lowering my hand to link my fingers with hers.

"It could be our second date," she says hesitantly, and I stop us by our joined fingers to kiss her again.

"I'd like that."

We walk the remainder of the beach chatting about surfing, volleyball, and whether Lily's ever kayaked before. As we reach the deck of our place, I set my board on the side of the house and head for the outdoor shower. It's protected by the house on one side and thin fence panels on two other sides, but one part remains open. Lily stands on the deck as I turn on the water, her mouth opening as she points toward the door. She's about to say something, but I'm not letting her get away. I reach for her and tug her under the spray with me.

"Oh my God, that's cold," she shrieks before my mouth crashes on hers. I can't stop kissing her.

"I'll warm you up, sugar," I say against her lips, then deepen the kiss and press her back to one barrier.

"The neighbors," she whimpers between kisses. "They'll see us."

"Let them watch," I growl, reaching for her soggy skirt and removing it, hearing the material slap on the deck boards at our feet. My fingers make quick work getting under her bikini bottom. "You're so ready for me, Lily pad."

She moans as she lifts one leg to my hip. I push down my swim shorts just enough and lower her bikini bottoms. She wiggles her legs, forcing the wet material to the shower floor. Bending at the knees, I scoop under her center and impale her with one swift thrust. Her head falls back as her nails claw my shoulders. We don't match in height, and I reach for the back of her thighs, lifting her upward. Her legs wrap around my hips as I bounce her over me. Still pumped from the game and the date she planned, something snaps inside me.

"Were you saying goodbye to me this morning when we fucked?"

Lily gasps. Whether from the force of my thrusts or the sharpness of my tone, I don't know, but her mouth lowers to my shoulder, and she nips me in response.

"I'm not saying goodbye, Lily pad. I'm not saying goodbye ever again. You got that?" My fingers dig into the back of her thighs as her heels press into my backside. I'm so wound up; I'm not going to last.

"This is going to be quick, baby."

"Come inside me," Lily pants in my ear, and I explode.

I stumble, releasing one leg as my hand braces on the backwall of the shower. My head lowers to her shoulder as I jet off inside her.

"Holy shit," I exhale against her wet skin, and then I pull back to look at her face. "You didn't." It's a fact. I was too quick.

"It's okay," she dismisses, pressing a kiss to my bicep.

"It's never okay." Pulling out of her, I skate my fingers over her hip for the promised land but her firm hand stops me at the wrist.

"We don't have time. Second date awaits."

While I don't want to leave her unsatisfied, I like the sound of that. A second date.

21
What If

[Lily]

Our second date is a twilight kayak adventure into sea caves. It wouldn't be my first choice of explorations, but it seemed different and something Brut might enjoy. I wasn't as strong as he was at kayaking, but I could keep up, or he held back. Either way, we stick together as we follow a guide into the ancient caves of La Jolla. It's pretty cool, and I try not to let my claustrophobia press in. I find the older I get, the more I develop strange issues I didn't have before—like a fear of enclosed places.

Brut is thrilled with the adventure and thanks me three times for planning the date. Of course, he refuses to let me pay again. I want to protest, and actually do, but then I finally acquiesce. It seems more important to him whose credit card covers the fun. When the tour ends, the time is late, and we grab fish tacos off a food truck near the kayak rental shop. I don't typically eat out—keeping up the healthy eating habits as he pointed out— but I also like to cook enough I don't need other people making food for me. Eating out appears to be a staple of Brut's life, and I wonder if he'd stay in if someone cooked for him.

Ironically, his kitchen becomes a conversation topic when we return to the house. He reminds me of how I promised to help him renovate his home while we sit together on the couch with our feet propped up on the ottoman. I'm nursing another hard lemonade while Brut downs his beer.

"So, here's the basic layout. What would you put in it if it was yours?" Brut sketches the outline of his kitchen, and I can see it's narrow. He admits it's old, dated, and underused lately.

"If it was *mine*," I emphasize, "I'd have a top of the line stove. Stainless steel. You need a large farmhouse sink. Double-door refrigerator." I pause, imagining my dream kitchen in a house. Besides the fact I don't own my apartment, my place is too small for luxury appliances. I've admitted to Brut I don't need *more* because I use the bakery for most things, but sometimes, I think it would be nice to have a home not attached to other places.

"What color is your place now?" I ask, still concentrating on the design.

"Brown."

My head rolls on the cushion to look at him, waiting for more details. "Brown? That's it."

"Yep. Brown cabinets. Brown appliances. Just brown."

"Brut"—I laugh—"that sounds awful."

"It is." His voice lowers as he takes a pull of his beer.

"I'm sorry. That wasn't nice. I'm sure it's fine."

"Nope. It's awful." He sets the beer on the tray on the ottoman and turns to face me. His arm comes over the back of the couch, and his fingers toy with my hair. "Tell me what color you'd make it. Tell me about your dream kitchen."

This seems like a dangerous game, but I'll play.

"White cabinets. White subway tile backsplash. Maybe black countertops. Granite actually. I'd love an island like this place has. Maybe an open plan with a living space like this house as well. In fact, if I could move this house, it might be perfect."

Brut nods. "Except there is no beach where we live."

"Not close enough, true." I'm on the northeast side of Los Angeles while Brut is in Pasadena.

"What if we bought this house? As a second home?"

I don't miss the *we*. "What if," I tease, wiggling a brow even though there's no chance I can own beachfront property. Everything I have is wrapped up in the bakery.

"And what if I gave you your dream kitchen?"

"What if," I joke again, growing slightly uncomfortable because the probability of my dream kitchen in a dream home with this dreamy man is zero. Yet my heart races within my chest.

"What if I asked you to move in with me?"

My shoulders stiffen as I stare at him. He can't be serious.

123

L.B. Dunbar

"Are you...suggesting future plans?" I pause a beat, my breath catching. "Hypothetically, if you asked me, I'd have to say..." *Yes.* "No."

"Why?" His brow furrows as his fingers stop twirling my hair.

"Because I own the shop, which includes the apartment upstairs."

"But what if...you moved?"

"I'm not moving my bakery."

"Not the shop, just you."

Suddenly, I'm not sure I like this game. He must be teasing me, and I don't feel like playing anymore. "I think we should stop," I say softly.

"Stop what?"

"Stop the *what ifs*." Because there are so many other what ifs we could address, but we also can't change the past. The pain would be like picking at an old scab. I'd bleed again and have to heal again. The process took long enough the first time.

His eyes search my face. "Okay, Lily pad." His arm shifts from my shoulders, and he reaches for the remote. "How about a movie?"

The request sounds strange. We haven't watched anything other than the ball game the other night. He's making this suggestion to fill the awkward tension suddenly between us. Hoping not to ruin our second date completely, I agree. Once he selects something, he returns his arm to my shoulder and tugs me against him. Unfortunately, I'm not focused on the rom com on the screen, but the *what if this was my real-life* scenario flashing through my thoughts.

+ + +

I'm the one to wake alone on the last full day of our vacation. A light blanket covers me on the couch. I'd fallen asleep during the movie. I thought Brut rearranged us so we both lay on the cushions, but I see that isn't true. Shifting to my back, I stare up at the ceiling until the smell of bacon hits my nose. I sit up, peering over the back of the cushions to find Brut working in the kitchen. I never purchased bacon, so he must have stepped out for the salty treat I deny myself.

He's wearing my Because Cupcakes baseball cap backward on his head again. I giggle at the pink against his skin but realize I like seeing him with it. I also like seeing him working in the kitchen.

What if he did give me a dream kitchen?

A whisk scrambles eggs in a bowl.

"Hey, sleeping beauty," he says as he notices I'm awake.

I'm sure beauty is the last thing I am with my hair all over the place, but Brut's smile tells me he means what he says. He thinks I'm beautiful.

"I slept here all night." I'm a little concerned we didn't sleep together. Maybe the *what if* game turned too serious for him as well.

"You did. I couldn't rouse you to save your life, so I just let you be."

"I'm sorry," I answer, crossing my arms over the back cushions.

"Why are you sorry?"

"Because I didn't want to sleep without you."

The whisk thuds in the bowl as Brut sets it down on the counter and rounds the island. Within seconds, he's cupping my face and climbing over the back of the couch, flattening me into the cushions as he straddles me.

"I don't want to sleep without you either." His mouth finds mine, tender and soft. "Good morning, sugar."

"Good morning." I sigh under him.

What if I woke to kisses like this each morning?

"Eggs?" he asks, and I nod. He presses upward, steps over the couch, and returns to the kitchen.

After breakfast, we spend the day at the beach. I follow Brut to watch him surf, and he returns with me to hang out in the afternoon sun. My heart breaks with each passing minute as we lazy through the day with soft touches and lingering kisses.

How will I say goodbye to this?

"Got any plans for tonight?" Brut abruptly asks me, and I laugh. A sheepish look fills his eyes.

"I think my calendar is clear," I tease.

"Then date three it is." His brows wiggle, and my heart sinks a little despite the playfulness. I don't want to keep counting dates like we're

L.B. Dunbar

counting down to the inevitable, but when evening arrives, I understand Brut's intentions.

Date three. The sex date.

After a dinner he prepared, which included grilled steaks but a hearty salad, he leads me upstairs to his room. Each bedroom is a mirror image of one another. Same double bed. Same French doors. Same small balcony with glass railings. And on Brut's, he's made a nest of blankets and pillows with votive candles lining the railing.

"What's this?" I breathe in the sweet, romantic setting.

"Date three. Making love under the moonlight." My brain races to the things I said to Brut on our first night watching the sunset. Dance in the rain. Plan *what ifs*. Make love under the moonlight. He's checking off the list of my youthful, romantic dreams.

Why? My heart aches.

Instead of asking questions, I turn to him and kiss him softly, savoring his lips and his sweet intentions. The long kisses heat, but Brut pulls back, beginning the slow tease of undressing me.

He removes my dress, unclasps my bra, and slides down my underwear. His hands explore my body, lingering on the back of my calves, the curve of my hips, and the roundness of my shoulders. I should feel self-conscious, and in some ways, I do.

His gaze is so intense as his eyes follow the trail of his fingers over my skin. "You're the most beautiful woman." His voice is serious, but for some reason, my reply is sarcastic.

"I'm getting old."

"You're aging to perfection."

My mouth returns to his, wanting to swallow his sweetness. I deftly undress him as well, removing the short sleeve button-down and khaki shorts he wore to "dress up" for dinner. He wears boxer briefs, and I take in his sexy appearance in the tight undergarment before removing them. Holding my hand, he guides me to the cove he's made on the balcony. I feel like royalty as he leads me among the blankets and pillows. A naked princess but also a treasured woman.

As I lie on the bed of covers and downy fluff, Brut continues to explore my body while the sky darkens over us. It isn't as if he hasn't touched me before. We've certainly been adventurous this week, but he takes his time, memorizing me with his hands, his fingertips. He outlines my arms, covers my breasts, and runs a flat palm over my belly. His fingers trace along my hips before he sits up and massages my legs down to my feet.

"Flip over," he commands softly, and I do as he says, relishing the brush of soft cotton under my naked body. He massages up my calves, over my thighs, and onto my backside.

"This ass," he moans, digging into the white globes accentuated by my tan lines. His fingers continue to my lower back, up my spine, and across the base of my neck. The full-body massage causes me to relax more than I can ever recall being. With a gentle press on my side, he rolls me to my back again. His mouth covers the cupcake tattoo on my hip, outlining the artwork with sucking kisses. His fingers skate over to my center, and he looks up at me with a devious glint in his eyes.

"Date three is for sex, but we've already done that." A finger slides slowly inside my core. "Tonight, we make love, Lily pad."

A second finger joins the first, stroking me, priming me, but I'm more than ready for this man. What I'm not prepared for is the slow intensity he uses to fill me. He's methodical, deliberate, and he's taking his time to push to the hilt and then pull back to the edge. The rhythm is languid and sweet, and our bodies move in a luscious dance that matches the beat of the tide lapping on the beach. The lullaby of the waves sets the pace for us, and Brut brushes back my hair while he rocks into me.

"On which date can I say I love you?"

"Brut," I quietly choke.

Tears prickle my eyes. *This one*, I want to whisper, but I don't. The statement can't be scheduled on a calendar. The announcement isn't measured in time. In fact, I've been holding those three words for him for twenty-two years. I'd like to think I'm ready to share them, but I'm too afraid.

Brut lowers his mouth to mine, and he kisses me with the same lazy, loving rhythm of his lower body. My skin tingles. My body at one with this man over me, filling me. A hum vibrates up my center.

L.B. Dunbar

"Getting there, sugar?" he asks as he curls to the side a little, slipping his hand between us and touching the sensitive nub as he slips deeper inside. The build-up is drizzled caramel. The release even sweeter. I'm coming in soft waves, light ripples, and dragging pulls. My hands clasp Brut's backside, holding him inside me as I clench around him. I don't want him to leave my body.

"That's it, baby." He exhales into my neck once I start to come down from the high. His pace quickens enough to take him over the edge next, then he stills inside me. I ride the pulse within, knowing his seed fills me. We haven't been safe this week—not even a little bit—but I couldn't be with him in any other way. If one week is all I get, I want everything and beyond as he said the other night.

Everything and beyond.

22

The Morning-After Effect

[Lily]

The next morning, I wake to dawning sunlight, the squawk of seagulls, and Brut's arms around me. After making love, we stayed on the balcony, talking halfway through the night as if we could fill the remainder of our stay with the years missed between us. I'd like to say I felt fulfilled, but instead, a hollow sensation burrows through my midsection. The inevitable is just around the corner.

A light kiss on my shoulder tells me Brut is awake.

"You stayed in bed," he teases against my neck. "It only took all week, woman."

"Good morning to you too, sunshine," I say as I twist to face him. Morning breath isn't pretty, but Brut does not seem to mind. He kisses me, lingering like the caresses from last night.

"What are those two doing over there?" The shrill voice of an older woman stops us mid-kiss. Brut lifts his head, narrowing his eyes.

"Shit." He chuckles as I tip my head back to see what he does.

"Oh my God," I groan, pressing Brut off me and wrapping a sheet around me as best I can. I crawl through the open screen door, not wanting to stand and expose us any more to the nosy neighbor peering over her balcony at ours. Brut crawls after me, completely naked, and tackles me to the floor of his room. I fall to my stomach in a fit of embarrassed giggles. He rolls me to my back and struggles to unwrap me from the sheet between us. Hands tug and pull at the material, eager to be reckless just as we were outside.

But suddenly, Brut's phone rings the annoying rap music with his son's name in it.

"Shit," he curses, holding still over me as if he expects the ringing to stop.

"You should answer that." I don't want him to ignore his son.

"I'll be home in a few hours. Can't whatever it is wait?" Brut groans into my neck, collapsing over me. The words pull reality even closer. We only have a couple of hours left. We need to be out by noon.

"Would he call you if it could wait?"

Brut's head pops up, and he stares down at me. "Probably not." He stands quickly, reaching for his shorts on the floor from our disrobing the night before. I roll to my stomach, watching him tug on his shorts while I hold the sheet to my chest. I prop up on one elbow as Brut calls his son's number.

"Hey," he snaps too sharply for a greeting.

I understand his frustration, but his son must need him.

"Hank?" Brut's voice croaks.

I draw up to my knees, observing the expression on Brut's face shifting. His eyes meet mine and hold as he listens a minute. His free hand wipes down his face and then combs back through his hair. His hand pauses on the back of his neck.

"Why the fuck did he do that?"

Brut nods as if understanding the explanation for whatever happened.

"He was arrested?" Panic fills his voice. His tan face turns to ash.

I stumble up to my feet, struggling with the long sheet while holding it around me like a dress.

"But you bailed him out?" Pause. "Thank fuck."

Brut listens again.

"I can be there in a few hours. I'll leave now." His eyes leap up to mine, and I nod, knowing whatever happened, he needs to go.

"Hank, I owe you so big, man. Thank you."

He pauses a second, chuckling without humor at something his brother said.

"Yeah, yeah. See you in a few."

As he clicks off his phone, I rush to him. "What happened?"

"Chopper got in a bar fight. Fucking punk," Brut grumbles, swiping down his face again and tossing his phone on the bed.

"He was in jail?" *Poor Chopper.*

"Hank got him out." He pauses a second, tipping his head back to look at the ceiling. "Look, Lil, I hate to do this—"

"Go. Of course, you have to go."

His hands come to my upper arms, stroking without thinking. "You know I don't want to leave too soon."

"It's only a few hours earlier than it would have happened."

Brut stiffens, his fingers stop rubbing and dig into my arms. "What does that mean?"

"I just mean, we'd be separating soon anyway, right? You need to go, Brut. We aren't important right now. Chopper is."

"*You're* important to me," Brut stresses, but I can't have this discussion with him. The week has been wonderful. A dream come true. A second chance with the one who got away. Who'd have thought? But I need to call this week what it is.

Brut and I can never be together.

"You're special to me, too."

"Special," Brut snaps, squeezing at my arms. "Special? Why the fuck do I feel like you're about to tell me we can be friends?"

"Isn't that what we've been? Friends with benefits. One week only."

"Lily, you know it's more than that." He sighs, clutching at my arms and dragging me closer to him.

"I don't think we should discuss this now. Chopper needs you."

Brut's eyes drift back and forth between mine as if he's looking for something. "That's it, isn't it? It's him. He's always going to be between us." Brut shakes his head, pursing his lips as he releases me.

I grasp the sheet at my chest. "It's never been him, Brut, and you know that. I don't fault that child for being born. It wasn't his mistake."

"No," Brut heaves. "It was mine. I did it. I fucked up."

My breath hitches. Twenty-two years come crashing down between us. But we can't do this again.

"You weren't alone, and it wasn't just anyone, Brut. You know that." I shake my head, my lips quivering. Lauren's name lingers between us. Brut stares daggers at me, and my heart shatters all over again.

131

L.B. Dunbar

"You said you forgave me." His shoulders fall, his expression defeated as he shakes his head, looking away from me.

"I do." My voice lowers as it trembles. I do forgive him, it's just—

"Just not enough." He looks beyond me to the balcony. "I should help you clean up." He's gone monotone—empty—like I suddenly feel inside.

"Just leave it," I say, refusing to look back at the love nest. "Just leave."

His eyes snap back to mine, and he points between us. "We aren't fucking over, Lily. Not this time."

"Brut," I groan before twisting my face away. "You need to go."

I don't watch him leave, but I feel his absence. And I don't move.

Not until I hear the side door slam do I fold to the floor and dissolve into sobs.

23
Wilting At Nineteen

[Lily]

Suddenly, I'm nineteen again...

Tears pour down my face, ugly and scalding.

"Is it true?" My voice choked over the question. The man, not a boy, but a man of twenty-three, had ripped out my heart like none other.

He hung his head in shame, aware of what I was asking without clarification. Was it shame? *Was I correct that he felt embarrassed, remorseful, apologetic, or was I projecting onto him how he should have felt?*

"How could you?" The question was so filled with anguish, so anchored in pain. I stared at the man I thought I loved. The man who touched me like no other, kissed me like no other, made me feel wanted, desired, and respected.

Respect. A terrible word yet I understood what he meant when he denied having sex with me, telling me he didn't want to ruin me. Didn't he see he'd already ruined me with his penetrating blue eyes and his soft sighs? As he told me things, taught me things about touching, accepting, and feeling?

But respect must mean something other than what I thought because of this, because of what he did to me...

"Say something." I didn't even recognize my own voice. Medusa or Maleficent or something evil had possessed me as I demanded he explain why, what, where, how.

"I didn't mean for it to happen." His voice cracked as his fingers squeezed at his eyes before pinching the bridge of his nose. "I don't know what happened."

L.B. Dunbar

"Try to explain," I'd demanded, finding a voice in me I didn't know I had. I needed to understand how. How he could refuse to sleep with me, but he fucked *her.*

"I was drunk."

The gasp falling from my lips could have been heard in Texas. I couldn't believe this was his excuse.

"Look, you don't understand. A lot has happened, sort of all at once, and I just...I had too much to drink."

I want to understand, *I screamed inside, my brain hurting from the vibration. I wanted him to tell me all that happened. I wasn't a kid, dammit.*

He went to night school. He wanted to be more than a mechanic.

He clearly didn't want me, though.

"When?" Still flabbergasted by his explanation, I needed to know. For some sick reason, I craved an explanation. Lauren had already said something, the gleam in her eyes as she revealed what they did and where...

"Two weeks ago."

My heart. Just claw it from my chest. Throw it on the ground and stomp on it. Watch the blood splatter as the pieces of the organ pumping life through my veins explodes like shrapnel over the floor of this fucking garage. We hadn't entered the office, our usual place of indiscretion. Our hiding spot for the dirty little secret of our affair.

That's what Lauren called me. His dirty little secret.

"You think he wants you?" *she'd hissed.* "A kid? One where a train already barreled through the station and didn't stop." *I was never with her precious Rick, but she's never believed me.*

"Like you're a virgin," *I'd argued childishly. I was, but I was ready to give myself to this man until she took him from me.*

"Two weeks," I repeated back to him, astonished that he'd kept the secret, the lie, for fourteen days. Fourteen days where guilt never crossed his features, his beautiful features. Tan skin, blue-as-the-sky eyes, clean jaw, edgy and hard.

Those lips, those lush lips that kissed mine, sucked my breasts, and tasted me for the first time.

I'd shivered, needing a shower, needing the hottest hot water to remove my skin, knowing we'd shared him—my sister and me.

"I didn't say anything because I didn't know how to tell you." He'd answered my next question before I'd asked. Suddenly, I was bone tired, knowing all the answers in the world won't erase what had happened.

"Say it," I demanded again, wanting to hear the truth directly from him even though my sister gladly told me.

His eyes pinched. "Lily pad—"

"Don't call me that. Just admit what happened!" I'd screamed.

"I slept with someone else."

Someone else? *I'd scoffed inside.* Someone else!

My boyfriend slept with my sister.

But we weren't dating, were we? He wasn't really my boyfriend, was he? We were each other's dirty little secret. We'd only been one place—his brother's concert at a bar—and he had to sneak me in, the underaged rulebreaker. My sister saw us there.

"What was all this?" I'd waved my arm around the waiting area of his father's garage. The question was rhetorical. I know what I wanted us to be.

Each time he fingered me, each time his tongue split me open, each time his mouth met mine. I love you.

But I had evidence I wasn't anything to him.

"We were having fun."

Slap. Punch. Kick. The words had taken the air out of me.

Fun. I've never hated a word so much in my life.

I loved you, *I'd screamed inside my head knowing the phrase would mean nothing to him.*

He didn't love me.

I can never forgive you, *I'd wanted to say, but I didn't. My rejection would have no effect on him. He won't care if I held that weight over him. He obviously didn't care about me.*

"I see," I'd said instead of all the emotions roiling inside me.

Brut's eyes narrowed. "That's it?" His expression puzzled me. The anger in his tone, the hard lines in his face. How was he angry at me?

And what else could I say? I understood? *But I didn't.*

135

L.B. Dunbar

Other than, I meant so little to him he could fuck my sister in some random bar because he had too much to drink.

"You aren't going to yell, scream, hit me?"

"Would those things make a difference?" I'd asked, an eerie calm overcoming me. "Would they change what happened?"

Brut swiped a hand down his face and then brushed it back through his hair. "I don't know how to make this right."

"Never sleeping with her in the first place might have helped." Sarcasm dripped through my veins. Then something else crept in. A cold rush. A deep awareness. He'd never slept with me.

Was Lauren correct? Did he think I was a kid? Was he not attracted to me? I refused to believe he wasn't. He touched me. He kissed me. He told me he craved me. But the contradictory evidence stood before me.

He didn't fully want me or he never would have cheated.

He's a cheater, *my heart screamed. A cheater and a liar because he withheld the truth from me. For two fucking weeks! My body trembled again. Disgust filled me.*

He'd kissed me after her. He'd touched me after... He told me...

Oh God! I broke, recalling what he said to me.

"You're everything to me, Lily pad. Everything and beyond. Don't give up on me."

Foolish. I was stupid to believe him, holding out hope he was careful with me because he wanted it to be perfect. We would be together forever, so why rush?

He said what he said, knowing he'd been with her already.

Don't give up on him? *He'd given up on me.*

"I don't think we should see each other again." I didn't even know why I said such a thing. Wasn't it obvious we wouldn't? My sister had come between us just as she'd threatened she would.

"Lily, I think—"

"You've done enough, Brut. Just...just leave." It was ridiculous to say. We stood inside his father's garage, the place of our secret rendezvous. I needed to walk away, but I couldn't find the strength. My knees still shook despite the desire to run away from him.

He'd stepped forward, reaching for my hands, but I withdrew them in revulsion. He'd caught them anyway, quicker than me, and he'd pressed his lips to my knuckles.

"Lily pad," he'd pleaded into my skin, but there was nothing to beg for.

He'd already ruined my heart.

We were over.

Dream destroyed.

L.B. Dunbar

24
The First Fight

[Brut]

I race through L.A. traffic as fast as one can with gridlock on a beautiful Saturday afternoon. My chest feels hollow because of the way things went with Lily.

You're special to me.

Fuck that. My hand pounds the steering wheel as I swear at another slow-moving driver.

Hours pass like days as I'm drawn back to my reality.

A fight. What the fuck was Chopper thinking?

He *wasn't* thinking, I surmise, just as I wasn't all those years ago. I'd received notice that I lost my scholarship due to a failed class. My attendance was poor because I had to cover for my dad in the shop. He drank too much, too often, and couldn't be roused. Then he officially fell sick, and I discovered the gambling debts.

I did what I shouldn't have done. I got drunk. Late night, a dive bar, and a girl with eyes like Lily's. My weakened state of mind and the angry energy within me fooled me into thinking I was losing myself in Lily. Sweet Lily. I hadn't gone to her because I didn't want to ruin her. I didn't want our first time to be under my hostility. I just needed five minutes to stew, and it changed the course of my life forever. I'd used the wrong sister.

Lily found out from said sister. After two weeks of guilt, the tears, the horror, and the accusations assaulted me—as they should have. Broken Lily. She disappeared. She wouldn't take my calls. I finally went to her house a week later, but Lauren answered the door. That was when she told me she was pregnant. I didn't believe her. I didn't *want* to believe her. I wanted nothing to do with the older Warren sister again. Heartbroken, I had no choice but to let the younger one go.

Then almost a year later, a present arrived on my doorstep.

138

Happy Father's Day, read the note atop a bundle of blankets over an infant in a car seat. I looked up to see the brake lights of a waiting car, which then sped off the second I acknowledged it. The weeks that followed included a paternity test, a formal appeal to rectify the name on the birth certificate, and a petition of abandonment to qualify for legal parentage. Born Brutus Joseph Warren, I changed the baby's name to Charles Henry Paige, giving him my father and my brother's name as well as my own. My father nicknamed him Chopper.

I'd never fault that child. That child sealed my fate. If I ever doubted Lauren, I had all the proof I needed growing before me for almost twenty-two years.

Lily's words linger in my ears as I pull into my driveway, taking note of the sadness of my house compared to the brightness of the beach house. Lily's dream home is nothing like my current home.

I want to give her a house.

I rub at the ache in my chest as I slam the SUV into park and rush for the front steps. Chopper sits inside the dark living room, his head resting on the back of the couch. Sensing I'm ready to lay into my son, my brother jumps from the chair he sits in. Hank is bigger than I am in stature—fuller, thicker—but we're the same height. I've always been the calmer of the two of us, but not today.

"Brut, just calm down."

"Calm down?" I snap. "What the fuck were you doing?" I narrow in on my son. His dark hair matches the color mine once was. His eyes however will match my greatest love and my biggest nemesis. Chopper rolls forward on the couch, his head lowering to his hands as his elbows hit his knees. He doesn't speak to me. He doesn't even look at me.

What the fuck?

"I think you need to relax. He's okay now. Nothing major. The cops hauled them each away to cool off."

I stare at my brother with his hands on my shoulders, nodding at me as if I'm a child who needs to understand.

"You pulled strings, didn't you?" I bark again. My brother was once a famous musician. After all the fights he's been in, all the bar mishaps from years of drinking, he has connections. His lip twitches, and he struggles to straighten it, proud of his behavior.

"You think this is funny? What if it had been Elston or Ronin?" Elston and Ronin are the older two of his new stepsons. A fight could have happened with either of them and the roles would be reversed right now. Hank would be losing his mind.

"Ronin wouldn't fight anyone." Hank huffs. "Elston might be another story. But this isn't about my boys; it's about yours. And he's okay, for the moment."

Hank's calm does nothing to soothe my frayed nerves. I fold to a squat before Chopper.

"Are you okay?" I push back his longer hair, tipping back his head so I can see his face. Instead of sorrow or remorse, there's an edge to my son's expression, along with a shining black eye. He hosts an empty glare while I scan his features. He looks just like me when I was his age, but he has *her* eyes. It's been hard to look him in those eyes over the years. They remind me too often of what I've lost.

"Get enough of a look?" I'm startled by the venom in his tone. My son and I have what I consider an open relationship. I've been both parents fluctuating between friend and disciplinarian. As he grew older, I also became a little too lax. Alcohol when he was too young. Girls at the house. Later nights than necessary. It didn't mean I didn't care about him, or worry he would be an alcoholic like Hank, or fuck the wrong girl and impregnate her, like me. I just let him loose too soon.

"What happened?" I soften my voice, hoping he'll talk to me. He usually does, but there's something in those hard eyes I haven't seen before.

"It was a fight. No biggie."

"No biggie? Chopper, you went to jail for this."

"It was only lock-up. Hank got me out."

"You know this won't be the end of it." He'll have community service or something. He can't possibly get off scot-free, not to mention he'll be paying his uncle back every dime.

"What's it matter?" With that question, he presses off the couch and brushes past me.

"Where are you going?" I stand to find his back to me.

"Out," he throws the single word over his shoulder and storms through the front door.

"What the fuck was that?" I turn to my younger brother.

"Growing pains?" Hank responds. He's always been the less responsible of the two of us. He shrugs, as if a fight was an everyday occurrence. My son runs wild, but a fight isn't in his repertoire of offenses. He's never raised a fist in anger to anyone.

I turn for the front door when I hear Chopper's car fire up, and then I spin back to face my brother.

A smirk graces his mouth. "So, how was your vacation?"

"Wouldn't you like to know? Are you fucking stupid? Why would you set Lily up to be there?"

"You liked that, didn't you?" Hank nods as if he pulled one over on me. His grin lighting up his face.

"Yeah, just great. Except she hates me just as much as she ever did."

Hank's all-too-pleased-with-himself expression falters. "She does not."

"Right. You're the one who just spent the best week of your life with her only to have her remind you in the last seconds of the mistake you made years ago to lose her."

"Did she really bring that up?" Hank stares at me, his expression like a confused child even though he's forty-three with a salt-and-pepper beard.

Did she? I reconsider. Nope. Actually, I did. I mentioned my mistake, blaming my son for what happened.

I'd never fault that child, I hear again, a tenderness to her voice when she spoke of him, defending him.

I fall onto the couch, covering my face with my hands. Hank returns to his seat on the chair to the side. My furniture sucks, I note, knowing without looking up that the room is like a man cave with old recliners and a lumpy, worn fabric couch. Dark drapes and deep wood paneling. *Brown.*

I stare at the carpet, threadbare and thin. Why am I thinking of these things?

141

What if…

"So, the best week of your life, huh?" Hank interjects. I look up at my brother, and his face pinches as he sees something in mine.

"Yeah, genius. It was fun."

"How fun?" Hank tilts his head, his brows dancing.

"I'm not kissing and telling you anything."

"So, there was kissing and things to tell?" Hank's forehead furrows with excitement.

"What are we, teenage chicks? I'm not telling you a thing."

"Just admit you enjoyed the vacation."

I sigh in exasperation, my chest aching. "I did. I enjoyed it more than I should."

+ + +

I only last until Monday morning before I break. I don't have Lily's number. We never exchanged them for the 739-code, and I don't want to call the bakery. I need to see her in person. The shop opens at seven, so I'm there fifteen minutes later. A sweet bell trills over the door, announcing my entrance like an old-fashioned, small-town bakery. However, it appears, I'm not the first customer.

I freeze as I see Lily embracing a young man in a leather jacket. She pulls back without looking up at me, cupping his face and looking him square in the face.

"I love you. We'll work this out."

Further stunned by her words, I speak. "What the fuck is this?"

Turning in Lily's arms is my son. My goddamn kid. His arms wrap around Lily's waist. Her hand still presses one of his cheeks.

"Are you fucking my son?" The question is totally irrational, and Chopper spins out of Lily's arms, placing his body in front of hers in a protective stance.

"How dare you?" Lily chides from behind him.

"Dad," Chopper growls. "That is just so wrong. She's my *aunt*."

The label lingers between us. Yes, Lily is his aunt. That's right. His mother is Lily's sister. Of course he isn't fucking her. My brain takes a moment to register the impossibility of Chopper and Lily together, but then a new question arises.

"How the hell do you—"

"Who the hell are you?" A short, cappuccino-toned woman with wild curls to her chin rounds past Lily and Chopper. Holding up two cake knives, she crosses them in front of her as though she's placing a hex on me.

Ignoring her, I address my son. "What the hell are you doing here?"

Before Chopper answers me, Lily steps forward, placing herself between my son and her feisty worker.

"Brut, I think you need to leave."

Her strong tone nearly brings me to my knees. We have so much to discuss, like how long has she known my son and when will I see her again. My heart races, but I'm not getting anywhere near Lily with ninja-bakery girl and my kid protecting her.

"We need to talk," I say, a plea in my voice.

"We will, but not now." Lily looks down at her hands, wringing them. I've never seen her so nervous. Unsettled by her words, I also accept when I've been dismissed. Turning toward the door, I slam it open with my palm and hear it rock back on the metal behind me.

Fuck. What the hell is going on?

+ + +

I'm shit at work for the rest of the day and leave the garage early, hoping to catch Lily again at the end of her hours. The front door to the bakery is still unlocked although the cupcake shaped sign reads: *Closed.* The blinds are lowered, and Lily stands with her back to the front door, wiping down the glass display case when I enter.

"It isn't safe to leave the door open."

Lily spins, holding a spray bottle and rag to her chest. "Jesus, Brut, you scared me."

I twist the lock myself and step toward her. She wears an apron over her pink T-shirt and some kind of knit skirt with pink and white stripes.

143

L.B. Dunbar

Her hair is in two pigtails like the day I saw her collecting shells. That moment suddenly seems like a lifetime ago.

"Lily pad." Her name clogs in my throat, and I swallow the lump suddenly there. There's so much to say, but I need to touch her first. She turns her back to me, setting the glass cleaner and towel on top of the display case. Her hands brace against the freshly cleaned glass, keeping her back to me.

"I can't do this, Brut."

"No, Lil," I say, choking again. Rushing up to her, my hands come to her hips, and I draw her back to me. "Lily, I'm sorry. I'm so sorry." I wrap my arms around her middle, and kiss her neck, pleading with her. "Forgive me for being an ass. This morning. Saturday morning. Any morning." Peppering her with more kisses, I tug her T-shirt to the side and nip her neck. Her head falls back to my shoulder.

"Damn it, Brut." I feel her body give against me, and my hands slip lower. I didn't sleep at all the past two nights without her in my bed. I'm crazed with need for her, to connect with her.

"It isn't over, Lil. It was never going to be one week. Everything and beyond. I want you. I *need* you." *I love you.* My hands come to her sides and begin gathering up her skirt. She isn't stopping me, and I take it as a sign to continue. Her fingers curl into fists on the display case, but she presses back against me.

"Brut," she groans.

"You still want me, sugar. I know you do." Her head shakes once, but her hips don't lie. Her backside curls into me. Scrambling for my jeans, I unbuckle my belt and unzip my pants. I'm frantic to be inside her. If she can feel me, she'll know we aren't over. With my foot between her feet, I tap at the sides suggesting she spread them. She allows me to hike her skirt to her hips. She's wearing a thong, and I tug the material, adrenaline giving me strength to snap the band. Scooping under her, I pull back by her hips and enter her with one thrust.

"Lily," I groan, filling her to the hilt. Her head falls forward to the display case. She meets me thrust for rushed thrust, pushing back to drag me in. Sparks dance before my eyes as we push and pull against one another. Grunting, growling, taking. It's desperate and raw. Within seconds, one of her hands lowers to touch herself and I grip her hips, guiding her in a frantic rhythm over me.

I'm sorry, I'm sorry, I'm sorry. I pound into her.

"Brut," she warns, stilling as her back arches and her channel clenches. I follow her within seconds, jetting off within her like a savage. Our ragged, harsh breaths fill the otherwise silent room while I collapse over her, sandwiching her against the case. My hands release her hips and raise to hers, linking our fingers together. She holds mine tightly as I squeeze her fingers in return.

"I can't lose you again."

Lily's body relaxes underneath me. "Brut, I—"

"Shh, baby. Not yet." We're breathing heavy, and I'm still buried inside her. I just want one more minute. One more week. One more anything.

Don't leave me, I plead, rolling my forehead against the back of her neck.

"We have so much to talk about," she finally says.

I know she's right. I know, this is it.

25

Letting Go

[Lily]

I just need a second to recover. I don't know where the moment of pure lust came from, but I somehow knew I needed it. I needed Brut inside me one more time because we didn't part on good terms when he left me too soon the other morning. In my fantasy, we'd make love again before we said tearful, heartfelt goodbyes and parted ways one more time.

I don't blame his early departure on him, but it still stung. My heart ripped open, and I'd cried as I picked up the lovemaking nest he'd made on the balcony. Washing the linens and packing my bags, I didn't bother to wipe the tears streaming down my face.

We couldn't be over, yet we couldn't begin again.

Lauren still stood between us. Now, more than ever.

Brut pulls out of me, and the combination of our release trickles down my leg. Using my apron, I swipe at the dribble and smooth down my skirt with shaky hands. Brut has picked up the scrap of material that was my thong but pockets it. I turn against the display case, using it to support my trembling legs as I watch Brut work at his belt buckle. He swipes a hand over his hair when he finishes and sheepishly looks up at me.

"I apologize. That was a bit rough."

How could I tell him I liked it? I wanted it. *One more time.* I've felt so discombobulated since Saturday morning, and then all this stuff with Chopper.

"Let me get us something to drink," I offer, knowing we're going to need something strong for all the shit we need to unbottle. I walk on quivering legs to the kitchen in the back of my bakery, looking in one of the upper cabinets for a bottle of Jim Bean that Esther keeps for toasting special occasions. Brut has followed me and stands on one side of the stainless-steel table in the center of the room. I should take him upstairs to my place because it would be more comfortable. But I'm worried if I do, I'll never let him go, and I can't take the heartbreak that will bring. My heart is already torn in two, and he's going to hate me after this conversation.

I pour us each a quarter of the short glass and slide his to him. He stares at me, waiting, and I slam back the liquid courage.

"Where do you want to start?"

Brut looks away for a moment, his fingers wrapping around his glass but not lifting it to his lips.

"I never meant to hurt you," he says, and my eyes close. This conversation is not the one I intended. It was twenty-two years ago. I was nineteen and horny, and the man I thought I loved didn't love me enough to have sex with me. Instead, he had it with my sister. It's over.

"Let's start with Chopper instead," I offer.

"Let's start at the beginning," he insists. "I'd lost my scholarship. My father was an alcoholic, who gambled more than I knew, and then became too sick to work. I was hardly holding the garage together, so he wouldn't lose it, and I was wildly mad about a girl I had no business touching."

I stare at him, wide-eyed. My heart racing. *I can't hear this.*

"You had so many dreams, Lily. You were larger than life. Larger than the life I had, and I knew I'd never be enough for you. You'd be my mom all over again."

"What are you talking about?"

"My mom was so unhappy with my pop. She didn't want to be a mechanic's wife. She wanted something more. I always wanted more myself and then it all went to shit. I was shit. I drank too much and gave into something I had no business giving into."

"Why didn't you come to me?"

"And do what, Lil? Take your innocence in my anger that I was a loser. That I was going nowhere, losing out on school and a different career, all to save my drunk father's ass and a garage I wanted nothing to do with."

"I'm sorry, Brut." And I truly am. Brut has been a caregiver all his life from the hint of things he's said the past week. His dad's garage. His

147

brother's career. His son's upbringing. Brut's life has been taking care of others.

"What are you sorry for?"

"That I wasn't enough for you. That whether you were a mechanic or not, a teacher or not, none of it made any difference to me. I was young and naïve, but I know how I felt." My voice shakes, and my hands clasp against my chest, trying to hold in the pounding of my heart. "I loved you, Brut, and you didn't love me." Tears fall, and I curse the traitorous stream.

"Lily." There's so much in my name, but not what I want to hear.

I swallow, finished with our past. I need to change topics because the present lays before us.

"I never liked knowing I had a nephew so close who didn't even know his family."

"I'm his family," Brut snaps, slamming a hand on the table. I flinch, taken aback by the sharpness of his tone, but his anger fuels me forward.

"When Lauren told me…my God, Brut, when she gloated about what happened, it killed me inside. Devastated me." I pause, collecting my breath. "But you are an amazing father. I see so much of you in him." My voice softens. "I just thought he might need a female influence in his life once in a while."

"So, you took it upon yourself to be it? And you never told *me*?"

I stare at him, puzzled by his tone. Is he saying I needed his permission? Maybe when Chopper was younger but not now. He's an adult.

Ignoring his question, I respond differently. "I'm sorry for what she did." Lauren. My older sister. She fucked my boyfriend to prove a point. *He doesn't want a kid for a lover.* Then she found out she was pregnant. A baby innocent of their decision. "It was cruel to both of you."

By the time Brut got Chopper, he and I were history. I wanted to offer my help, but I didn't know how. The wound just grew deeper and deeper for me.

"I went to your home after she left Chopper with you."

"You what?" Brut shakes his head, his voice rising.

"Lauren had disappeared. I thought you might know something. Your dad interceded. He told me flat out you didn't need her or any other relatives related to her. That's when I knew you had him, and he was at least safe with you."

"Why didn't you come to me at the shop?"

"I just...I couldn't face the place." So many memories of sneaking off to meet him—as his little secret. He broke my heart, and I couldn't return to the scene of my crimes. "I was young. I made mistakes." I don't need to remind Brut he made them, too.

"How did you meet Chopper?"

"He came into the bakery with some other kids. He was about fourteen or fifteen. I recognized him instantly. It was so surreal. He looks so much like you. I just went up to him and said, 'Hey, I'm your Aunt Lily,' without even thinking." I remember the day with complete clarity. He was with a group of guys and a few girls, who I assumed were the reason the boys were even in a bakery. One girl called out his name, and when I looked over at him, I saw a younger Brut instantly. Brown hair like soft leather. A smile that would break a girl's heart. Blue eyes shaped like my sister's but brilliant like his father's.

"Fifteen?" Brut's gaze searches my face for answers. "That was seven years ago." His voice fades, questioning the timing.

"He decided to keep in touch with me. He'd come here to visit, or he'd call me to talk." The truth falls between us and hurt etches into Brut's wrinkled brow. Guilt holds my throat, and I swallow at the pain I'm causing him.

Brut shakes his head in disbelief. "He never told me."

"He said you never talked about his mother or her family, as if we didn't exist. I told him I would respect your wishes, and leave him alone, but if he ever needed anything, as a friend, I was here for him." Chopper took me up on the offer. We've chatted about girls, friendships, and even a few life decisions, but I never asked about his dad, and he never told me anything about their relationship.

"Why didn't he tell me?" Brut questions, his brows pinching. My heart aches at the betrayal he must feel his son caused him. Brut's expression morphs, and I practically see another thought form. "Why didn't you mention it? All week, Lily. A *week*," he stresses.

"I wasn't thinking of Chopper last week." My voice lowers. I *wasn't* thinking of him. My head was only full of Brut and me, and the promise of our time together. No past. No future.

"Why was he here today?" Brut's tone sharpens again, and the news I'm about to share will be even harder to accept, especially as I'm sensing from the question Chopper hasn't mentioned anything. I'm betraying Chopper, but Brut needs to know what's happened. This will be the final fissure between us.

"Lauren contacted Chopper. On Friday." Brut's brows rise, surmising the same as me. Chopper's fight stemmed from Lauren. "She claims she's dying and wants to see him."

"Abso-*fucking*-lutely not." The threatening venom within Brut's tone is uncharacteristic of him, yet totally understandable. I don't know what Lauren could be playing at, but she's sent her son into a tailspin of questions. "She has no claim to him."

"I agree with you in every way, I do, but she's Chopper's mother, and if she is dying, *he* has so many unanswered questions that only *she* can answer."

Brut glares at me, disagreeing with me without speaking.

"Did you know? Are you still in contact with your sister? Did you know she was dying? Is this one more thing you kept from me?"

I want to reach for him and assure him I had no idea. Lauren hadn't contacted me.

"No." I shake my head adamantly. "The day we...I...when...I walked away from her too. I went to L.A. and took a job in a bakery to learn the business. I haven't spoken to her or heard anything other than a few hints from my mother about the baby being born and then Lauren went missing. I feared for him. But she's never contacted me."

Brut stares at me, struggling with whether to believe me.

"No. Just no," he blurts. "She will not see him. She abandoned him. That's all he needs to know." Brut scrubs a hand down his face. "The paternity test. Do you know what kind of hell that was for me? What if he hadn't been mine, yet here was a baby sitting on my front porch? And finding out he was mine added a new layer of fuckup with that bitch."

I flinch despite my agreement.

"Then waiting out the abandonment process and legally changing his name." Brut throws his glass toward the sink, whiskey raining down across my pristine kitchen. Thankfully, the glass ricochets within the stainless-steel basin where it lands and doesn't break.

"He's my son," Brut shouts, pointing at his chest. "Mine."

My heart breaks in two. Brut is correct. *He* raised Chopper on his own. Lauren has no right to her son. She walked away from him. And I didn't think I should be involved until Chopper stood in my shop with eyes so much like my sister's and the rest of him one-hundred percent Brut.

Brut stares at me. His face is confusion and disbelief, a broken heart and a damaged spirit.

And when he walks out my bakery door, I'm certain he'll never be back again.

26

Death Becomes Her

[Lily]

"I guess my dad is pretty mad, huh?" Chopper sits on a stool drawn up to my stainless-steel table, watching me fill cupcake tins. With his elbow perched on the edge of the table, he casually leans forward as though he isn't as filled with conflicting thoughts as he is. He watches me, dressed in his typical jeans and a faded T-shirt with the Restored Dreams logo on it. The process of filling cake cups is usually methodic and soothing, but today, I'm out of sorts, my rhythm is off, and I'm making a small mess.

"He has a right to be."

"But he shouldn't be mad at you. You didn't do anything."

I sigh. "That's actually why he *is* mad, honey. I didn't say anything. I didn't tell him we knew each other because I promised you I wouldn't. And I didn't tell him about your mother although, truthfully, I'd just heard the news myself." I was still struggling with the fact that my older sister, the one estranged to me for almost twenty years, wanted to see me as well as her son.

A friend of Lauren's named Crystal had contacted me on Sunday evening. The call included a short rundown of Lauren's health history. My sister had abdominal pains she'd blown off for too long as indigestion. Instead, it was colon cancer. She was given only months to live although a more recent evaluation moved up her end date. She was in the hospital, and Crystal thought things might decline through the week. She informed me that Lauren was holding out hope for Chopper and me to come see her before she gave up.

"Tell me how you hooked up with Dad again?"

I freeze, an extra dollop of batter overfilling the cupcake dish. Chopper doesn't mean he wants the details of sex with his father, but I'm still shaken by the question.

"We saw each other last week. On our vacations."

Chopper's head twists, his expression puzzled as he thinks of something. *Please don't recognize my voice from the time you called.*

"Huh, so weird he didn't mention it when I spoke to him."

"Really?" I mumble, removing batter from the overfilled wrapper as a diversion. I scrape out the mixture as best I can and throw the wasted wrapper in the trash.

"So, you and Dad...just ran into each other. Two old friends?"

I'm not certain how much Chopper does or doesn't know, but I won't be the one who tells him the sordid history of his father, my sister, and me.

"Yep."

Chopper nods once, and the movement is so similar to his father it pains me. His lips crook in a smile like his dad as well.

"You know, Lily, you can't bullshit a bullshitter."

With my back to him, I stiffen as I've moved to the sink. "What do you mean?" I ask, reaching for the faucet handles to rinse my hands.

"I mean, my dad walked in here guns blazing, ready to carry you out of here over his shoulder like some caveman freak. I'd say my dad has a thing for you. Isn't that interesting?"

I continue to wash my hands, keeping them under the spray. *Who knew how dirty they were?*

"Interesting, definitely."

Chopper's waiting me out, and I have no choice but to turn off the sink and dry my hands. Turning to face him, I see one eyebrow cocked, an expression I recognize as well, and pure intrigue written on his face. As though he knows a secret, but he isn't going to share it with me.

"Anyway. What did you decide?" I hate to circle back to less pleasant things—like his dying mother—but it's better than continuing this song and dance about Brut and me. There is no Brut and me. I don't want to pressure Chopper to make a decision about his mother, but I do think time is of the essence. If he wants to see her, the clock is ticking. He looks over his shoulder at the large digital timer by the entrance to the bakery as if he reads my mind. He has to make a decision sooner rather than later.

L.B. Dunbar

"I've got to go to work." He hops off the stool, and I sigh as he avoids answering my question. He takes two steps before stopping, his back to me, his voice soft. "Lily, if I go, will you come with me?"

My heart shreds from the fear in his voice, sounding so much like a child instead of the rugged young man he is at twenty-one, almost twenty-two.

"Of course, I'll go with you."

"I'd ask Dad, but he never wants to see her again. And I get it, but still…"

"I think if you asked your dad, he'd go with you regardless of his feelings. Whether he wants to see Lauren or not, he'd go to support you." I'm speaking for Brut, but I don't think I'm talking out of turn. He'd do anything for his son. I have faith in him in that regard.

"He's pretty bitter about her."

"With good reason," I defend. "But he's never been sour on you, Chopper. He loves you."

Chopper turns back to face me. "How do you know?" He's back to questioning me, seeking answers about my relationship with his father more than questioning his father's love for him.

"Once upon a time, I knew your dad, remember? He was a good man then, and I'm certain he's a better man now." I'm not bullshitting. Brut has been through a lot in life, all for others. He'd do the right thing for his son, no matter how he feels about my sister.

"Why wasn't he with you instead?" It's a rhetorical question, yet I still catch my breath. I don't even think Chopper knows his dad and I were a thing. I'm just the aunt, the sister of the woman who bore him. Still, it's something I've asked myself again and again in the past twenty-four hours.

Why wasn't it me? Why wasn't Chopper mine?

However, we can ask ourselves some questions until the end of time, and there's never going to be an answer.

+ + +

154

By evening, Chopper calls me to say he's decided to see Lauren. He picks Thursday as it's his day off and we make plans for him to meet me at the bakery. Then we'll ride together in my car. I trust myself to drive more than him, especially if he gets emotional. He isn't crying over his mother, but the hurt is still real.

Thursday isn't a good day for me as we have three weddings on Friday night, but Esther can manage them, and the new girl we hired at the beginning of the summer, Julia, has come in handy. She's a natural at baking—ironic, right?—although she's quiet and a little innocent. Esther frightens her with her loud voice and brazen talk about sex. Julia blushes each time Esther speaks, but she's listening with ears open, learning. A sexually curious girl resides inside the shy body of my little worker, and I recognize myself in her.

Unfortunately, I can't tell Chopper no, so I rearrange some things and confirm the address with Crystal. Lauren's been staying in Sun Valley, California, a twenty-five-minute ride northwest of Pasadena. If she wasn't dying, I'd kill her for being so close yet so inaccessible to her son. I have no idea how long she's been living in that area or why. Our parents moved to Texas long ago, and my mother claims she wasn't aware Lauren had been so close to our original home.

"I think it's nice she finally got in touch with you," my mother mentions when I call her to ask if she knew about Lauren. Mom didn't seem as surprised as I would have expected, so I have my answer. Ironically, she wasn't breaking any speed limits to rush to the side of her eldest daughter who lay dying.

My sister is dying. I mull the words over in my head and find I feel strangely numb about this information. We might have been sisters, but we were never friends. Rick started the wedge between us. By the time I was eighteen and Lauren was twenty, we weren't enemies but definitely did not want to be near one another. She drank. She snuck out. She hung with a rough crowd, and when she found out about Brut, she went ballistic.

"He's older than you by four years."

"He doesn't seem to mind," I recall saying.

155

L.B. Dunbar

"He'll mind when he sees you're a child. Has he taken you out? Why haven't I seen you at parties with him?" Those valid questions stung, but I didn't feel the need to justify Brut to Lauren even though I'd had the same quandary myself. He didn't include me in parties with his friends or find me a fake ID, as I'd heard other guys do for girls, to get them into a bar. Then one time we went to hear his brother's band. That's when Lauren found out about us.

Knowing I couldn't go the places she could, Lauren took advantage of Brut. I'd like to think he was strong enough to resist her, be a man and all that, loyal to me, et cetera, but I also had my eyes opened from the experience. Brut didn't love me enough to commit, and I'd never felt more like a child than when everything happened. Neither here nor there now, the fact remains my sister and I were estranged from the moment she told me about Brut and her. She became nonexistent to me. You can't miss what you don't have, and I didn't have sisterly love to pine over. I didn't know this person who was dying in Sun Valley. She was a stranger to me.

+ + +

On Wednesday night, I'm busy in my apartment kitchen which doubles as my office, working on finances. My cell phone rings under a pile of papers, and I almost ignore it, not wanting to lose my place in my calculations. When the phone rings a second time, vibrating some of the future party orders, I scramble to find it.

Two missed calls from Chopper and one from Crystal.

Quickly, I call Chopper.

"She's dead," he announces into the phone, a choking sound in his rough male voice.

"What? Who, honey?" The second I ask, I know who he's speaking of, and my stomach drops. I don't know if I feel sorrier for Chopper or the passing of my sister. *Chopper,* I realize instantly. I don't know my sister. I haven't since I was nineteen, which is more than half my life ago.

But Chopper, the sweet young man on my phone, has a new set of loss to deal with in life.

"She died this evening. Crystal called me." Chopper swallows so loudly I hear it through the phone. "I didn't get to see her."

"Chopper, honey, where are you, baby?"

"I'm just driving around." He swallows again, and suddenly, I'm worried he's drinking and driving.

"And where's your dad? Does he know?"

"I called you first. He's at the shop."

"Why don't you come here? Let's talk."

"I don't really want to talk," he says gruffly.

"Okay, let's just hang out. I can teach you to make cupcakes," I suggest. He isn't a child, but I need to distract him somehow. Making cupcakes always works for me.

Silence follows a moment before he whispers, "Why didn't she love me?"

My heart has no answers. I want to say it shouldn't matter. He had Brut, and an uncle and his late grandpop, but I know that won't be enough. A boy wants to know why his mama didn't keep him. Brut certainly had those questions about his own mother, who ran off when he was still young but old enough to remember her. It's another reason I wanted Chopper to know me. I was a woman who would stick with him, if he wanted me.

"I don't know, honey. I'm sure she did in some way. But you were better off without her." I pause, hoping I'm not overstepping with what I'm about to say next. "Her dying is sad, but this might be a sign. You weren't meant to reunite or make amends or whatever she was hoping would happen. It wasn't on you what happened to her. She'd already been gone from your life."

I'd like to think he was nodding as if he agreed, but I couldn't see him, and he remained too quiet to be heard through the phone.

"So, you're coming here, right?" I close my eyes, hoping he'll say yes.

"I'll get there, eventually," he says, but I don't like his answer.

"I'm open all night for you, honey."

L.B. Dunbar

"Okay. I'll be there in an hour."

Relief envelopes my shoulders. I don't want to betray him, but there's someone who needs to know what's going on. I inhale for courage and resolve to call Brut after I hang up with Chopper.

158

27
Reaching Out

[Brut]

The shop phone rings. Yes, we still have a landline although Midge has been trying to convince me it would be cheaper to use a cell phone for the business line. It's after hours, and I shouldn't answer it. We have a service that collects the messages, but when it rings a second time within a matter of seconds, something tells me to pick up.

"Restored Dreams," I bark, annoyed before any conversation has begun.

I need to go home. I've been spending too many hours in the garage, hoping it will keep my mind distracted from the clusterfuck of my life at the moment. The loss of Lily. The discovery she knows my son. The news of Lauren.

I don't know how to feel about Lauren's prognosis. I lack feelings when it comes to her, yet I don't wish death upon anyone. I want her to live, knowing her son had a decent life without her. I want her to understand he was happy, healthy, and cared for by a loving parent, if only one. Selfishly, I want him to refuse to see her, but I'd heard Chopper tell Hank his plans. He's going tomorrow to see Lauren…with Lily.

I'm upset he didn't ask me, but then again, I don't know how I would handle seeing her again. Twenty-two years ago, that woman ruined my life in some aspects. I instantly remind myself she enriched it as well by giving me Chopper. Even more so, she completed the blessing when she disappeared. We might have shared custody, and I shiver at the thought of being tethered to Lauren Warren for the rest of my life. Raising a son alone wasn't always easy. He missed out on having a mother, but I can't say I wish Lauren had been present. I fear the influence she would have had on him.

"Brut?"

I startle at the female voice, soft and hesitant, through the phone and exhale her name in strained relief. "Lily pad."

Lily kept things from me and while I could beat myself up for keeping things from her years ago, that was the past. The current deception with Chopper is more relevant. I'm hurt she's had a relationship with my son for the past seven years and hasn't included me.

Silence falls between us until I remember she called me.

"What's up?" My voice is too casual, too flippant, as if I couldn't care less that she's reaching out to me, but my heart hammers in my chest, knocking on the inner wall and scolding me for being a dick.

"Chopper called me."

"Oh, yeah?" Sarcastic again, but now my heart pinches. I'm jealous, I admit it. In the past week, my world with my son has turned upside down. A decent relationship has twisted to nonexistent.

"He told me Lauren died." The words hang between us, a weight dropped, causing a solid thud, like a car falling off the lift.

"I'm sorry to hear that." A strange sense of emptiness surrounds me, like when a customer mentions their spouse's mother's cousin died. The news is sad but doesn't affect me. Death *is* sad. Cancer sucks. But I didn't know Lauren even twenty plus years ago. She was the sister of my sexy secret, who seduced me when I was drunk and vulnerable and stupid.

I want to ask why Lily's telling me, why Chopper didn't call me, but I bite my tongue, the bitterness filling my mouth.

"Well, thanks for letting me—"

"Chopper's just driving around. I'm worried he's drinking. I asked him to come here, to talk, to hang out, and I thought...I thought I'd let you know, in case you might worry."

I rub my forehead. I am worried, but more so, I want my son to come to me. Still, I appreciate what Lily's doing, informing me of her concern and her intervention, and I exhale in relief. At least he'll be safe if he goes to her.

"Thanks for letting me know." I have so much more I want to say, but I hold my tongue. I'm ready to dismiss Lily. If I don't, I'll end up begging her to explain things to me. I want to understand. How did things get so out of control? How did I lose her again so quickly?

160

"If you want…you're welcome to join us. I can't promise a party, but we could just be here for Chopper. I told him I'd even let him make cupcakes."

I snort. "Haven't you already taught him how?" Admittedly, I'm a little upset to learn he might have done such a thing with her, and without me. A vision of Chopper in my kitchen as a child comes to mind—scooping out ingredients and dumping them into a bowl—only added to the visual is Lily, and she's laughing. I miss her sounds. Shaking my head, I rid my mind of things that never were.

"Nope." She giggles without humor. "I just didn't know what else to offer him."

"Well, thanks, Lil. I'm sure he'll enjoy the distraction." Instantly, I recall Lily making cupcakes at the beach house and how we got distracted together, smoking out the kitchen. Then I remember the night I frosted her neck and nipples. Caramel will never be the same to me. Within seconds, I'm hard and cursing myself.

"Okay, yeah, he said he'd be here in an hour. I can call you again if I think things look bad, like he's drunk or something."

"Maybe we could just have a code for it." My lip curls as the words leave my mouth, and I wait to hear if Lily recognizes what I'd said. A second passes, and then she snorts. The snickering sound stiffens me, and I have to lean back in my chair due to the uncomfortable strain behind my zipper.

Dammit, I miss her.

"I'll keep you posted, unless, again, you want to come here, too." Something lingers unsaid in her invitation, and I want to believe she wants my presence, but I can't give in. Anger still hums under my skin.

Only, once we hang up, I find myself reaching for my keys, knowing where my SUV is going to lead me.

28

Because Cupcakes

[Lily]

Chopper stirs batter with the efficiency of a Kitchenaid mix master. Beating the crap out of the ingredients has given him some focus. His steps faltered when he initially arrived, raising my concern. Despite his general swagger, his pace was that of someone who'd been drinking, and another breath of relief fills my lungs that he's presently sitting in my bakery kitchen instead of out driving.

I probably shouldn't have called Brut. Chopper will think I betrayed him in some way, but I also thought Brut needed to be informed of what had happened and how *I* handled things. I wasn't Chopper's parent—I wasn't a parent period—so the respectful thing to do seemed like giving Brut a heads-up. The decision whether to come here or not would fall on Brut, but I offered my place as a haven, a neutral territory of sorts for father and son.

Lost in concentration on Chopper's eager stirring, it takes a second to recognize someone is rapping on the back door to the kitchen.

"Special delivery?" Chopper asks, his brows raised in the familiar way of his father. Glancing at me with his teasing grin and his relaxed face as he mixes batter in a bowl, I see the child inside the man, and my heart breaks a little for him.

Under normal circumstances, I wouldn't open the kitchen door this late, but I have a suspicion of who it could be, and a smile graces my face. Instantly, Brut admonishes me for opening the door without peering through the peephole.

"You know it isn't safe to open your door this late." His eyes narrow as I step back, allowing him entrance. "Unless you're expecting someone." The hesitant drop in his voice suggests I'm waiting for someone else and sends cartwheels spinning inside my belly. *Does he really believe I'd already be onto another man?* Brut Paige has ruined me once again, and I won't be dating or anything else for a long time.

"I was only hoping it was you." The statement might have come out a little too breathy, a little too desperate, so I clarify. "For Chopper, of course. I was hoping you would show for Chopper." With that, I turn and lead Brut farther into the kitchen.

"What the…?" Chopper stops his rapid swirling to peer up at his father, and then he looks at me, the depths of confusion unmasked in his eyes. "Lily?"

"He needed to know about Lauren. And we're both concerned about you."

Brut hesitates beside me, slipping his hands into the pockets of his jeans. The two men stare at one another. I marvel at the unspoken exchange between father and son. Brut's jaw twitches with the sting that his son doesn't want him here and I'm crushed for him. Chopper's expression states all his own hurts, which he's struggling to compartmentalize.

Thicker than the batter in the bowls, silence falls between us.

The first to speak is Brut, his tone calm, his body language shifting. "Whatcha making?"

The ease of his voice suggests this is how Brut mastered taking care of others. He isn't yelling or screaming, or threatening to hit something, which might have happened in my family. As if he can handle this situation, he's calm and confident, at least in appearance.

In response, Chopper's shoulders settle, and he looks down at the bowl before him. "Monster cupcakes," Chopper replies, his voice lowered.

Brut steps forward, keeping the steel worktable between him and his son. "What's in those?"

"Oatmeal and M&Ms and peanut butter. It's like a cookie on crack."

Brut laughs at his son's explanation. Then, his body stiffens, hesitating as though he'd like to help, as if he can't *help* himself not to offer, but he holds back, just watching his son who is no longer swirling the batter but mashing the whisk into the thick mixture.

"Sounds delicious." Brut nods at the bowl where I've been experimenting. A bottle of liquid caramel sits to the side. His lips twist in recognition. "And what's that one?"

"Lily says it's Midnight Nibble, but I think Midnight Nipple sounds better. She's going to cover the top with drizzles of caramel."

Brut's gaze jump to mine, but I look away quickly, feeling heat in my face.

"Sounds even better."

The corner of my lips curl, though I still can't look up at him. I hate that I'm responding to Brut when he hurt my feelings the other day, accusing me of sleeping with his son and then angered that I have a relationship with Chopper without Brut's knowledge. I also think back on the sex we had against my front display case. Desperate. Raw. Edgy. We were saying goodbye forever, taking the one last chance we didn't get when we were interrupted Saturday morning.

My grin grows heavy as I realize I may never touch this man again.

"Want to help?" I offer. Cupcakes can be the solution to many unanswerable questions, and we all have our own private thoughts to grapple with tonight.

I push the bowl where I've been blending chocolate and salted caramel toward Brut. "Mix."

For several minutes, we stir and fold before we bake. With the cupcakes in the oven, I reach for whiskey in an upper cabinet.

"Let's toast." In the Irish tradition, you take a shot in honor of the dead and turn the glass upside down on the casket. We won't be doing such a thing for Lauren, but something should be said in honor of her. Chopper warily peers at me while Brut's edge has returned.

"To fathers and sons," I begin. "For love and understanding. Patience and kindness. Dedication and devotion. Relationships that—"

"Can we just drink?" Chopper interjects.

"Don't interrupt Lily," Brut replies.

Chopper defiantly slams back the shot, and Brut watches, his anger slowly brewing. I sigh, taking my shot for liquid courage. Chopper lowers his glass with a sharp thud on the steel tabletop and hops off the stool he's been sitting on most of the night.

"I'm out of here," he announces, swiping at his lips.

But before he takes two steps, Brut asks, "Where are you going?"

"Out," Chopper snaps, turning for my front door.

Without thinking, I reach for Brut's forearm but direct my voice at his son. "Sit," I snap, and Chopper freezes.

Slowly, he turns his body to face me, fists clenching at his sides. Before he can even question me, his father speaks up.

"I have something to tell you."

Both Chopper and my head whip up to Brut. He lowers his head, twirling the shot glass between his fingers.

"I have a story to tell you."

"I'm a little old for story time," Chopper snarks. Still gripping Brut's forearm, I see Chopper's eyes trained on my hold. Slowly, I release Brut who watches my fingers slip from his skin.

"Well, this is a story I should have told you a long time ago." Brut takes his shot, then lowers the glass with a gentle tap on the steel top.

To my surprise, Chopper slides back onto the stool.

"When I was twenty-three, I loved a girl."

My breath hitches, and Chopper's eyes shift to me.

"She was full of promise. Excitement. Life ahead of her. And her laugh. God, her laugh was the best sound in the world."

I tremble.

"Lauren was like that?" Chopper interjects, and both Brut and I glance over at him.

"Not your mother," Brut clarifies. "I've already told you before, what happened between your mother and I was a one-night decision." Brut peers at his son, and there's an entire conversation I'm not hearing. "I'm talking about your mother's *sister*."

A second passes before understanding crosses Chopper's face, registering my relationship with his mother. Confusion scribbles over his expression as he glances from his father to me and back. "Lily." My name whispers between us all.

"She was younger than me. Nineteen to my twenty-three. And so pretty. So sexy," Brut adds, and I watch as Chopper makes a face. "She had plans and so did I. I wanted to be a teacher, maybe a professor one

L.B. Dunbar

day. But I lost my scholarship, and my pop couldn't afford the tuition. His drinking and debts had driven the shop into the ground, and he was slipping after it."

Brut swipes through his hair as he looks up at his son. "I wanted to give this girl her dreams. Be her everything. But I lost focus. For one night, I lost focus." Brut exhales heavily.

"Lauren," Chopper mutters. His brows pinch before he glares at his dad. "Your girlfriend's sister?" The label echoes through the kitchen, bouncing off the steel and ricocheting back at us.

Brut holds his head high, but his shoulders bear the weight of so many things. "That decision changed the course of everything, and I regret every moment of it."

Chopper sucks in a breath. "But that means I—"

"Am the only positive thing to come from that night." Brut pauses. "You are one of the best parts of my life."

Tears fill my eyes at the admission Brut has given his son.

"You are the only thing I have *never* regretted."

I swallow back the lump in my throat and quickly swipe at my eyes.

"But I could have been her son." Chopper points at me, and I turn my head to Brut, wondering what he'll say next.

"You would have never been her son. A son with her would have been someone else. *You* wouldn't have existed without Lauren. And because I'd never give you up or give up who you are, I don't ever wish for you to be anyone else's."

What Brut says makes total sense. If *we* had children, they would have been a different combination of genes and personalities, which means scientifically speaking, Chopper wouldn't be Chopper even if we named a son the same thing. It doesn't mean I wouldn't have raised this boy as my son if Brut had ever asked me. No, Chopper was destined to be who he is *because* of who his biological parents were and the result of their actions after his birth.

I understand the reasoning, but Chopper seems to be struggling.

"How could you do that to her?" he questions, his gaze shifting to me.

"I've tortured myself the same question for twenty-two years."

166

My heart rips at the honesty.

"How can you even look at him?" Chopper directs to me, his face horrified by what he's learned. "It had to have hurt like nothing else."

"It did hurt, more than I can ever describe." My eyes shift to Brut who has closed his. His fingers curl to fists as they rest on the steel table. Then, I gaze back at Chopper. "But it's called forgiveness, honey. I had to forgive them, if for no other reason than to allow myself peace and move on."

Chopper's forehead furrows as he ponders what I've said. Then, his eyes widen, filled with their own well of pain.

"You must hate me," he chokes on the quiet declaration.

Instantly, I circle the island, reaching for his face and cupping it gently between my hands.

"I've told you before that I love you, and I don't say those words lightly. You are part of me by the nature of being my sister's son. But you've grown into someone very, very special to me. I do not, nor have I ever, held what they did against you. Like I said...forgiveness. Bitterness can eat you up if you let it, honey. I've seen it in so many people. And bitterness isn't good for anyone, especially the person who bears it. I...I just don't live my life like that."

Chopper nods within my clasp, and I lean forward to kiss his forehead despite his manly size.

"You'll need to forgive her as well," I offer. "If you resent Lauren...her leaving you, her death before you could see her...that resentment will only fester, and Lauren wins a victory she does not deserve."

Chopper tips his head again, his eyes closing at my words. A tear slips from the corner of one, and my thumb is quick to brush it aside.

"I just wanted to know why."

"Some questions we never have answers for. Call it destiny or fate or a sign. It just is what it is, and we can dwell, or we can move on. You decide. You can only live your life, honey, and not worry or wonder about the reasons behind others."

Chopper's eyes remain closed, but another tear leaks out. Wrapping my arms around him, I pull him to me. He doesn't embrace me back at first, and that's okay. He needs my comfort, and I'd give him anything he asks of me. Eventually, he slowly lifts his arms and encircles my waist. Then, he shudders against me.

I can't see Brut because he's behind me. I have no idea how he feels about what I've said or how I'm acting toward his son. All I know is a young man is hurting, until a hand comes to my lower back. Peeking around Chopper's head, I see Brut's hand cupping the back of his son, stroking through his hair in a soothing manner.

While I don't want to let go, Brut needs in, and Chopper needs his father. As I slide back, Brut's hand on his son's head tugs him to his chest. Chopper falls to the side, leaning into his father. I release Chopper, allowing Brut to take over. Chopper tugs at his dad's tee, willing away the tears but unable to tamp down a sob or two.

Normally, I'd expect a hug between two men to be awkward—one between a father and his grown son potentially strained—but Brut is holding his son like he's had a lifetime of embracing this boy, no matter the age. He kisses the top of his head without hesitancy.

"I love you," he mutters to his child, and my heart breaks all over again from the tenderness and sincerity. "We'll get through this." The collective *we* proves Brut's solidarity with his son. I sense Brut has said this statement too often in his life. He's gotten *through* so many things, but at some point, you wish for more than merely getting by.

Watching in wonder at the display of affection before me, I'm shattered again by the love of father and son. There is a rightness to Brut and Chopper. They need one another.

Brut turns his head to rest against his boy's and looks at me. "Thank you," he mouths.

Brut might feel he owes me, but I want to tell him he owes me nothing. Witnessing him with Chopper puts everything into perspective for me.

Life has happened as it should.

29

Funerals Aren't Supposed to Be Sexy

[Brut]

The past two days have been hell. Lauren made Chopper the executor of her estate. *What a crock.* Did she even own anything? This news further enlightens us that he's therefore responsible for her funeral. I'd like to find a cardboard box and set her out to sea, but I keep my comments to myself. Instead, I go with Chopper to the funeral home in Sun Valley. Lily joins us.

Chopper seems to be relying heavily on Lily, and after the other night in her bakery kitchen, I see the connection between my son and her is strong.

"I love you," she'd easily told him. As if the words were so simple. As if he were her child.

Myself, I find quiet relief in Lily's presence although we keep our distance. Without speaking about it, we both agree the focus needs to be on Chopper. He needs our support in any manner to get through this bizarre twist of events.

Chopper has the awful experience of picking out a coffin but declines decisions about the service. Crystal has been rather forthcoming to explain Lauren had few friends, and she doesn't suspect the funeral will be large. Chopper's agreed to an open casket viewing for a half-hour with a brief prayer service followed by a short funeral procession to the closest cemetery. Whatever Lauren's reasons were to go to Sun Valley, she will rest here eternally.

I'm rather proud of Chopper. He's acting like an adult while I sense the child inside him. He's freaked out by his decisions but keeps his calm. He doesn't understand why he has this responsibility from someone he never knew or who never wanted him. If she wasn't already dead, I'd kill Lauren and pay whatever consequences.

L.B. Dunbar

The morning of the funeral, Hank drives Midge, Chopper, and me to the funeral home. My brother and his wife decided to attend as moral support. Knowing our whole past, Hank understands this is a crazy situation, one I still don't fully have my head wrapped around. He's turning into a good brother—not like he wasn't before—but he's stepping it up with Midge by his side.

The funeral will be the first time Chopper has ever seen his mother, and his nerves show in how he jiggles his knee in the back seat next to me. I'm tempted to tap him, to make him stop like I'd do during parent-teacher conferences or when I was once called into the principal's office, but I don't dare touch him today. *Let him have his anxious moment.* I'm scared out of my mind, as well. I haven't seen Lauren in twenty-two years either. This isn't exactly how I pictured meeting her again.

When we arrive at the funeral home, I feel strangely numb as though I'm doing something I don't want to do but have no choice. I have no desire to attend a service commemorating the end of a person's life. Surprisingly, I was able to find my suit still fits although I'm certain it's outdated. Chopper and I agreed he didn't need a suit if he didn't want one, so he wore a black button-down with black jeans and his heavy boots. I'm fidgeting with the buttons on my coat as we approach the front doors.

As we enter, everything hits me when I see Lily. She's dressed in a shapely black dress, cutting just above her knees with short cap sleeves over her shoulders. Her neck is exposed, and my mouth waters to kiss her at the juncture I know will turn her to putty. The thought is inappropriate, but she looks amazing and even offers a weak smile when she sees me. Then her attention shifts to Chopper who walks into her open arms.

Like the night at the bakery, I want to hold them both. The other night, I held off on touching Lily other than a hand on her back, signaling my presence, but my body hummed to envelop them collectively. Eventually, Lily relinquished Chopper to me. Today, I want to wrap them in my arms and get us the hell out of here. Instead, I step forward when Chopper steps out of her embrace.

"Lily." I address her too formally as I choke off the second half of her nickname, swallowing it back. Hank knows I spent my vacation week with Lily. He also knows we fought and have come to an unspoken truce during all that's transpired for the sake of Chopper.

"Lily," Hank says a little too loudly and a little too enthusiastically. "How was your vacation?"

Forget the funeral, he's going to drag us back more than a week to when life was good. *Has it really been ten days since the beach house?*

I want to take Hank out with my fists and then throw him in the coffin next to Lauren. *Asshole.*

"It was wonderful," Lily replies, raising a brow at him before looking over at Midge. "One day, we'll need to share how it all happened." Her other brow rises, emphasizing her knowledge that these two pulled some kind of stunt and somehow arranged our vacation together.

Hank chuckles and Midge flushes, but now isn't the time for answers.

Hank interrupts my thoughts when he speaks to Lily again, touching her shoulder. "How are you holding up?"

My head pops up as if the question is a riddle. In all the chaos, something I haven't considered is Lily's emotions, and now, I want to punch myself instead of Hank. *Lauren was her sister.* I have no idea if they've spoken over the years. She told me she knew nothing about Lauren's condition or her whereabouts, but that doesn't mean they hadn't talked at some point. Either way, Lily must have her own demons and torments about this day, and I've been so absorbed in Chopper I haven't paid her the attention she's due.

Is she grieving? Is she confused like Chopper? Does she need me?

"Oh, I'm fine." She waves off Hank and brushes a piece of her butterscotch-blond hair behind her ear. Her hair has a curl today as if she did it up for a special occasion. *Some special occasion.*

Watching my brother lean forward and kiss Lily's cheek, I'm back to wanting to punch him.

Midge steps up next and embraces Lily, speaking low into her ear. Lily nods against my sister-in-law, and a pang of jealousy courses

171

through me. Everyone's touching her when I want to be the one comforting her. My anger at first learning Lily knew Chopper and then the reveal of Lauren's death has dissipated to respect for Lily's kindness toward my son. Then my emotions returned to longing. I've missed her something fierce.

Still as a statue, Chopper waits just inside the viewing room. I nod at Lily to excuse myself, fisting my fingers in my pockets so I don't reach out and drag her to me. Nearing my son, he turns to me, and the panic in his eyes breaks me. He looks wounded beyond anything I can fix, and my heart rips to shreds. *Damn Lauren.* That's right, God damn her to hell for what she's doing again—abandoning Chopper.

Reaching for his shoulder, I squeeze. "It's okay. You don't need to go any farther if you don't wish."

Chopper nods, his eyes searching for Lily. She has stepped around me, standing close enough I can smell her fresh-air fragrance. Summer rain. Sunshine. Something fruity. My thoughts leap to ten days ago and us dancing on the deck of the beach house. I've never wanted time to roll backward more than I do at this moment.

Lily holds out a hand, and Chopper curls his fingers within his aunt's. It's strange to think of her in this manner. Stranger still that Chopper knows her relation to him, but a twinge of comfort comes to me as Lily leads my son to see his mother for the first and last time.

"She doesn't look how I imagined her," he says.

Lauren was very opposite her sister with her once raven black hair, cold blue eyes, and more angular features than the roundness of her younger sibling. Her hair has grayed, and her face looks swollen. I can't see her eyes, and I'm thankful.

Lily looks up at Chopper. "What did you think she would look like?"

"In my head, I envisioned you." His voice breaks.

I'm not certain if it's sorrow or relief, but I'm glad Lauren looks nothing like Lily. The contrast is refreshing, and hopefully, Chopper will continue to separate the two women in his head...and his heart.

Lily smiles weakly, her mouth falling open like she wants to tell him something, but then she changes her mind. We step aside as an older woman comes forward. Lily stays to the right of the coffin, greeting the woman who introduces herself as a nurse. She doesn't have much to offer about Lauren other than she didn't suffer much.

I take no comfort in what I hear. I don't wish pain and injury on Lauren, but I don't have any sympathy for her either. Instead, all my thoughts circle around Lily and my son.

Minutes later, the funeral director comes to the opposite side of the coffin and begins a short prayer. I admit my mind wanders off, drifting with the lull of his monotonous voice. I'm slammed in the chest with the vision of Lauren sidling up to me and seducing me. Her mouth near mine, telling me Lily won't mind. *She was a woman, and Lily was a child.* I remember fighting her off, but later, I'm in a back room with her. I recall whimpering Lily's name as I did what I shouldn't have done, and all the while Lauren encouraged me to take what I need.

"That's right. Think of Lily." Her slurred voice rattles through my head like ice cubes in an empty glass. Cold surrounds me, and I shiver.

Midge's hand comes to mine, but I don't respond to her touch. Instead, I look over at Lily sitting on the other side of Chopper. My heart hammers. Sweat trickles down my temple despite the chill. I want Lily's hand on me. I need her warmth to still the coolness covering my flesh. I'm staring at her, unabashedly, ignoring what's happening around us. My eyes refuse to tear away from her as if Lauren might rise up, cackle like the witch she was, and steal Lily away from me, steal my son. My gaze shifts to him, taking in the outline of his face, his floppy dark hair, his thick nose like mine, and his blue eyes, thankfully soft and sorrowful like his aunt and not penetrating like his mother's.

Quickly, the service ends, and we stand. The director asks if we'd like to say a final word before they close the casket, and Chopper declines. We're ready to exit the main room when the director announces he needs pall bearers. The funeral attendees number only a few with the nurse, Crystal, and a man no one asks about. The rest of the people are my family. Hank, Chopper, and I step forward although the last thing I want to do is touch the coffin. I don't want Chopper to either, as if holding the handle will somehow bring him into contact with Lauren on some level.

We wait outside as the coffin is prepared and then assist in lifting the wooden rectangle into a hearse. Hank says he will follow in his car, which places Lily behind us. Alone. I don't like this setup.

"Lily, ride with us," I say with a sternness to my voice, practically demanding her.

"I don't want to leave my car here." She dismissively waves while emotion fills her voice.

"You should go with her," Chopper states, and I find myself stuck between knowing I should comfort my son and wanting to be near Lily.

"No, I'll go with you," I offer, but I'm still looking back at Lily's car behind Hank's.

"Why don't we both ride with Lily?" Chopper suggests, and I want to tackle-hug him. Instead, I nod and stalk toward her car. She's already in the driver seat, but I open the door without permission.

"What the…?" She curbs her tongue as Chopper rounds her car to the passenger side.

"I'll drive." I hold out my hand to help her out of the car, and Chopper climbs into the back seat.

"This isn't necessary," Lily mutters, standing in my space and holding her ground.

Leaning forward, my lips near her ear. "Don't make me spank you in front of these people to get my way."

Her breath hitches, and I pull back to see her eyes dilate. She'd like it, and my dick jolts to life. This isn't the time nor were my words appropriate, but it gets her moving. I shuffle her around the vehicle, keeping my hand on the small of her back until she slips into the passenger seat.

I'm honestly wondering if anyone would care if I just gunned it out of this parking lot and sped back to Pasadena instead of following the hearse to the cemetery.

When I return to the driver's seat, the dazed glaze in Lily's eyes returns, telling me she'd never understand if we left abruptly. Her elbow perches on the edge of the door. Her head rests in her hand. She's a million miles away, and I'm grateful I demanded to drive. I don't need her getting in an accident.

We arrive at the burial plot and stand under a gloomy sky as the funeral director reads another prayer. My hand returns to Lily's back as if magnetically pulled to the spot, and I don't remove it even as we stand on the edge of the grave. Chopper remains somber, hands folded before him with his head lowered as we await the final words.

When all is over, Hank steps forward and shakes the director's hand, and I follow suit. We walk as a group, sticking close but not touching while we near our cars once more. Lily stops a few feet from hers and turns back to the gravesite. Like Lot to his wife, I want to tell her not to look back. I want the past to be the past and hopefully be buried with the woman who changed everything, but Lily remains frozen, a pillar of salt rooting her to the earth as she stares.

I slow my gait and follow her gaze.

"I just want to make sure she goes in the grave." It's an odd statement, and we pause as the cemetery workers begin lowering the casket. The scratch of shovels against dirt echoes in the silence around us, and Lily begins to visibly quake.

"Enough," I whisper, reaching out for her arm, stroking a hand down her pebbled skin. She remains still as if unaware of my touch. "Let's go."

Lily turns to look at me, her eyes sparkling with unshed tears. I don't want her to suffer sorrow for Lauren, yet the pain in those misty blues express so much more is going on in her head.

"She was my sister," she whispers. "But I did not know her."

I nod, taking a second to peer back at the workers filling the pit in the ground. My gaze then swings to Hank, standing near his car. I'm truly blessed, I realize, as I love my brother, and he loves me. He stands with his wife, vigilant over her but supportive of me. I'm staring at him when Midge says something to Hank, and then she steps forward.

"Lily, honey," she speaks softly, like a mother to a child. "Come to the house. We're going to have dinner as a family tonight."

This snaps Lily's focus. First, she glances at me, and then over her shoulder at Midge. Smiling weakly, she puts on a brave face with false bravado. "I don't want to intrude on family time." Her voice cracks again, and she swallows.

175

L.B. Dunbar

"You're not intruding," Midge offers. "You're family, too."

Lily stares at Midge, and then the tears fall. Big tears at first. Silent and swollen, plopping like drops of rain. One here. Another there.

"I don't have a family." Her lips quiver, and I realize Lily's on the edge of shock. She's trembling again, and the tears plop down to her dress. I reach for her cheeks. She doesn't flinch, which I take as a good sign, but I also don't think she's aware of my touch.

"I'm your family," I say, forcing her to look at me. "Chopper, too."

The tears fall harder, and Lily's hands come to her face. I can't take the heartache vibrating off her and wrap my arms around her. She crumples against my chest, her hands still covering her cheeks as she sobs against me.

"Shh, Lily pad. It's okay." I stroke her hair as my other hand firmly holds her waist to keep her pressed against me. "We'll get through this."

I don't actually know if we'll ever be okay, but I'd like to think we have the future before us.

The past has finally closed the door.

30
Family First

[Lily]

My system shut down for a few moments and emotion overtook me as we stood on the drive, watching the men lower my sister's casket and cover her with dirt.

Dust to dust. An eerie sensation crawled over my skin, and I couldn't stop shaking. I also couldn't look away. I'd like to say a hundred images flashed in my head of Lauren and me when we were children, when we had been playmates, but my memory remained blank.

Ashes to ashes. The whole process left me cold, not so much from my emotions but from the experience. One day, I'll die, and who will attend my funeral? I have no family.

When Midge told me I was part of their family, and Brut gave me reassuring words that I had him and Chopper, I crumbled like a too-dry cupcake. I fell apart against him, needing his strength while knowing I didn't really have him in my life. The past week plus has been filled with so much strain I feel as if I've lost a year of my life instead of ten days in the late summer. I don't know what steps to take next, and that's how I find myself in my car with Brut driving me to his brother and sister-in-law's house.

Brut remains silent, and whether the intention is to give me space or be alone with his own thoughts, I appreciate the quiet. I want to know what he's thinking and how he's feeling, but I don't ask. I don't have the energy for his answers. We've come to a strange understanding of don't-speak-and-we-won't-know. We've huddled around Chopper for two days, supporting him through decisions someone so young shouldn't have to make as he dealt with the death of a mother he never knew.

I curse Lauren again, but I also realize nothing can be done about her decisions. Some answers will never be had. I worry for Chopper, but he seems to be handling everything in stride. Maybe he's just become numb like the rest of us.

When we arrive at Midge's, the first thing she places in my hand is a drink. It goes down a bit rough, but I instantly feel warmer than I've felt in days. I relax a little within the chaos of her home. Her sons are present—Elston, Ronin, and Liam—and I marvel at the fact Midge is going to have another child. Eighteen years difference from her oldest to the future baby, yet she glows like a youthful woman. Her hand occasionally caresses her belly, and on more than one occasion, Hank stops to do the same thing.

A sadness mixes with the warmth of alcohol and settles within me. *Resolve.* I'm not relaxed; I'm resolved to the disappointment of never having what Midge has—love and children. Family.

I don't want to blame my sister. Even though I spent tears on the lane near my sister's burial site, my remorse is not for her, but the absence of something greater. Recent events have been a reminder of all she took from me, yet I can't look back with confidence and say she took anything. Brut never claimed to love me. Marriage was certainly not on his bucket list. He was a vibrant young man, under the weight of life, struggling to push through for a dream. He was having fun. Nothing more.

A plate of veggies is placed before me as I sit on a stool in Midge's kitchen, and I take a bite or two before the house erupts in boisterous greetings near the front door. Tommy Carrigan and his wife, Edie, have arrived. I had met Tommy Carrigan—a long, long time ago—when Brut's brother, Hank, ran off to play for a band, and Brut snuck me into a club where they were playing. Chrome Teardrops was their name then with Kit Carrigan, Tommy's sister, as lead singer. Brut had Hank pull strings to get me into the bar as I was underage. It was one of the only times Brut and I were outside the garage office or the back seat of a car. It was also the night my sister discovered us.

"Darlin'," a Southern drawl addresses me, and dark eyes widen as Tommy Carrigan looks at me before shifting his eyes to Brut and back. His once dark hair has transformed to sleek black and bright silver. He even sports a heavy scruff of salt and pepper. Glancing over at Hank and comparing the two men, I can see them as young heartthrobs on a stage, playing songs to make women pant. Hell, even in their forties, women would toss their bras to them.

"She's more beautiful than I remember." Tommy winks at me and then shakes his head at Brut as though he's disappointed in him.

I don't know what any of this means, but his gaze is a reminder that Brut has not left my side. He lingers beside me where I'm seated on a stool. I'm certain he's the one to offer me a drink and set food in front of me. It's comforting yet unnerving at the same time.

"Edie, meet Lily Warren. She was the love of Brut's life."

Was. My sore eyes narrow as a pixie-haired blonde reaches for my hand and swats her husband at the same time.

"I see you're still a dick," Brut mutters behind me as Edie covers my hand with a second one, holding on a moment longer than necessary.

"Edie Carrigan," she says, smiling warmly. "And that was certainly awkward." Her eyes flit to Brut behind me.

"Nice to see you again, Edie," Brut says, stepping forward to place a chaste kiss on her cheek and a brief hug. As Brut pulls back, Tommy's already got an arm around his wife's waist, and I'm curious what the possessive move is all about. I'm sensing Brut and Tommy don't care for one another although I don't remember stories of their animosity.

I'm more curious why the house is filling up for a funeral luncheon when no one attended the funeral. Sadness returns at my lack of family, and I excuse myself to find the restroom.

As I'm returning from the powder room, I hear gunfire and shouting sounds coming from a room near the staircase. I peek my head inside to find a light-brown-haired ten-year-old, his tongue wiggling outside his mouth as he presses a controller with two thumbs.

He doesn't look up at me but addresses someone through a headset. "Go left, go left."

Hearing another gunshot and an explosion, I turn to the monitor to see blood splatter across the screen.

"Jesus," I say aloud and turn my head, finding Liam looking at me. Midge's youngest son is the male version of her in little boy form. Matching eyes, same hair color, warm smile.

L.B. Dunbar

"Hey cupcake la—" he begins but gets interrupted as he continues with the directions from his fellow player. We met when I made cupcakes for Hank and Midge's wedding dinner and another time when Midge wanted cupcakes for some clients. She's become quite the regular, and I appreciate the business.

After stepping inside the room, I take a seat next to Liam on the small couch.

"This is kind of graphic." I flinch as more blood splatters on the screen.

"Nah," he quips. "It's *Assassin's Creed*. It's historical, so it's all good."

I don't think I agree as another person is taken out on the screen. I'm mesmerized for a moment at the monotony of the movements in the game, though, and understand how gamers get sucked into hours of playing. Something happens, and Liam groans. He slaps the controller against leg and throws his head back on the cushion.

"I'm dead," he mutters into the headset, and then his eyes widen as he looks over at me. "Sorry."

"For what?" I chuckle.

"For saying dead. I'm sorry your sister died."

The condolence seems rather formal from a little kid, but I thank him for his sympathy.

"Mom said we didn't have to attend the funeral, but we had to be here for lunch. Said family first or something like that." He picks up the controller again.

"Well, you have a great family."

"Elston can be a jerk because he's older, and Ronin used to be my friend, but now he's too cool because he's in *high school*," Liam singsongs with mocking emphasis. "But Chopper's awesome." His tone shifts to full admiration.

"Yeah? What do you like about Chopper?"

"He doesn't treat me like a little kid. He's like Brut. They act like I'm someone, not like I don't know anything. Chopper's been showing me how to fix things on a car, and Brut keeps bringing me these kits where I can take stuff apart and rebuild it, but it all works mechanically."

180

I nod as if I have any idea what he's describing.

"That sounds…cool."

"It is cool. Mom says we're a clan of men, but I don't see anything wrong with that." He shrugs indifferently.

"Your mom's pregnant." This is no secret because she's definitely showing. "What will happen if you have a sister?"

Liam shrugs again. "I guess she'll learn to play baseball, do video games, and fix cars, too. That's what we do in this family." He's so cavalier and honest in his answer that I laugh.

"Sounds perfect," I mutter and look up to find Hank curled around the doorframe, looking at his youngest stepson with warmth in his eyes.

"It is perfect," he says softly, wiggling an eyebrow at me. He tips his head to the side, directing me to follow him, and I stand, excusing myself from Liam. Hank waits for me just outside the kitchen entrance.

"How are you doing?" he asks, peering down at me with playful eyes. They are the same blue as Brut's but not as edgy or serious as his older brother's. Hank is also more solid than Brut, so his crossed arms and imposing stare demand I answer.

"I don't know how to feel, I guess. I'm a little…out there." I wave a hand to imply anywhere but the present.

"Well, I want to reiterate what Midge said. You're our family, too. It's a weird, twisted connection, I get it, but Chopper knows who you are, and Brut's told me how amazing you've been toward my nephew, who happens to be your nephew too, so you have to know you're one of us."

Tears prickle my eyes again, and my nose burns. I blink a few times. "Thank you." Those are the only words I can find. I don't deserve their open arms although I didn't ever do anything directly to them. Still, I appreciate the earnest firmness of Hank's statement. I'm one of them.

"What's going on?" Suddenly, Brut stands at my side, holding my upper arm. "Why is she almost crying?" he snaps at his brother.

"Chill. I'm just reminding her that we're her family." Hank motions between the three of us, and Brut's eyes narrow at his brother.

"No wonder she wants to cry," Brut mocks, and like a pressure of air bubbling up inside me, I release a snort-laugh, before covering my

L.B. Dunbar

nose and giggling more. Brut's lips slowly crook up on one side, and his eyes dance. "Well, there she finally is."

My brows pinch as I watch his grin grow.

"I've been waiting for some of those sweet noises."

"Sweet?" Hank jokes. "Did you not just hear that honk?"

I'm giggling harder, like a complete loon, while Brut's mouth opens to a wide grin.

"Sweetest sounds I've ever heard come from Lily pad."

My breath hitches along with another giggle, and now it sounds like I've hiccupped.

"Cripes, get a room," Hank mutters, running his hand down my arm in comfort. His smile says he's teasing.

"We already had one, thanks to you," I mumble, and Hank freezes.

Brut's smile falls, and Hank watches me a second. Then his eyes twinkle, and his mouth opens. "Oh, you're definitely part of the family."

31

The Party Is Over

[Lily]

Brut drives me to the bakery although there's no reason for him to do so. He claims I've had too much to drink, which I deny. I'm warm and fuzzy but not buzzed. He also decides it isn't safe for me to go home alone so late. I've lived here for years and come home later than nine without worry. I understand people's concerns. This neighborhood, on the edge of Los Angeles, isn't a great, but the area is trying to revive itself. The rent is cheap for now, and I feel perfectly secure living here, but I don't argue with Brut. I don't want to be alone yet, which is only prolonging the inevitable.

Not only does Brut insist on driving me, but he's also adamant that he escort me to the back door, and then tells me he's going to walk me up to my apartment. The entrance to my place is within the bakery and one reason the apartment came with the space. The studio layout isn't much, but the owner did the space up nicely with exposed brick on two walls. It might have been a loft office for the original business, but it's been converted to include an open concept living area, and I do mean open. As you walk up the stairs, a low privacy wall encases the stairwell, but immediately at the top you see everything. A double bed in front of you. A couch and television to the left, and a four-seater kitchen table which doubles as my desk centering the L-shaped kitchen area. I'm able to write off the space as my office.

With a sheer curtain hanging as a divider between my bedroom, aka the bed, and my living area, consisting of said couch and T.V., but my place looks more Bohemian than homey.

"So, this is it," I say to Brut, crossing the short distance to my nightstand and removing my earrings. I hear Brut shuffling behind me, and it sounds as if he's placing his suit jacket over the back of a kitchen chair. I turn to face him and find him slowly taking in my studio. "It isn't much. I guess you probably have a nice house."

There's a little snip to my voice, and I don't know where the sarcasm comes from. He's already told me his house is run down, so I don't know why I'm thinking of it as none of that matters to me. Maybe it's that I don't want him sizing me up because I live in a tiny, unsafe apartment over the bakery, which is all I have in life. On the other hand, the way he stands in my place causes me to have a flash of our lives as if it were a different time. With his shirt sleeves rolled up and his collar unbuttoned, he could have just returned home from work—teaching. I might be dressed like this because I'd served dessert a party. The image is haunting, and I turn away from him.

"Thanks for the ride. Do you need to borrow my car to get home or call Chopper to pick you up?"

"I don't think you should be alone tonight." His low voice comes from directly behind me. T

he words tickle down my neck. In many ways, he's right. I don't want to sleep with my thoughts, which I know will bring no rest. When thick fingers come to my shoulders and squeeze, I tense up without meaning to. Then the tip of one finger strokes down the back of my neck, and my head lolls forward. My eyes close, and I give into the shiver rippling over my skin. Brut finds the zipper to my dress and slowly slides the closure downward, exposing my back.

"Brut." His name whispers like the caress of his hands on my skin.

"Let's just be, Lily pad. Let me be here for you."

I don't reply, just feel the warmth of his palms as he presses the sides of my dress until the fabric falls off my shoulders. Fingertips tickle down my spine and stop at my lower back. Brut pushes at the waist of my dress, forcing the remaining material to the floor.

"God, I love your back." He kisses my nape. "You are so beautiful."

I'm trembling again, only this time it's with need—need for his touch, his mouth, him inside me. I want to forget everything just for a little bit.

"So sexy," he murmurs as his hands cover my lower cheeks, smoothing his warm palms over the firm curves. I'm wearing a lace thong, and Brut slips a finger under the strip of fabric but doesn't remove it. "Keep the heels on and step forward."

With his hand on my hip, he guides me, moving me two feet to face the wall beside my nightstand. He drops his hold on my hip and lifts both my wrists.

"Keep your hands up," he mutters into my shoulder as he nips me, hard. My back arches at the sting, and my backside brushes against his silky suit pants. He moans against my skin as his tongue follows the trail of my neck to my shoulder. He reaches forward, dipping under the narrow lace covering me and combs through the thin strip of coarse hair.

"Let me take your worries," he says as he slips a finger inside me, and I moan like a porn star.

We've been together, obviously. We've had our week worth of sexcation, but this…this feels different, intimate, intense. Brut's finger slides slowly in and out before adding another and then a third.

"Oh God, Brut," I moan again. I'm full like this but not full enough.

"Like this first," he hisses into my neck, nibbling my skin, taking his time to linger with each bite and work his magic lower with each stroke. His movements are languid and luscious, and my body tightens. I press back, wanting friction with the stiff length in his pants. He thrusts forward, mimicking how he'll move, but not yet. For now, his fingers slide in and out of me, and the wet sound fills my apartment.

"You're so wet, sugar, and you're going to come so hard." His command makes it happen. I still, the rush flowing out of me as my knees give. Brut presses forward, flattening me against the wall.

"There she is," he says like he did earlier when I laughed. "Give me all your sounds."

I don't even realize I'm making a keening noise, a whimper at the relief. I'm outside myself, a million pieces, like confetti floating in the breeze, and it's heavenly.

"Are you still coming?"

I nod because I am. I've never felt anything like this, this longing, this lasting, this desire. With no purchase to grab anything, my hands slip from the wall, and I reach back for Brut's hip, holding him against me.

"I want you." I'll give him anything if he can make that kind of orgasm happen again.

"On the bed, on your knees."

I step over to the bed, ready to step out of my heels, but Brut demands I keep them on. I'm also still wearing the black lace at my ass and a black bra, which seems to turn him on. I feel sexy and alive, and I kneel on the edge of the mattress, spreading my thighs while I hear the release of his belt and the shimmy of his pants hitting the floor. He slips his shirt over his head in one tug and steps forward. He forces aside any lace obstructing him. Holding himself, he drags his tip between my seam, down to my entrance, teasing me, working me up again. I press back, eager for him.

"Do you have any idea how sexy you look like this?" he says, reminding me again how much he likes me, at least in this sex kitten position.

I arch my back and stretch my arms like the kitty cat he wants me to be, and that's all it takes before he slides into me—slow, deliberate, satisfying. He presses forward until he's to the hilt, and then he pulls back, torturing me with a leisurely tug-of-war that makes me ache. My body begs to keep him inside as he drags to my entrance as if he plans to exit me. After a few moments of slow push and pull, his patience breaks. His pace quickens, and our skin slaps as he pummels into me.

Holding both my hips, he grunts with each thrust, working harder, deeper, faster.

"God, I've missed you, Lily pad." His voice stammers as his movements chop the rhythm.

"Get there again," he commands, his tone steadier despite the hurried motions.

I don't know if I can, but before I speak, his fingers come around my hip and delve over folds slick and needy. Within seconds, I'm screaming his name, pushing back to force him deeper, afraid of losing this feeling, this connection, *him*. As I'm falling to pieces once again, fluttering to the bed with my release, he pulls out and flips me over.

Tugging my thighs, he spreads me wide, lowers so his knees hit the edge of the bed and impales me once again. I cry out at new sensation.

Brut holds each leg under my knees, rocking into me, watching himself enter my body and disappear.

"This is how it always should be," he says, staring at himself frosted by me, coating him so we work like a well-oiled machine. His eyes move up my body to my face. "Everything and beyond."

Right now, I almost believe we could have everything and beyond. I can pretend this is how it's always been. My mind races back to the image of him coming home from a day at school and me undressing after a social function. I allow myself to fall into make-believe for a few more minutes.

Brut reaches a pulsing orgasm, pushing me near the edge again as he fills me. Then, when he finishes, he collapses over me, covering me like a blanket. His weight pins me in place, and I take the heaviness of him as if I can hold this moment forever. *Everything and beyond.* But just as quickly, he stands, pulling out of me, and pulls up his boxer briefs and pants. He never stepped out of his clothing. He enters my bathroom as the door is just next to the nightstand and returns with a towel. I can't move and realize I'm still wearing my bra, thong, and shoes.

Brut helps me sit up and then squats down to slip off my heels. *Isn't the prince supposed to glide on the glass slipper, not remove them?* But I don't believe in fairy tales, and our night is only a fantasy.

Brut reaches for the covering on my bed and pulls it back, implying I should crawl in, which I do. I'm suddenly bone weary with exhaustion combined with sated sex.

"Brut," I whisper in question as he folds himself behind me.

"Don't think. Not yet." The command reminds me of the beach house.

We're going to need to think eventually, though, sooner rather than later.

+ + +

I wake to find I'm alone in my bed. Rolling to my side, I see Brut standing next to the mattress, staring down at me. He's dressed, and his hands are deep in his pockets.

"I thought the rule was you weren't allowed to leave the bed in the morning."

Brut chuckles softly, lowering his head, and I know what's coming. My heart races as I consider the way we were last night. It appears the finale has arrived.

I reach out my hand, and Brut lowers to squat next to the bed. We keep our eyes on one another.

"Thank you," I whisper, working to keep my voice steady.

Thank you for a second chance at the first time.

Thank you for making me feel alive and sexy.

Thank you for a dance in the rain and playing what ifs and making love under the moonlight.

"Why do I feel like you're saying goodbye?" Brut lowers his lips to my knuckles.

"Aren't you?" My question lingers between us, and when he doesn't look up, I have my answer. "I want to be there for Chopper, but I don't want us to be in the way. We had a second helping, Brut. The vacation was a little cupcake carved from the larger cake of life. It was sugar-sweet and delicious, but now it's been devoured. I'm satisfied and full and—"

"Can't move on without you," he mumbles into my skin.

"You will, Brut. You did before." I don't mean to be cruel, just honest.

"Jesus, Lily." His head shoots up, and his brows pinch. His eyes glisten. "Why are you doing this?"

Because I'm scared. Because I'm terrified you'll leave me again after...

"I think Lauren's death was a sign. She's come along again while we were together and tore things apart. It's a message from a higher power that we aren't meant to be everything and beyond. More like once upon a time..."

"You don't really believe that?" Brut's blue eyes shine despite the dimness in my apartment.

No, no, I don't. But I don't know how else to protect myself. I'm overwhelmed with the sense I'll lose Brut if I give into him again, and I find the only way to save myself is to let him go.

"I think I must," I lie. We had our tryst. Now, we move forward. Strangely, I feel at peace as I watch him kiss my knuckles one more time, stand once again, and then reach for his jacket on the chair where he placed it last night. He doesn't look back as he descends the stairs, and I watch him walk away from me. Again.

If only it were so easy to convince my heart I meant what I've said.

32
30-Day Grace Period

[Lily]

It's been a long month since Brut walked out my door. Seven weeks since the vacation. We circle one another without ever crossing paths in our mutual desire to support Chopper.

Chopper had some complications at first: reading the will, registering her death, and cleaning out Lauren's few belongings. Thankfully, Lauren was renting and had no property to sell. Chopper tossed out the few items she had owned after asking me if I wanted anything. I didn't. It was sad to me. Her life was over, the end of her line finished. Chopper denied her in all ways despite the unwanted responsibility she placed on him in the end. Eventually, there was no trace she ever existed other than him.

My mother and stepfather were a huge disappointment. I'd closed that door on them so long ago nothing should have surprised me, but the fact they neither came to Lauren's funeral nor called to offer support astonished me. Who leaves their child like that? But then I reconsider. These people were Lauren's role models. No wonder she walked away from her own child. I always knew I'd take the opposite road. If I had a baby, I'd never leave him behind.

At the doctor's office, I need to pee for the millionth time. I tell myself it's residual aftereffects of Lauren's passing, but in truth, I'm sick. Chills. Nausea. Achy breasts. It's mid-October, and minus the heaviness in my breasts, these symptoms seem typical of a fall cold. My complaints led Esther to prompt me to go to the doctor. I could have gone to an immediate care clinic, but I have an unsettling suspicion about what my real illness is.

Esther did too and bought me a test. *Two actually*.

I step out of the doctor's office bathroom, leaving behind the requested urine sample, and return to the waiting room.

"Lily?"

Mother of all things. "Midge?" I exhale after her name. This is not good. I haven't seen Midge since the funeral.

"What are you doing here?" She beams at me, her skin practically glowing.

"What are you doing here?" I ask, trying to sound chipper like her, but I know her answer.

"I'm pregnant," she says, stating the obvious. At forty-one, the same age as me, Midge will have her fourth child. I'd be blessed to have one at my age. Tears burn the back of my eyes at the thought, and I blink. This is another new development. I'm so emotional lately.

"Are you okay?" Her warm hand comes to mine as I sit next to her.

"I'm just here for a checkup." It's not a total lie. On top of all my other symptoms, I seem to have an actual cold. I sniffle disguising the prickle in my nose. "I haven't been feeling well lately."

"This is an OB/GYN, though."

I nod at the obvious, and her fingers tighten around mine.

"Are you pregnant?"

Giving in to some strange instinct, I cradle by belly with my right hand. *I don't know.* I mean, I know. I took the tests, but those can be wrong, right? I'm still in a state of disbelief, but each time I think about it, another emotion occurs. Hope.

Midge's fingers cover her lips, her face glowing brighter. "It's Brut's, right?"

Good Lord. "Midge, I don't know." For a second, I focus on the purple streak in her still auburn hair. It's long and full looking. I've read that pregnancy can do wonders to your hair.

"You don't know if it's Brut's?"

"No. I mean, I don't know if I'm pregnant. I just..." *I want to be pregnant.*

Midge's probing eyes scan my face.

Tears well again, and I blink rapidly. I swallow back a lump in my throat. *If* I am pregnant, I've been reading up on the risks of pregnancy at an older age. It's all so scary.

"Oh, honey. This is good news, right?"

191

I twist in my seat, covering Midge's hand with mine. "Midge, you need to promise me you won't tell Brut. You won't intervene. No tricks like the rental." We still haven't discussed how Midge and Hank pulled off Brut and me being in the same vacation home at the same time. My trip had been planned for months, once Midge told me about the location, but Brut had the time off sprung on him. *How had they coordinated everything?*

"I don't know what you mean." She winks.

"I know you meant well, but Brut and I...it just isn't meant to be."

"Why would you say that?" Her brows lift, and her expression would be almost comical if I wasn't on the verge of crying.

"Look, we had a great time together. I won't say it was a mistake or that I regret it, it's just...Lauren's death was a sign that Brut and me were never meant to be."

Midge pats my arm and nods toward my belly. "Honey, this might be a sign that you are."

+ + +

Two days later, I'm lying in my bed. I can't seem to handle some of the smells in the bakery kitchen without feeling nauseous. The doctor says I'm only halfway through my first trimester. I'd feel better if I made it to three months before telling anyone, but at the rate I'm going, I'll need to hire another worker. I can't stomach the stench of combinations I typically love.

Footsteps pound up my stairs. Esther has heavy feet for a little thing, and I've often teased her about not knowing how to walk lightly for such a small stature. I should really have a door installed at the bottom of the staircase for some privacy, but I've never considered it before. The open concept of my loft allows me to hear most of the workings of the bakery below.

"How's it going down there?" My back remains to her as I mumble toward the wall. I've left her in charge again after trying to make it through another unproductive morning.

"What's the matter with you?" The sharp male voice makes me spin on the bed, and I stare up at Brut.

Midge! She needs a cupcake in her mouth to keep it stuffed.

"I'm not feeling well. Just needed to lie down a bit." I sit up slowly, allowing the room to spin a moment. I reach for a tissue. I seem to have developed allergies as well as growing a human inside me. My hand hovers toward my stomach, but I force it down to my knee. I'm not ready to tell Brut.

To my surprise, he squats beside the bed. His hand comes to my knee without thought. I've missed his touch so much. The innocent act of his palm on my kneecap prickles my nose, and I blink at the moisture threatening my eyes. I use the tissue to disguise my emotions.

"What's wrong?"

I wave him off. "Just a cold."

His brows pinch as he searches my face. My fingers twitch to reach out for his stubbled jaw.

"Can I get you anything?"

"What are you doing here?"

"Midge told me you were sick. Said I should check on you."

Scooting to the edge of the bed, I stand with some effort. The room sways a little, and I hold out my arms to steady myself. My stomach roils.

"Thank you, but I don't need you to check on me because Midge told you to. I'm fine. I can take care of myself."

"So you once told me."

My head snaps up, but he's teasing me. His hands slip into the pockets of his jeans as he watches me. I move to step around him, but the nausea comes fast.

"Oh shit," I mumble, covering my mouth and racing for the bathroom just behind him. I crumple to the floor before the toilet, heaving though I know nothing will come up. My stomach suddenly has a force like no other, but nothing inside it to release.

"This doesn't look good, sugar."

My eyes close at the endearment as I face the inner bowl. *Please God, don't torture me anymore.* I mentally will Brut away, but instead, he's crowding me in my small bathroom.

"I'm okay," I lie, shaking from the retching reflex. I struggle to stand, using the seat to hoist myself upward. Thinking of what I've just done, I immediately reach for the sink and wash my hands. As I stand, scrubbing, scrubbing, scrubbing, the tender heat of Brut's hand comes to my lower back. I blink several times, forcing back more threatening tears. He needs to leave before I'm even more of a mess.

"See, I'm good," I say to my hands, avoiding the eyes I feel searching for mine in the reflection of my mirror.

"You don't look so good."

My head shoots up at the insult to discover he's right. I'm ghostly pale. My lips too light. My eyes too large. I need to lie down again. *It will pass.* It just takes a little bit.

I try to stand taller, but Brut's hand doesn't leave my back. He walks me to my bed and guides me down to the mattress.

"Let me get you some crackers…or some tea."

"I'm good," I mutter, motioning toward a small bowl on my nightstand. I keep the saltines handy although the thought of eating one makes me feel nauseous again. Brut squats staring at me. I can't handle the intensity, and my eyes close under the pressure. A cool hand comes to my forehead, brushing my hair back, tucking it behind my ear.

"That feels nice," I murmur, though I shouldn't be encouraging him.

He continues to stroke my temple and around my ear, and as I'm slowly drifting off, I imagine I hear, "I miss you, Lily pad."

+ + +

When I wake, Brut has brought a chair to the side of my bed. Tea steams in a mug on my nightstand.

"Hey," he says, looking down at me. His elbows perched on his knees, and his clenched fingers hold up his chin.

"How long was I out?" I lift my head drowsily and search for my phone for the time. I've got to get back downstairs. We have orders for a wedding and a grand opening party. Esther can't do it all alone, even if she has Julia to help her.

A hand comes to my shoulder, pressing me back. "Esther said you normally sleep for an hour. I made you some tea."

I lie back, staring up at him. What is he still doing here? Why is he being so nice? Does he know? Did Midge tell him when she promised not to?

"I'm okay," I murmur.

Brut nods his head, twisting his lips as he peers over at me. "I'm not."

My head rolls on the pillow. "What's wrong?" I ask, immediately sensing a deeper meaning to his words. His gaze turns away from me.

"Chopper misses you. The irony is finally catching up to him. Lauren left him behind but then left him responsible for her. He needs his aunt...his friend."

Most things were settled. Now Chopper waits. Bills need to be paid and a public announcement released about her death. After six months, he will be free of that responsibility.

"He hasn't come to see me lately." I haven't had much contact with him as the weeks pass. I assumed he had things under control and was possibly avoiding me. Maybe *I* am too much of a reminder of his mother. The thought makes me sad. If I lose Chopper as well, she's really taken everything from me.

Brut's hand comes to my shoulder, rubbing over the joint and startling me from my thoughts. Lauren might have taken everything from him, too, but she also gave him his son. That's one thing she did right.

I reach for my lower belly as if to protect what isn't more than a lima bean inside me.

Will he think I've done the same thing as my sister?

I've loved Brut Paige most of my life, and I view the little lima bean as his gift to me. I'll always have a piece of him to remember our week together.

"Maybe you should call him to check in."

I nod, agreeing. I've been a little preoccupied myself, and avoiding Chopper means keeping the truth from them for as long as I can. "I'll do that."

"Maybe you could call me to check in, too."

L.B. Dunbar

"Brut." I sigh. I'd love to do that, but where would it lead? Stolen moments? Another vacation? One week? I just can't envision us going anywhere. Then again, I often dream of being with Brut, especially in my condition. I don't want him to feel trapped, though. I won't do to him what Lauren did.

"Fine." He exhales. "I'll call you." There's a determination behind his voice, and my head tilts in question. He nods, growing more adamant with each bob. "You'll see," he adds. With this, he stands abruptly, leans forward to kiss my forehead, and removes himself from my apartment.

33

All Jokes Aside

[Brut]

Seeing Lily sick restores my faith. Not in a negative way, but in a determined manner. I'm a putz, and I chickened out when she rejected me the night of her sister's funeral. Instead of accepting she was hurting and might need my support, I gave her space. The longer the time spanned, the greater the distance, and I didn't know how to retrace my steps. Instead of sticking to my original plan—win Lily back—I lost focus. After finding my son in her arms, learning of his mother's death, and then struggling to help him through a situation I could hardly wrap my head around, I could no longer see straight. My end goal was Lily, but the finish line blurred.

When Midge told me she saw Lily at the doctor's office and hinted I might want to check in on her, I wanted to chastise my sister-in-law for meddling again. Then I thought twice. This was the push I needed and an excuse to visit her. She really is sick. I didn't think someone could turn that shade of green, and I'm a dad. I've had my share of sleepless nights with a vomiting child. Still, Lily looked different. Maybe it was just that I missed her—and her body—because her tits definitely looked bigger. Her curves perfectly fill my hand, but somehow, she looked a little fuller up top. I'd dismissed it as the way she lay on her bed.

With her brows pinched after the retching, and her face clammy, I'd watched her rest.

I didn't want to surmise what might be going on in her pretty head, but her sister's death threw Lily for a loop as well. After our night together, I didn't want to say goodbye, but I'd seen old fears written in Lily's face. In fact, her expression looked very similar to the night she told me to leave her way back when.

Everything in me wanted to pull her tight and refuse to walk away when she was nineteen. The same feelings occurred a month ago when she told me goodbye in her apartment. I could leave her alone if that's what she wished, but I didn't wish it, and I didn't really believe Lily did either. She wouldn't let me touch her, kiss her, or slip inside her if she could so easily dismiss me. We might have needed some space after Lauren's second intrusion into our lives, but this time, Lauren would not win.

It's the afternoon of my sick-call visit, and I'm putting into place what I said—if she wouldn't call me to check in, then I'm checking in with her instead. It's only been an hour, but I need contact.

What did the cupcake say to the muffin? I text.

Three dots appear and disappear. When they pop up again, I hold my breath waiting.

I don't know, what?

I'm just a cupcake looking for a stud muffin. It's cheesy, no further food puns intended, but I need to reach Lily on some level.

That was really bad. 😊

I picture her laughing, and it brings a smile to my face. I sit back in my desk chair and try another one. **What did the frosting say to the cupcake?**

Three dots again, and I envision the curl of her mouth as she thinks about it.

LOL. IDK.

I'm not good at text acronyms, so I shout out to Midge in the outer office. "What's IDK mean?"

"I don't know."

"Is Chopper out there, ask him?"

"No." Midge laughs. "It means I don't know."

Oh. I laugh at myself and text the answer. **I'd look good on you.**

This one's a bit risky because—I won't lie—I'm trying to flirt with her.

Brut! ROTFL.

Jesus, Lily might be over forty, but she's texting like a twenty-year-old, and I don't know what she's saying.

"Midge, help. What's ROTFL?"

"Rolling on the floor laughing."

I nod as I stare at my phone, relieved but slightly disappointed. I miss Lily's sounds, and her laughter is at the top of my list. My smile grows, though, and my cheeks heat with pleasure.

"What are you doing?" Midge says, her voice close. It's her day to come in and check my books, and she stands at the entrance to my office. I toss the phone on the desktop and sit upright, turn to my computer and place my fingers on the keyboard, but my eyes wander back to the phone. Waiting.

"Nothing," I snap a little harsher than necessary.

"Mmmhmm...Tell Lily I said hi."

My gaze jumps up to my sister-in-law who props herself against the doorframe. She has the slightest baby bulge with her arms crossed over her breasts, and it makes me curious once again what Lily would look like pregnant.

"How did you know I was talking to Lily?"

"Is there someone else who would make you smile like that?"

I lower my head, slowly shaking it back and forth and chuckling. I've been caught.

"What's going on with you two, anyway?" Her voice draws near as she's closed the distance from the doorway to the edge of my desk.

"Nothing at the moment, but I'm working on it."

Midge twists her lips and tweaks up an eyebrow. "Sounds promising."

"I hope so," I say. "Promises are all I can give her."

Midge's face falls a little, and she bites the corner of her lip. "You know, I'm not good at dispensing love advice."

Now *my* brow tweaks as my brother and his sneaky wife, the woman standing before me, played matchmaker and rekindled the flame for Lily and me with their stunt.

"But I think Lily needs more than promises this time around, Brut. I understand what happened between you two, and it's a hard story to swallow. Lily needs time, but then again, I think she's had enough time to reflect and forgive."

L.B. Dunbar

I keep my eyes focused on Midge. Has Lily really forgiven me? She says she has. She acted as if she did, but with Lauren's death, I feel something between us as if Lauren's ghost has been placed there again.

"She's forgiven you, Brut, or she wouldn't let you touch her."

My face heats. Hank must have told Midge about my week with Lily. I admitted too much to him one night after he coerced me with beers. For a man who no longer drinks, he sure knows how to add peer pressure and get information out of me.

"But maybe—"

"Before you go all *man* on me and conjure up some story of how she did it to get back at her sister, or she was with you for her own chance, I want to tell you what I see as an outsider."

I wasn't going to go to the extreme Midge suggested, and I'm not certain where she's come up with the elaborate idea Lily slept with me to get back at her sister, but...

"That woman's in love with you."

My head rocks back.

"And I dare say, she always has been. I bet even when you ripped her heart out, she still loved you and might have taken you back had you ever gone after her. Did you go to her, Brut?"

"Of course not. She told me to leave her alone, and I did. Why would I chase her?" Forget that I did call for weeks, even showed up at her house, but after my confrontation with Lauren, I didn't persist. I should have asked Lauren how she could so coldheartedly tell her sister what happened, but my own guilt ate at me. Fighting with Lauren wouldn't change what we did. Or how it hurt Lily.

"Maybe she needed reassurance that you really did want her. That you picked her. I'm even going to go out on a limb and say she might have taken you back and been willing to raise Chopper with you, had you let her."

"Why would she ever do that? I cheated on her." I pull my head back again as my hands settle on my desk. My heart begins to strangely race. Midge has lost her mind, and she's staring at me like I have two heads. However, Midge's husband cheated on her, so I'd think she'd have more understanding of Lily's position.

200

"Because she loved you. She *loves* you, and she sees your transgression now as a mistake from someone young, vulnerable, and a little messed up. She loves Chopper and wishes she'd had more time with him when he was younger. And it's called step-parenting technically, but in her case, it would have been called being a mom."

I stare at Midge, her brown eyes boring into mine. *What is she saying?* My stomach twists. I don't even want to consider the possibility that Lily would have taken me back when she was only twenty, her age at the time Chopper came to me, and accepted him as her child to raise along with me. It's a crazy thought.

"How do you know Lily loves me? Has she said that?" I hold my breath, knowing Midge has become closer to Lily over the past month. She makes an effort to spend time with her, going to lunch with her and having her over to their house. I assumed it was all that you-are-part-of-our-family stuff she and Hank told Lily at Lauren's funeral.

"She doesn't have to say it, Brut. It's how she looks at you. How she looks when she talks about you."

My eyes lower, and my fingertips digging into my desktop. Sweat pools on my palms.

"How does she look?" The quiet question resonates loud in my office. I know how I want Lily to look at me, the expression I'd like to see on her face.

"Like she's in love with a good man who made a poor choice one night, and who might need to get his head out of his ass and forgive himself." Midge's brow rises. "Go after her, Brut. Stop letting time slip away."

My phone buzzes, and I immediately turn my attention to it. The text appears instantly.

You bake me crazy.

I burst out laughing.

"Tick-tock," Midge says, pointing at her bare wrist.

I'm smiling too big to glare at her, and she returns my grin. "I'm on it," I say although this makes me think dirty thoughts of being *on* Lily, which I miss.

You make the world a batter place, one cupcake at a time.

201

OMG! Stop. LOL.

While I envision her bent over laughing, and I can almost hear her sound in my head, it's not enough. I need to see her, hear her, touch her.

I quickly find an image of two cupcakes holding hands and send it to her. Cupcake lovers is the caption.

It's gonna happen, Lily pad.

Three dots appear and then disappear. I'm afraid I've gone too far, but she needs to know I'm coming for her.

Tick-tock as Midge says. I'm not letting any more time pass.

34

24 Hours Really Can Change Everything.

[Brut]

"Don't panic. I'm sure she's fine." Hank greets me as he stands inside the doorway to my office the next morning. I don't know who he means, but the look of fear on his face tells me it isn't good. He motions for me to come into the waiting room.

"I'll keep calling," Midge says to Hank, her eyes shifting to me and back to the television set. It isn't Midge's day to be here, but sometimes they grab coffee together, and she drives him to work.

The TV is a new addition to our waiting room, suggested by Midge as a way for our customers to pass the time. I don't really want customers hanging out all day, but we have a few who need minor services like oil changes or tune-ups, and Midge contends the television is a nice touch. I warned her if I caught the guys taking breaks to watch soap operas or porn, the set goes.

Something in the tone of the news report catches my attention.

"And on Sacramento. A series of break-ins occurred in the early morning hours. Crews rushed to the block to find several small businesses vandalized. The extent of the damage includes broken windows, smashed doors, and one minor fire. Police are still searching for a suspect, possibly two, and a motive. Gang initiation is the current suspicion."

I freeze, staring at the image of the torn awning of Because Cupcakes dangles in front of the window, which hosts a giant hole. Firetrucks are parked outside Lily's place. There's no sign of anyone.

"Brut," Hank calls my name, but I'm racing out the front door without looking back. Jumping in my SUV, I pound the steering wheel as I weave through the streets of Pasadena, hoping to get to LA in a timely manner.

The last text on my phone to Lily reads: **What's up, cupcake?**

203

Muffin much, was her response.

I want to smile at the playful silliness, but my chest squeezes my lungs too much. I can't breathe.

Please let her be okay.

The thirty minutes to her place are the longest thirty minutes of my life. When I reach the crime scene, I argue with two firemen before they let me inside Lily's shop.

"We haven't been able to move her," one tells me, and my heart races. Is she trapped? Is she hurt? Did they get her? If someone shot her in this godforsaken neighborhood, I'll kill them.

I push a policeman, sprinting through the missing door to find Lily kneeling among the broken glass. Giant shards and smaller chunks litter the faux wood flooring. Her main display case, the one I had pinned her against and fucked her hard, is missing all the glass. The shelves are broken, falling in on one another. The place looks like the crime scene it is.

My eyes bolt to Lily, rocking back and forth. Her arms cross her chest as if she holds something to her. The shards crackle under my feet as I take slow steps to her side. Squatting down, I gently say her name. "Lily pad."

My hand automatically goes to her back, rubbing her spine a second before she registers someone near her. Her head turns in my direction, and my chest feels like someone stabbed me as I see her grief-stricken, tear-stained face.

"Brut," she whimpers. Her eyes are glazed, and her lips quiver. "Why would they do this?"

Now isn't the time to remind her she's located in a terrible neighborhood, one rather unsafe. Instead, I wrap an arm over her back.

"I don't know, sugar." I wish I had answers for her, wish I could erase the heartache she feels. The garage was broken into once, and the violation is hard to explain even though it was never physical.

Another thought occurs. "Lily, are you hurt? Were you here when this happened?"

God help whomever if someone touched her.

"I was upstairs when I heard the crash. I ran downstairs without even thinking. I startled him." Her gaze returns to mine, staring blankly at me, confusion and frustration filling her expression. I shudder to think she was upstairs, remembering the entrance to her loft apartment has no security door. What if someone had gone up there?

"Lily, sugar, come with me, okay?" I'm asking, but I'm not leaving her any room to refuse me.

She absentmindedly nods but returns her gaze to the floor strewn with large chunks of her window and the broken display case. Relief fills me when I consider the brick that caused such damage did not hit her, nor did the punk she'd startle shoot her. Thankfully, nothing worse happened other than broken objects that can be replaced.

"Where's Esther?" She comes as an afterthought, and I'm hoping Lily's catatonic state isn't from something happening to her co-worker and friend.

"I gave her the morning off. She wasn't here."

Telling me this brings a new set of silent tears.

"Okay, baby. I'm going to pick you up." We don't need to talk. We need to get out of here.

She kneels upward, and I hear glass crumble underneath her. My chest pinches with the pain she must be experiencing. Keeping my arm around her back, I scoop under her legs and hoist her up. Jostling her a moment, I see the large cuts along her shins and wince. Glass is stuck to her skin, and I'm certain some has dug into her.

"Oh, baby." I kiss her temple as I carry her out of the store. An ambulance is waiting to inspect her.

As the medics look at Lily's shins, they suggest a visit to the hospital. Lily agrees but doesn't want an ambulance ride. "My insurance won't cover it."

I'm stunned by the admission. Does she not have medical insurance? A million more things run through my mind. Does the business have insurance? Does her landlord? My heart races with the knowledge Lily could lose everything because of some asshole kids trying to be part of a defunct group so they can feel like someone. I might complain about the garage, but I understand that if something occurred—

a fire, a theft, a natural disaster—destroying the place would not break me because I have insurance. These thoughts riddle my mind as I drive Lily to the emergency room where I then sit and watch as my brave girl endures them numbing her skin and working with astute attention to remove each minute piece of glass.

For a moment, Lily makes me leave the room as she answers some personal questions about her health history. I don't question it, allowing her privacy, but later I wonder if something greater is wrong. Edie, Tommy's wife, is a breast cancer survivor, and new concerns fill my already packed mind. Does Lily have some condition that prevents her from taking certain pain medications? Does she have a pre-existing condition that conflicts with this emergency? Is she suffering from something extreme?

And my greatest concern—why won't she share anything with me?

Lily and I had gotten a little lost when our vacation ended and we returned home, but I want to be there for her. I walked away because she asked me to, but I knew it was only going to take one look, one touch, one moment, and we'd be together again. Somehow. Some way.

When Lily gets the okay to leave with instructions for aftercare and a prescription for pain relievers, I drive her to my home. She doesn't speak much other than an occasional hum to agree with me or a snort to disagree. I typically love all her little noises, but right now, I want her voice. Instead, she remains silent. There are a million questions to ask, but I decide tomorrow will be a better day to tackle all the necessary issues of filing insurance claims and confirming the police report. For today, she's going to settle in my bed, and I'm not leaving her side...ever again.

+ + +

Lily sleeps in my bed, and I sit watching her from a chair I pulled up next to it. For all my fantasies of her being in my place, this isn't how I envisioned it happening. She's curled around a pillow which seems to be her custom for comfort. I recall her doing such a thing on our vacation. She's a stomach sleeper, and I don't mind as long as she lets me wrap an arm over her. At the moment, she lies on her side, and I notice once again her lush breasts, fuller as they are exposed under my T-shirt. I assured Lily earlier that I'd go back to her place when we were allowed in and retrieve some of her belongings.

She let me undress her and redress her like a child. I wondered if she wanted a shower or possibly a bath, but her lids closed, signaling her exhaustion. She appears drained of energy and purpose, but I don't believe she's defeated. She'll resurface to be the survivor she is, but for tonight, she needs to process. She needs pampering, and I'm here to pamper. She's a wonder, and I marvel at her resilient strength. She'll get through this—*we'll get through this*—but not tonight.

"Brut," she whispers in the dark. It's after midnight, and I can't sleep. I'm still too wound up from the paranoia of something happening to her—something extreme, something life-ending. I don't want to imagine such things, but my brain won't shut off. I can't lose her. And once again, I recognize my chance is here, whispering, waiting. Like Midge admonished me, I need to stop stalling. Tick-tock. If I had lost Lily, if it had been too late… I shudder with the thought.

I don't want to consider if I never had this second time with her. *What if.*

No more waiting, I decide.

"What, sugar?" I've been sipping whiskey to release the demons and loosen my brain, so I'll eventually sleep. I notice her eyes open in the dark room.

"Thank you for coming to get me."

I lean forward, setting my glass on the nightstand and balancing my elbows on my thighs. "You don't need to thank me for anything. I'll always come when you call." Although she didn't call me for this emergency. How could she? If I hadn't seen the television report, would she have reached out for me? I don't ask these probing questions, wanting again to let her process what's happened. I also don't want to turn things around to me and my emotions. I need to think of her.

Her hand reaches across the space between us, lingering in the air a moment as her fingers wiggle in my direction. I quickly clasp them in my hand and raise them to brush my lips over her knuckles. I linger, a wave of relief I've struggled with all day suddenly crashing over me. My eyes close, and I swallow the lump in my throat. There's so much to say but not tonight.

"Brut, honey." She pauses. "Will you lay next to me?"

My heart leaps to my throat, choking along with the thickness there. This woman is about to bring me to tears.

"I'd do anything for you, Lily pad. Anything." My eyes open slowly to find the intensity of hers glistening in the darkness. I kiss her knuckles once again and quickly stand. My shoes and socks are already removed, so I shuck off my jeans and remove my shirt. Climbing over her, I'm careful of her legs and wrap my arm over her waist. She doesn't curl into me but allows me to curve around her.

This is where I want to be. This is where I want her to stay. Forever.

35

Handle With Care

[Lily]

I wake wrapped around Brut. Literally. During the night, I shifted in my sleep and burrowed my head into his chest, hoping to drown out the sound of the brick breaking my bakery window. The noise ricochets in my mind, and I remember thinking the building was going to crumble. I'd pressed against Brut, scared at first, but now I'm awake and...horny.

With one leg hitched over Brut's hip, I rut against him like a shameless, lazy dog.

"Lily pad," Brut whispers.

"Oh God, Brut," I mutter, embarrassed by my behavior but unable to remove my leg from over his body. My achy breasts press against his firm chest, and I realize once again how they've grown. My clit pulses, desperate for friction from the morning wood against it. Brut's hand comes to my hip, slipping under the T-shirt he'd dressed me in last night.

"What's going on here?" He's not complaining, just confused by my sudden display of unashamed wantonness.

I'm confused, too, but I've become a hot mess of pregnancy horniness. *Tell him.*

"I just..." I pause, retracting my leg, but he catches the underside of my thigh.

"Tell me," he demands, and then he tugs my leg, drawing me tight against him again.

With no shame, I moan. "This."

"This?" he teases, slipping his hand farther under the tee and cupping the weight of one breast. He squeezes, and I moan again, arching my back, forcing the heavy globe into his palm.

"Yes, please."

"Or this?" He brushes his hand down my body, traveling my curves until he slips a hand into my underwear, grabbing my ass to pull me

209

L.B. Dunbar

toward him. I'm on the verge of losing my mind, and then my stomach rumbles. Brut stills.

"Brut," I whimper, desperate tears prickling my eyes. My body hums with sexual need.

Then my stomach rumbles again.

"Lily, I won't deny you anything. But first, I think we need breakfast."

Noooo. The rejection stings. But Brut is right. I haven't eaten in twenty-four hours, and maybe food will add perspective. I shouldn't be humping him like this. However, I haven't seen Brut in a month, and I'm practically ravenous for his body. In my heart, I know Brut will have sex with me if I want him to, but something holds him back and it isn't just my stomach calling. We need to talk, and I have no choice but to agree to a delay.

I nod, and Brut kisses my forehead.

We need breakfast…and I need to tell him a few things before anything else happens between us.

+ + +

Promising to make waffles, Brut left the bedroom to give me a moment to freshen up before coming downstairs. He had mentioned his home was run down and in need of a facelift, but what I notice seems like a freshly painted house. The stairway leading down to his living room is light gray with white trim around the windows and dark hardwood risers. The banister and railing matches. The look is beautiful and classic.

The floors in his living room are the same rich tone as the stairs and the furniture is manly and modern. Light brown leather chairs sit across from a dark gray couch. But the item I notice first is a matching ottoman. A flat screen television hangs above a fireplace. The mantel holds black and white images of his family—Chopper, Hank as a rock star, Brut, his father.

"What's going on here?" I ask as I enter his kitchen.

I enter the kitchen to find white cabinets missing a countertop. A large Viking stove, industrial and stainless steel, graces the center of the main wall. My heart skips a beat at my dream appliance. I turn slowly, finding a farmhouse sink under a window. My eyes take in a double-door refrigerator, also stainless steel. The protective film still covers the outside.

"Are you in the middle of a renovation?" I ask, taking in the full expanse of his small kitchen. A circular table with four chairs around it centers the space. The table doesn't match the updated décor, but it's obvious Brut has been improving his home, and it looks strangely like the kitchen I described in our game of *what ifs*.

"Someone once told me if I didn't like my house, I should rehab. I decided it's time for a change." Brut shrugs. He turns to face me, his back to the waffle iron which rests on a piece of plywood over the cabinets acting as a makeshift countertop. "Maybe I'll sell when I finish."

He turns back to the iron and removes a waffle, plating it and then motioning for me to sit at his table. A glass of orange juice awaits me.

"It's like you're nesting," I say without thinking as I take my seat and thank him for the waffles. My mouth waters, and I suddenly feel like I haven't eaten in weeks.

"What's that?" He chuckles as he turns back to the iron and pours more batter into the grid.

"When a woman who is…" My voice drifts. *Oh God*, I choke on my words. Then I swallow. I don't know how to tell him.

"What is it, Lil?" His voice softens as he looks at me over his shoulder.

I shake my head, signaling nothing, but my heart knocks in my chest. *Tell him.*

"I don't want you to be afraid of anything," Brut begins. "You can stay here. You shouldn't return where you live, Lily. It isn't safe. I don't want you working in that location either, but first things first. Insurance claims and the landlord before any other decisions are made."

Ignoring his list of demands, I fill my mouth with the first bite of delicious waffles and mutter, "It's not that."

"Then what is it?" Brut takes the seat nearest mine, setting his plate on the table while he looks over at me.

211

L.B. Dunbar

"Nesting is when a pregnant woman prepares her home for having a baby. She cleans and reorganizes in preparation."

"Oh." Brut laughs nervously. He scrubs the back of his neck, staring down at the waffles on his plate. "Well, I still want you to stay here."

Tears blur my eyes, and I swallow the suddenly sticky mess of waffles in my throat.

"Lily pad, it wouldn't be that bad, would it?" He looks up with hurt etched in his expression.

"It's not that, Brut." *All my life I've wanted to be with you.* Taking a deep breath, I blurt out the bomb. "I'm pregnant."

My voice lowers along with my head. I can't face him. My skin prickles, waiting on the rejection he's going to give me. He's trapped all over again by the *other* Warren sister. But I've already made up my mind. This lima bean will be born and loved.

Brut's chair scrapes on tile floor, and I hold my breath. My chair moves next by his hand on the seat. Suddenly, Brut is in my view, squatting before me.

"Mine?" His question chokes him, and he swallows hard.

"Yours." Panic fills me. Does he think it could be anyone else's? Then another thought occurs. Was he with someone else in the time we've been apart?

"Lily pad." He scrubs a hand down his face, and I'm hyperaware of the scruffy scratch to his jaw. "How? When?"

"When we were on vacation. We didn't exactly practice safe sex." I take a deep breath. "I'm due in early June."

Brut's lips twist while his eyes lighten, almost dancing. "You *have to* stay with me now." His voice is nearly giddy.

"I don't want to be in your way. I don't want you to feel trapped or feel like I did what my sis—" A large hand clamps over my mouth, and those sparkling eyes darken.

"You will never be like her. Never compare yourself. I don't feel burdened or trapped or anything else. Lily, with you, I've always felt…"

The momentary pause makes my heart skip a beat. "What?"

"Everything."

A tear slips down my face. I understand what he means because I've felt the same.

"Lily, stay here. Be with me." His voice softens as he cups my face, begging me with his eyes, but I can also sense his heart. He wants me here. After a moment of his silent plea, he releases my face and lowers his head to my stomach. He kisses me over his T-shirt, lingering on the cotton before his gaze leaps upward.

"May I?" His hand already grips the hem of the shirt, lifting the material. When my stomach is exposed, Brut leans forward, pressing a longer kiss to my belly. His eyes close as his mouth remains on my abdomen, as if he's speaking to Lima Bean without words.

My trembling hands come to his hair, brushing back the tendrils and combing through the white color.

We aren't young anymore.

As if reading my thoughts, his head pops up. "Are you okay? Everything's okay, right? I mean she's—"

"You mean I'm not young?" I tease.

"You aren't old," he admonishes. "But being over forty, there can be risks."

"So far so good. I'm having an ultrasound for the baby's heartbeat next week." A perk of being an older pregnant woman is the doctor requested this test a lot sooner than she might for a younger mother-to-be.

"A heartbeat," he murmurs, laying his warm palm on my belly skin. He hesitates. Then, Brut abruptly stands, startling me. "Let me get the bathroom in my room set up for you. You must want a shower."

I'm surprised by the suggestion especially since I haven't finished eating, and Brut hasn't even touched his food. However, I can't deny that I need a shower and maybe we both need a few minutes. Brut looks like his brain has gone into overdrive and maybe this excuse to set up his bathroom is a means to give himself some space.

He's having a baby, later in life, with me. It's a lot to process.

He excuses himself, and I wait a few minutes before climbing the stairs to his room. Compared to the lower half of the house, the upstairs needs some attention. I don't know why I'm thinking these things other

213

than my brain speeds forward. Tempting fantasies fill my thoughts. I haven't lived in a house in a long time. Could a nursery be set up in one of these bedrooms? Brut has offered for me to stay here, but it's only temporary, right?

Stepping into Brut's bedroom, I find him standing in the middle. He's clutching the back of his neck again, and I don't know what to say. Suddenly, I feel awkward around the man of my dreams. Maybe because I don't want to lose him. Maybe because I've just dropped something huge on him. Maybe because I want to help him process, but I also want to give him space. I don't know what to do.

"Everything you might need is in there." He tilts his head toward the bathroom.

I nod because I don't trust the scratch in my throat. After entering the bathroom, I close the door behind me, taking a moment to look at myself in the mirror. I'm a mess. My hair is wild. My eyes too large and melancholy.

What was I thinking? That Brut would love me a second time? That he'd want to marry me?

My hands come to rest on the counter, and I look down to find Scrabble tiles on a towel.

Stay with me, they spell.

I gasp, shaky fingers coming to my lips. My other hand scoops up the pieces, and then I turn for the door.

Brut sits on the edge of his bed, his hands folded between his thighs.

"Brut," I whisper, clutching my hand filled with tiles to my chest. He glances up at me. There's another silent plea in his eyes.

"I mean it, Lily. Stay here, okay? We'll work everything out." This is his line. I've heard it before. Something in my stomach sinks, warning me to pay attention to what he isn't saying, but my racing heart overrules my thoughts.

I pick a few tiles from my palm while Brut's gaze probes at me. Then, reaching for his hand, I open it palm upward and lay three tiles against his warm skin.

Y-E-S.

Restored Dreams

Instantly, I'm tackled to the bed and drop all the game pieces. A little squeal escapes while Brut climbs partially over me.

"Did I hurt the baby?" Worry fills his tone when his hand covers my stomach. He's already lowering his head and lifting my shirt, like he can visibly see anything. He presses kisses to my stomach again. Soft suction caresses over my entire belly, warming me, baptizing me. Brut seems rather excited while still a little shell-shocked. His hand follows the kisses, gently caressing my abdomen as if he can feel Lima Bean inside me.

"How are your legs?"

The question startles me, and I chuckle. "Better, thank you." The numbing cream the hospital initially swabbed on my skin has worn off, and I have other medication to take for pain. My shins are still covered in bandages, but I didn't need any stitches. The large swatches of gauze up my legs add to my disheveled appearance.

Brut scoots lower on my body, traveling over my underwear, and my breath hitches as most of his body rests between my spread-eagle legs. I'm instantly where I was this morning on the horny-meter, and I dig my fingers into the bed covering.

"Explain to me what was happening earlier?"

I'm embarrassed to recall how I dry-humped him and was practically begging him for sex. His rejection put things in perspective. I needed to get this huge secret off my chest. Now that I have, more truths seem necessary.

"Pregnant women can be horny. I'm off the chart. I'm craving sex more than ice cream or pickles."

Brut's head pops up, a look of shock on his face at my brutal honesty.

Okay, maybe I'm being too truthful this morning.

"Did I just say that out loud?" I guffaw to cover my humiliation, but my tongue winds up to ramble more. "That's another thing. I'm losing my mind a little, like misplacing my keys and not remembering I took out the trash to find I already did it."

"What you're telling me is you need a little 739?"

215

I stare at him a moment, uncertain what he means. Then, I gasp, and recall the ridiculous code we established at the beach house.

"Oh. My. God."

"You know, I'll always answer that call from you," he says, his voice lowering to a deep rumble before he exhales with a heavy breath over my hot core. The rhythm beating there is faster than my heart.

"That code was for booty calls," I whimper. I don't want to be a booty call to Brut, but right now, I'll be anything he desires. I'm just desperate for his mouth.

"You'll never be a booty call to me, Lily pad. Never." His mouth covers wet cotton, and he exhales again, increasing the warmth down below. "Let me satisfy your hunger, Momma."

My eyes roll back at him calling me the title, and then my back arches as he kisses me over the cotton. He tugs the material to the side, and his tongue swipes up my slit. I moan, my knees coming upward to brace on either side of his head. I don't miss that one of his hands remains on my belly while his tongue pays me homage.

A strange thought occurs to me. "One day, you're not going to be able to get on top of me because I'm going to be so fat."

Brut pulls his mouth back and peers up at me. "I can't wait to see it, but let's practice now then. Hop on pop."

I laugh as Brut leaves me hanging once more and flips to his back beside me. I climb over him, straddling his hips and landing my eager heat over his hard length.

"Wait." He places a hand on my hip. "Your legs."

"Just lay back," I demand, pressing on his shoulders to keep him in place. My body is going into sexual overdrive. I'm willing to kneel on glass again just to get him inside me. In fact, if I don't get his dick soon, I might spontaneously combust. Slipping off the bed, I whip off Brut's tee and remove my underwear. Brut perches up on his elbows to watch the hasty show.

"My God, you are so beautiful, Lily pad."

I barely have a bump, but Lima Bean is in there, between us, joining Brut and I together forever. I crawl over his calves and reach for the waistband of his jeans, tugging forcefully to remove his clothing. I'm a

216

woman on a desperate mission, and I groan with the effort to undress him.

"I love your noises," Brut mutters, sitting up to help me by tugging off his tee. Falling to his back again, he meets my gaze. "Are you sure about your legs?"

"I've got it." I grasp his swollen shaft in my hand and tug, reinforcing I'm about to have my way with this man's body. Ripples dancing over my skin with excitement, I'm obsessed. My brain has a mission—Must. Have. Brut.

I lower for a swift lick up his smooth, hardened shaft and then open my lips for a deep suck.

"Sugar," Brut growls, digging his hands into my hair. Moistening him is only a tease. I release him with a pop and crawl to squat over him. With my feet flat on either side of his hips, I lower in one quick thrust.

"Fuck," Brut grunts.

"Did I hurt you?" I ask, concerned at my aggressive, needy behavior.

"Hell no," he mutters, gripping my hips. I remain still only a moment before I move, literally bouncing up and down in my frog-like position. I lift enough to slam back down, swallowing him whole, feeling him tap an undiscovered slice of heaven inside me. So sweet, so ripe, so ready to come undone.

"Brut," I choke on his name, overcome with emotion and hormones and everything about us. I'm not going to last long, feeling the intense friction in just the right place, filling myself with his amazing dick. But also, my heart is full with relief that Brut isn't upset. He still wants me. He wants *this*.

His thumb comes between us. After a few quick, circular rubs, I'm done. My orgasm hits me hard. I have no idea if Chopper is home, so I bite my lip to keep from screaming Brut's name.

"Don't you dare keep those noises to yourself. Scream," he commands.

And I don't as my body unwinds. His thumb continues to stroke me, and my legs continue to power thrust over him. Almost instantly, I feel the tightening again.

217

L.B. Dunbar

"I'm going to go again. Brut. Again." I'm huffing in total surprise that I'm going to come a second time so soon. My bouncing body no longer feels under my control. I'm a spring let lose.

With his thumb on the sensitive nub and his dick tapping the sweet spot within, I unravel again. This time, I slam down on Brut to catch my breath while my body clenches. My head falls back like I could howl at the moon even though it's roughly midmorning.

Brut bucks upward and jolts within me. I ride out his wave of release. Our breaths mix in heavy pants. I've clawed at his chest, and I soften my touch to soothe his reddened skin. Leaning forward, I kiss the marks I've made.

"I'm sorry," I quietly say, and Brut lifts his head to peer at his pecs.

"You can mark me anyway you want." His voice is thick, struggling from the exertion of what we just did.

"You need a tattoo," I say although I have no idea if that's something he'd consider.

His hand instantly comes to my hip, palm flattening over the large cupcake tattoo coloring my skin.

"I know just what I'd get," he teases, squeezing me, and I respond with a laugh, thinking how sweet it would be if he had ink to match mine.

36

The Right Thing Said The Wrong Way

[Brut]

After our sex-a-thon, Lily decides she needs a shower. I suggest a bath and get up to run one for her. I need a moment anyway. The morning has been a whirlwind. Lily in my house, waking in my bed, announcing her pregnancy. I'm happy. I mean, I'll be happy, but I'm still in a state of...stunned.

I'm forty-five.

Can I really start over again? Can I do it right this time? Will it be different?

These thoughts fill my mind as water fills the tub. One big difference this time around is Lily. I won't let her go, and we'll do this together. I'll be her partner, and it will make all the difference. *We'll get through this.*

I had no issue raising Chopper alone. I had family support, but I still would have liked someone to share the experience with me. I would have liked my son to have a mother. Not Lauren, but someone feminine and maternal to care for him. I recall how hard the past few months have been, opening up the wounds of not having a mom who loved him. Lily would have been good for Chopper.

I consider what Midge hinted the other day. Could Lily have been Chopper's stepmother? Did I miss an opportunity when I was so caught up in the mayhem of everything else?

As I sit perched on the closed toilet, waiting for the tub to fill, I scrub both my hands down my face. Funny how life is. Funny how I recognize Lily's pregnancy as a second chance—a golden opportunity to make things right—and I want to do it right. For Lily. For the baby. I want to give her all the things she wanted all those years ago.

Love. Marriage. A baby in a baby carriage.

We have to get married. It's the right thing to do. I need a ring, and the date, and a license, and…

"Hey." Lily's soft voice turns my head to the bathroom door. Her naked body leans against the doorjamb, and her blue eyes fix on me.

"Hey." I sigh although the list rolls on in my head. Her looking at me like she is mixes my panic with pleasure. We are going to be good.

I reach out a hand for her, willing her to step forward. She does.

"I wonder if it will hurt."

Marrying me? I stare up at her but find her gaze on the water in the tub.

"I'll help you get in." The water isn't too deep yet, and I guide her as she gingerly steps into the tub. She sits and lifts her feet to balance on the edge of the porcelain. I need a new bathroom, I decide, and add it to the list. Lily can decide how to rearrange my bedroom.

Our bedroom, I think with growing excitement.

We're going to get married, a little voice in my head announces. My heart jumps in response like an animated creature looking around in confusion. *Who? Us?*

I stare down at Lily, at the space on her belly that will grow and stretch to accommodate life. I missed this stage the first time. Lauren told me she was pregnant, but I didn't believe her, and I didn't believe her baby could be mine. I didn't know my child until she dropped him off at the door.

I scrub a hand down my face. *Jesus*. It will be different this time.

"I can almost see the wheels spinning," Lily says from the tub.

I want to join her. I want to hold her. "We should get married."

Lily's head rocks back, her lids rapidly blinking. "What?"

"We need to do this right. *I* need to do it right."

Lily stares at me as if she isn't seeing me or hearing me. Her mouth gapes, then her lips clamp shut. She pauses another moment and then says, "Okay." The simple word hesitates while it echoes off the bathroom tiles.

"Look, you were worried about the ambulance ride yesterday. I know how expensive independent insurance can be. I can take care of you."

Her mouth falls open again, then snaps shut. "I have insurance." Her tone is a little defensive.

Still independent small business insurance is pricey.

"As my wife, you can be on my insurance. The baby will be covered as well." I pause. "You've been to the doctor, right?"

"Brut," she admonishes. "Yes, I've been to the doctor. I have an ultrasound for the heartbeat next week. I already told you this."

"Ultrasound," I repeat. *Baby images.* We will see the baby. "I'm coming with you."

Lily's expression tightens, and she glares at me. Something isn't adding up but I'm too lost in my head, steamrolling forward with my thoughts.

"I'd like to know your doctor schedule, and I'll add it to my calendar. I won't miss a thing."

"Brut, it isn't—"

"We already discussed you staying here. The kitchen countertop should be here within the week. I still need to do the backsplash and maybe you could help me choose a new kitchen table." I'm rambling as I tick things off in my head. "We could get married by the end of the week, and we could—"

"Brut. Stop."

Her harsh tone makes me snap up my head. "What? What's wrong?"

"It's just...this isn't exactly how I saw things happening. I don't want you to feel obligated. There's no rush for kitchen countertops and insurance coverage." She pauses. "I already know you'll be a great father. I'm sure you'll always be present for the baby, but..."

Does she doubt I'll be a decent husband? "Look, nothing is happening as I thought it would either, but I want us to marry. For the baby."

Lily's face pinches. She glances at her toes on the ledge of the tub. "But what about us?" Her eyes immediately close after asking.

"What about us? I want you here." I sit straighter, emphasizing my enthusiasm. Still, there's something in the lines on her face. I've cataloged her noises. I've memorized expressions. But I'm missing something, and I don't know what it is.

Then the truth hits me.

"You don't want to marry me." Everything inside me rushes to my stomach, and in another second, I'll need to open this lid and vomit.

"That's not it." Lily's voice remains monotone, too quiet, too lacking in emotion. "I just thought one day I'd have a wedding...and..." Her pause leaves me hanging. What am I missing? She scrapes her nail along the porcelain, scrubbing at a tile like she can chip it away.

"We can do that." My voice is too high, while my shoulders lower. My body language shows the added weight of one more thing. My list grows longer. *A wedding*. "Okay, we can get Midge to help and contact a minister—"

"Brut, can you slow down a minute? We don't need a wedding, especially a rushed one. I'm just saying I thought I'd have one...one day." Her hand comes to her still small belly. "But like you said, nothing happened as you thought it would."

Something in her tone doesn't settle well with me. I don't like the sound of the words I said repeated back to me.

"I take care of things, though. This is what I do." I inhale and exhale heavily. "But okay, you're right. I don't mean to push."

"You're not pushing," she says softly. "We just don't need to do everything today."

I chuckle, rubbing the back of my neck, then nod to agree.

"What I would like to do today is check in with the landlord and contact the insurance company."

The bakery. I almost forgot. I plow forward again. "I don't think you should return to work."

"Excuse me?"

"You stand all day, which can be stressful in your condition."

Lily sits forward in the tub, her arms resting on the edge while her feet still angle on the opposite ledge. She's flexible, and my mind flashes back to the frog-like position she took over me on my bed. My God was she horny and I loved it. I love her.

"I'm pregnant, not dead. So, I will continue working, and I *will* reopen my bakery." The determination in her voice reminds me of a nineteen-year-old Lily telling me about her future.

"Okay." I hesitate. "But I think you need to reconsider your location."

"The bakery is located on Sacramento Street. And that's where it will stay. The location works best as I'm just outside LA. I need to be close to the city for events."

I sigh, exasperated. "Lily pad."

"*Brut*," she exaggerates.

I take another deep breath. "Okay, let's just take it one step at a time."

Taking baby steps is going to be difficult, though, when I want to run to the finish line.

+ + +

"What is she doing out there?" Chopper asks a few days after Lily told me the good news. He stands before the back door leading from my kitchen to the backyard. I stand inside as well, staring at the wall behind the stove. I should have bumped out the entire room which is long and narrow, and added an addition to make an open-concept space like the beach house.

I sigh, worrying for the millionth time I won't provide Lily with all she wants, all she needs.

"She's doing yoga," I reply without having to look out the door. The October morning is pleasant, and my girl claims yoga is good for the baby.

Lily and I have slowly established a routine of living and working around one another. I got back to the garage, and Lily's been elbow deep in insurance claims and working with her landlord. She's in a panic with the holiday season coming. The police have cleared her business for normal operations in the kitchen area, but the storefront still needs some repairs.

L.B. Dunbar

Hank gave me a hand, and we cleared out the damaged display cases and cleaned up all the glass. After a scrub down and industrial vacuuming, the place didn't look too bad despite the boards across the front. Lily should have new windows installed any day. I'm still not happy she insists on remaining in her current location, but we settled on her living space. She's with me. We moved her personal things to my house—*our* house—and she'll use the space above the bakery as an office. She's even considering subletting the studio to the right tenant.

After Hank and I finished cleaning Lily's place, I asked him to bring Midge over for dinner tonight. Lily and I have something to discuss with them. We've already told Chopper about the baby, and he seems excited enough. As enthusiastic as a twenty-two-year-old can be when he's getting a sibling.

When we told him, he told us he was moving out. "The timing's perfect. With Lily moving in, I don't have to worry about you being alone, and with the baby, you'll have your hands full."

Lily worries she's forcing Chopper out, but he assures her she can't get rid of him even if he lives elsewhere. I was touched he worried about leaving me alone. The comments made Lily cry. I've never pegged her for an emotional person, and she admits it's not her typical behavior, but pregnancy has made her a hot mess of emotions. Tears result from television commercials, reading a social media post, or something she witnesses—like an old man hugging his kid—which is what happened between Chopper and I after he told me he was moving out.

I also know Lily's dealing with a lot. The damage to her business rattled her despite her brave front and survivor attitude. She's also pregnant. She's moved in with me. It's all been an adjustment, but I'm concerned she isn't adjusting like I am. I'm so happy. Waking up to her each morning causes me to nearly burst. I stare at her form next to me in our bed, where she finally lingers each morning instead of rushing to get out of it like she did at the beach house. As her body shifts and the baby grows, she tires easily. Still, I marvel at the changes. I follow her movements as she crosses a room or sits on the couch absently holding her stomach. She glows from the early stages of pregnancy, and her light warms my insides.

Yet something's still missing.

When Hank and Midge come over for dinner, I'm hoping to finalize the marriage plan and get something checked off my list. I'm still waiting on the countertop, but I plan to grill, so it won't be too much of an inconvenience with a half-finished kitchen.

When Hank and Midge arrive, I'm the only one nursing a beer as my brother doesn't drink, and Lily and Midge can't. I'm a little perturbed to discover Midge knew Lily was pregnant before me. I thought Lily and I were sharing some big news when we announced the baby to my brother and his wife.

"Seems I'm the last to know," I mutter, lifting my beer to swallow down my irritation along with the cool liquid.

"Don't be upset," Midge admonishes. "It wasn't my place to tell you. I just nudged you in the right direction."

"How so?" I look at my sister-in-law as I lean against the counter-less cabinet. We're gathered in the kitchen despite the disarray. Midge and Lily sit at the table that needs to be replaced while Hank stands behind his wife, leaning on the back of her chair.

"I told you Lily was sick. Remember, I saw her at the doctor's office. I figured if you worried about her, you'd go see her, and her being sick was a good excuse. Not that you needed an excuse but…"

"You needed a kick in the ass," my brother adds, finishing his wife's thought.

Lily giggles. "So that's how it happened?"

Midge is noticeably more pregnant than Lily, but I smile inside, knowing my brother and I will have children roughly the same age this time around. I'll also have someone to commiserate with me as we'll be two old guys with young kids.

"Speaking of how things happened." Lily clears her throat. "How is it that Brut and I ended up together at the beach house?"

"Oh, about that." Hank coughs, and I watch as my brother swipes his fingers through his hair before he answers. "I own the place."

"What?" I snap, my irritation level rising at another thing I seem to be the last to learn.

L.B. Dunbar

"When I learned I still had some money, and my wife wouldn't let me invest in her business..." His hand comes to Midge's shoulder. "I wanted to buy something. Something I could own alone."

Hank's eyes drift to the side. He technically doesn't own the garage. He just works at it. When he went through his rock star years, and his rock bottom phase, decisions needed to be made. He gladly gave up the garage when our pop died, and the will left the place in equal shares to both of us. I've offered over and over to make Hank a partner, no financial transaction necessary, but he doesn't want it.

"Anyway, I thought rental property might be a good investment. I found the place, made an offer, and took possession around July. You and Lily were our first and only tenants so far."

"How did I get involved?" Lily questions, looking at Midge.

"When Hank first looked at the property, you had mentioned wanting a vacation. It was around the time of our wedding dinner." The mention reminds me Lily made the cupcakes for their celebration but declined the invitation to attend the meal. Midge continues. "I simply suggested the location, and you seemed eager to go. Hank had already decided to hire a property manager as the place is too far away for us to supervise. You were our first customer."

A thought occurs. "You made Lily pay." I'm pissed and realize I'll be paying my brother for Lily's share. She was obviously bamboozled a bit, and I don't want her paying for things when we are family. Or she will be. This reminds me of my purpose in inviting Hank and Midge to dinner.

"Actually, the money is in an escrow account. We planned to give it back to Lily." Midge looks sheepishly at Lily and reaches for her hand. Her eyes shift up to her husband and back. "I'm sorry we've held the money for so long. We were waiting for the right time to come clean."

"It was a romantic thought," Lily says, surprising me, and my lips twist in a smile I don't feel. I'm still reeling a little from the deviousness and the lack of information.

"Don't be upset," Hank adds. "Seems keeping things from one another runs in the family."

I glance up to meet my brother's gaze. He's watching me, and I know what he's referencing. It's a long story, but I kept from him the fact I'd put his money in a trust before he'd hit rock bottom.

"Well, speaking of sharing things, then…" I preface. "Lily and I have other news."

Lily's head comes up while Midge's swings in my direction. Midge still holds Lily's hand.

"Lily and I would like you to be witnesses for us. We're getting married."

A weird expression crosses Midge's face, but Hank presses back from the chair he leans on. "Congratulations, man. That's amazing." Hank rounds the table and comes for me. A strapping bear hug embraces me, and Hank pounds on my back forcefully.

"When is the wedding?" Midge asks, not moving from her chair. She's still holding Lily's hand.

"We're going to the courthouse, like you did," Lily explains, her voice off, quiet and hesitant.

"But we'll have a wedding after the baby comes," I announce. Lily and I discussed things. Insurance purposes. Proper birth certificate. She knows it's important to me that I do things right this time and take care of her, take care of the baby. She agrees a wedding can come later.

"How did you ask her to marry you?" Midge inquires, which I find rather strange, personal, and none of her damn business.

"In the tub," Lily says, her face pinkening.

"How romantic," Hank states dryly.

"Well, it might have been," Midge suggests, and her face flushes as well as her eyes shift to Hank. "Bathrooms can be."

I catch Hank glancing back at his wife, and I decide this is one story they can keep from me. Instead, I notice Lily's head is lowered, her eyes stuck on Midge's hand still holding hers.

"We'd love to be witnesses," Midge offers, her smile tight while she looks at Lily. Lily glances up and something transpires between the two women. Lily nods. Everything feels off. Maybe this is some strange both-pregnant-voodoo between them, and I decide to brush off my unease.

Suddenly, I need some air. "I'll go check the meat." I set my empty bottle on the table and head for the back door.

"I'll go with you," Hank says, following behind me into the yard. We're barely outside before my brother lays into me. "What the fuck, man?"

"What do you mean?" I ask, spinning on my brother before I near the grill.

"Tell me this isn't just Brut doing what Brut does, taking care of things. Tell me you asked her romantically. Tell me this is what your heart wants. Tell me you *love* her."

"What the fuck?" Facing off with my younger brother who's bigger than me, I'm ready to take him out in the yard like we did as kids.

"Well?" Hank waits, crossing his thick arms.

"I don't owe you an explanation," I say, reaching for another beer from inside the cooler set next to the grill. I filled the cooler earlier to keep the steaks at a steady temperature and placed a six-pack under the ice. I pop the top of one and practically pour the contents down my throat.

"No, you don't, but you owe that woman everything. You do realize she doesn't need to marry your sorry ass."

"What the fuck?" I say again, glaring at my brother.

"I know you like to take care of shit. It's in your nature to control, but that's an independent woman in there, and I have no doubt she can raise a baby alone."

"Do you think that's what she wants?" I swallow hard at the thought. I don't want her doing it alone. I want to be with her.

"No. I think, by some grace of God, she still loves you like she did all those years ago. She certainly looks at you the same way, like you walk on water. But something's missing in this scenario, Brut. You're doing the right thing, but are you doing it for the right reasons?"

"What in the fuck are you saying?" He's talking in riddles, and it's adding to my piss-poor mood.

"Do you love her?"

"Of course I love her," I stammer, my voice rising.

"Does she know that?"

"What the…?" I stop. *Does she?* Have I told her? She hasn't said anything of the sort to me, but I feel it. I feel how she looks at me, like Hank said. She looks at me like she did when we were young. I'd hung the moon for her, but only because she looked at me like she wanted me to. She wanted me to be her everything. And I want her the same way. She knows this.

"Brut, you can't be this dense." Hank runs fingers through his hair. "And this marriage thing. What's the rush?"

"I want her as my wife."

"Then do it properly."

"I am," I yell, before downing the rest of my beer. Then I remind him, "This is how you did it."

"Don't compare your relationship with Lily to Midge and me. Our situation was different. I've waited twenty years for love like Midge, and I didn't want to wait any longer. She also had other things in place, like her sons. We couldn't live together comfortably. Midge has already had a wedding, and she didn't need the formality of a second one. And I didn't need one."

"Lily doesn't need one either."

"Brut, man." Hank stares at me, and I don't get it. "Lily's *agreeing* with you, but this is her first marriage."

"Mine too," I remind him again.

"Then do it right for both of you, too."

I sigh, reaching for the back of my neck and cupping my hand around my nape. "I am. I want to marry her. I want her to be my wife." I pause, roaming over my brother's face. "I've waited a long time, just like you, Hank. I didn't have the interim relationship like you." The jab at Hank's past with Kit Carrigan hits below the belt, but he needs to understand. "I've been waiting my whole life for a second chance with the one who got away. And now she's sitting in my kitchen with my baby in her."

"Then do it right, now that she's willing to stay."

I stare at my brother more confused than ever. Isn't that what I'm doing? I asked her to stay, and she said yes. We're getting married. We're having a baby.

229

L.B. Dunbar
What am I missing?

37

Love Is A Necessary Ingredient

[Lily]

"Are you happy?" Midge asks me, her voice softening. She squeezed my fingers at Brut's rushed announcement, and she hasn't let go since. Or maybe I've been the one holding onto her, needing something strong and stable to help me *get through this,* as Brut would say.

"Of course." My other hand moves to my lower belly. It's becoming instinctive to reach for Lima Bean even if I can't hold her yet. I don't even have as much of a bump as Midge does to justify touching myself like I do, but the touch brings me comfort. As a reminder I'm doing the right thing.

I'm old enough to recognize I'm not so young. However, I don't need to panic that I'm having a baby. I can do this. I also accept that people marry for all kinds of reasons. I don't need to be in love to get married, but I want to be. I mean, I am in love with Brut, and I have no doubt Brut cares a great deal about me. He also seems genuinely excited about the baby. But love *me?* That hasn't been determined yet.

From what Brut has told me, he takes care of things. His personal history proves it. I understand wanting the baby on his insurance. And I appreciate his desire to be on the birth certificate from the start, considering the issues he had with Chopper. Both of those things are a reminder of what Brut went through the first time, and I want to do it right for him this time.

Which is how I suddenly find myself engaged to the man of my dreams but feel a large gap in my heart. I could have everything with Brut—*everything*—but I'm missing the beyond he mentions.

I want *his* heart.

"You don't seem very...excited." Midge speaks softly like she might spook me.

"I just thought… I hoped it…it would be for love, not insurance purposes and certificate names and Brut being *responsible* like he always has been."

"Brut might be responsible, but marriage? That's such a huge step. It's pretty spontaneous of him." Midge's expression confirms her surprise.

"Which still isn't love and I shouldn't even be saying this to you as his sister-in-law." I give Midge's fingers a squeeze before releasing her hand. My palm is sweaty with anxiety yet cold with the truth of things. Brut isn't in love with me.

"I'm about to be *your* sister-in-law, too, but I'm your friend first. You and Brut are being stupid."

"I know, right?" I exhale with the relief that she understands. "This whole arrangement is out of control."

Getting married is a big deal. We don't need to be joined in such a way. We both agree about the legality, but I'm not going anywhere. And I know Brut intends to stick for the baby. We don't need to get married.

Except I'd like to marry him, if he loved me.

"No, what's dumb is you *are* in love. With each other."

"Did he say that he's in love with me?" I don't know why I ask as if I'm a love-sick teen. I hate that I sound desperate for reassurance.

"Hasn't he?" Midge's brows pinch. "Don't you feel it? He's changing his house to give you a home. He wants to be there for you financially. For your business, your baby, your heart." Midge's voice rises with her enthusiasm. "Sorry, I'm excitable lately."

"Why doesn't he tell me how he feels, then?"

Midge stares at me a moment. "He hasn't said he loves you?"

I shake my head, feeling the burn in my nose and prickle in my eyes. I'm so tired of the tears.

"I'm so sorry, Lily. I know he does. Men can be so…stupid." She reaches out for me, but this time it's for more than my hand. Midge hugs me, and I melt under comfort. I need her friendship. I want her as my sister. Maybe I'll gain something else I've never had, through Midge. Family.

"What's going on in here?" Hank chuckles as he stands inside the kitchen. Brut stands behind his brother with a plate full of steaks and grilled vegetables in his hand. I quickly swipe away the tears, keeping my back to Brut, and Midge speaks with a dismissive wave of her hand.

"Girl stuff."

The plate practically slams on the table, and I jump. Brut is before me instantly, pushing back my chair so he can squat in front of me.

"What is it?" he asks, softening his tone as his thumb wipes at the corner of my eye, catching a traitorous tear before it falls.

"Nothing," I lie, cupping his face. I'm on the verge of having it all in the palm of my hands. I'm happy. I am. Almost.

+ + +

"This isn't a good time. I'm so busy at the bakery," I say as October shifts to early November.

Brut and I still are not married. I've been putting him off as best I can. He set a date, and then the insurance adjusters wanted to inspect the bakery. He picked another date, and Esther played sick for me, so I had to work.

The bakery is my everything. I need to be here for orders and deliveries, and with the holiday season in full swing, I'm too busy to take an afternoon off, head to the nearest courthouse, and sign some paper binding myself to Brut...when he doesn't love me.

"Why do I feel like you're brushing me off?" he snaps as we stand in the kitchen of his house. The beautiful kitchen is finally finished with a black countertop, white subway tile backsplash, and a fountain faucet over the farmhouse sink. It's everything I could have asked for in a kitchen.

"I'm not," I lie.

"Don't you want to get married?"

Such a loaded question. If I say yes, Brut will push for immediacy. But while I've wanted marriage my whole life, I've also wanted it to be for love.

L.B. Dunbar

But, if I say no, Brut won't understand...it's because I want to marry him for love. As in, he loves me.

Tell me you love me, and I might feel better. I can't say that to Brut. I won't force him to respond to a love-sick question or make him feel obligated to say something he doesn't mean.

He's only having fun with me. I heard him tell Hank such a thing this morning on the phone.

"We're good," Brut said to his brother on speakerphone while he was in the bathroom trimming his scruff.

"Never figured you for someone who'd like playing house," Hank replied.

"We're not playing house. We're having fun."

The statement crushed me.

"Lily, we need to get married," Brut speaks, restoring me to our conversation. The demand in his tone doesn't sit well with me.

"We don't *need* to do anything, Brut. It should be that we want to get married."

"Well, that's the question I asked you. Don't you want to get married?"

"I do. It's just..." My voice fades as my eyes close. I want to feel like an equal, not an obligation.

"What?" he snaps. The tone of his voice is the tipping point.

Over the edge of the cliff, I go. "I just think I got caught up in the rush. I mean, Brut, honestly, I've loved you since I was nineteen, and I just always thought...hoped...dreamed...you'd come back to me someday. I knew all the reasons we didn't work, and I still wanted you, and then Midge and Hank had to play matchmakers and set us up on that godforsaken vacation."

"Godforsaken," he murmurs.

I don't know if he's mocking me or stunned by the implication of a mistake, but I barrel onward. "And everything seemed so perfect. One week. No past. No future. Everything and beyond, right? But you know what, Brut?" My voice rises as do my arms, flailing out as my irritation grows, and I find myself imploding. "The past is always there to haunt us, isn't it? There comes Lauren again. Even from her deathbed, she can't let us be. And then the future. Boy, I bet you never thought *beyond* meant another baby. A baby!" I shriek. I'm on a roll. "I mean, how ironic."

Tears have joined my tirade, and I don't even bother to wipe them away. I almost feel sorry for Brut as he's seen too many from me lately, but I'm nearing the bottom of the ravine I've jumped into, and it's going to hurt when I hit the hard surface.

"You're so honorable and responsible. You just step right up with solutions for everything. And I admit, I got caught up in it all with you. I mean, look at this kitchen. It's beautiful, and I want to feel like you did it for me—"

"I did," he interjects, his voice low, his brows pinching.

I hold up my hands to stop him. I have so much to say, and I need to get it out. The negative energy leaves me, and I didn't realize how heavy the burden has been until I start feeling lighter the more I let go.

"Would I even be here if it weren't for Lima Bean?"

Brut's beyond excited for the baby, kissing my belly and helping pick out colors for a nursery. He tells Lima Bean—her unofficial nickname and because he's convinced the baby is a girl—he loves her often. When he does such sweet things, I'm lost in the fantasy of a future with him. A good man. A great father. But what about a loving husband?

He remains silent, and I have my answer.

When Lauren died, everything shifted, and Brut disappeared, just as he did when she first destroyed us. Reality settled in. Brut wouldn't have come to me if Midge hadn't told him I was sick. He's been continually put in a position to see me—the vacation house, Lauren's funeral, the pregnancy—but he hasn't taken the initiative himself to seek me out.

Twenty-two years of silence.

I'm such a fool.

"This is my fault," I say, shoulders falling in defeat. "I fell for you just as I did when I was younger. I thought I meant more to you, and I let myself be swallowed up again." A sob interrupts my words. "Brut, I want everything for you. Everything and beyond, but I want it for me, too." I swipe at the snot dripping from my nose. "Remember when we

L.B. Dunbar

talked about what would be fun for you, Brut? At the beach house? Sexy Scrabble?"

Brut stares at me as he's been doing for the past few minutes. His expression remains hard, no emotion in his eyes, a twitch to his jaw.

"I don't want to be your fun, Brut. I want to be your heart. I want to be the love of—"

I stop abruptly as Brut steps into my space, his hands cupping my cheeks.

"Don't kiss me," I whisper because I realize my problem with Brut. I'm attracted to him beyond normal. My body reacts to his like no other. One taste of his lips, and I'm going to give in. *And I can't.*

"What the fuck?" he mutters toward my lips just as the back door opens.

"Get a room, you two." Chopper laughs from behind his dad, but Brut releases me, twisting before me. I'm grateful for his body-block as I spin for the sink, reaching for a paper towel to wipe my face and blow my nose.

"Hey," Brut says, his voice strained.

"What's going on?" Chopper quickly responds. I don't have to turn to face him to feel his eyes on my back.

"I forgot I asked you to pick me up," Brut replies.

But Chopper ignores his father and addresses me. "Lily, what's wrong?"

I turn to him, my face red and splotchy from the too-many tears I've shed. My eyes still burn, and I struggle to blink away more moisture.

"Just pregnancy stuff," I mutter, waving a hand to dismiss the mess I am.

"Jesus, good thing I never plan to have kids."

For some reason, this statement sucker punches me in the gut. Being nothing other than a flippant comment by a twenty-two-year-old, the thought still hurts. Brut will soon have two children, both out of wedlock both unplanned. No wonder he's never written a bucket list. The unexpected keeps overtaking his life.

Suddenly, I'm so drained I just want to return to bed, but Because Cupcakes needs me, and right now, I need to work.

An awkward moment passes between all of us before I brush past Brut. He doesn't follow me, and for once, I'm grateful he doesn't chase, but deeper sadness settles in.

He never follows me.

+ + +

Standing too long, my ankles swell, and my feet puff up to the point of pain. Esther is militant about making me rest, but today, I need to keep busy. I'm thankful I still have the apartment upstairs where I can lie down for a nap, but I refuse to use it until I can't stand anymore. It's nearly seven o'clock in the evening, and I have one more batch of cupcakes to make. Cranberry orange, one of my favorites.

Over the years, I've spent Thanksgiving in a variety of manners—friends, vacations, alone, baking. I looked forward to this year being the start of what I hoped would be a new tradition—spending time with family.

"Girl, what are you doing?" Esther admonishes as she comes out of the bathroom. Her apron is removed, and she's staring at me as I set out ingredients.

"I'm just going to—"

"No, girl, what are you *doing*?" Esther's accent comes thick with her emphasis.

"I'm going to stay here tonight." I speak quietly, preparing for Esther's wrath.

Instead, she steps over to me. "You've worked too hard today. What happened?" Her warm hand covers my arm. She didn't miss my red-rimmed eyes earlier, and she wanted to talk, but with Julia present, we just didn't. Esther has had a rough relationship in the past. I sense she fears something she shouldn't.

"We just had a fight. Or more like I dealt out words, and Brut said nothing."

"*Chica?*" Esther presses.

"I said some things I shouldn't have said. I told Brut I didn't want to marry him."

237

Her dark brows pinch but her voice remains soft. "You what?"

"Not in so many words. It was more like I don't think I *should* marry him." *Wanting* to marry him was a different definition.

"Why?" There is more than a question in Esther's tone.

Keeping my eyes on the recipe before me, although I don't read a word, I answer her. "I've already told you. Brut likes to do the right thing, and in his head, the right thing is to marry me. And I'm being a romantic fool at forty-one and wanting him to love me instead." I shrug as if it's that simple.

"But he does."

"He hasn't said that." Another month has passed, and the man still hasn't expressed any feelings about me.

"Lily, anyone watching that man as he looks at you knows he's all over you like flour on fresh bread. He loves you."

I stare at my friend and her strange metaphor.

"Why do I question it then?" Is it just the hormones? Am I really an emotional mess? Do I *need* the words?

"A lot has happened so fast." Esther holds out her hand, ticking off the items on her fingers. "Your sister. His son. The pregnancy. Moving in together. Mind-blowing sex. Or at least I assume you have that kind of sex, but you refuse to tell me details, and you know this girl is desperate over here." She lets out a deep *phew* and an exaggerated swipe at her brow to finish off.

I shake my head with a humorless chuckle. She's always probing for details about sex between Brut and me, but Brut and I haven't connected sexually over the past week. I've been too busy avoiding the marriage discussion, which means avoiding him.

"Maybe it's the pregnancy hormones." I laugh it off although I don't want to use the pregnancy as an excuse. Lima Bean is already the reason Brut wants me to marry him, and therein lies another sliver of the issue. Brut didn't actually *ask* me to marry him. He suggested we get married, and then hit the ball for a home run without popping the question. And we're far enough along in the game now that I'm too embarrassed to call foul.

I haven't told anyone he didn't officially proposed to me, and that missing piece of the puzzle bothers me as well.

"You need to go home," Esther says, looking at the containers spread around the prep table. "Talk to him."

She's right, but I know I won't go.

"Avoiding isn't healthy," she tells me.

Again, I know she's right, but still… "It's just one night. I just need a little break. Things always look better in the morning." The saying is cliché but appeases my friend.

She pats my arm and picks up the container of flour. "No more cupcakes," she says, returning the jar to the counter where we store our dry goods.

"Bed." She points to my staircase, and I acquiesce.

With feet that feel weighted with lead, I climb the stairs after locking up and fall on the couch. My feet are so swollen, I don't trust myself to stand in the shower, so I lie on the cushions sweaty and sticky. Propping my elephant looking ankles up on the armrest, I reach for my belly, rubbing over the barely-there swell.

"We'll get through this," I mutter, my heart clenching at the words. The truth is, we will. Brut won't let the baby lack, but I can't live without him loving me.

My tired eyes finally have no more tears, and I close them with relief. I hear my phone ring from somewhere in the apartment but lying on the couch feels so good. I'm too exhausted to get up, so I ignore the second parade of ringtones, quickly following the end of the first.

I visualize a happy place in my mind.

The beach. Lima Bean. And sleep.

38

Man Up Or Go Home…Or Both

[Brut]

"Why isn't she answering?" I grumble to myself as I cross the bar. I'm heading back to the table where Tommy Carrigan has joined Hank and me. Hank doesn't drink anymore, and I blame a lot of his prior wayward behavior on the man to his left, Tommy Carrigan. He's a charismatic character with his Southern drawl and his permanent rock star status—even though they aren't rock stars anymore. That ship has sailed, and with its absence came a huge relief for me. I'd watched my brother spiral downward too many times. Hank claimed the band was his family, but the only family picking him up when he hit bottom was me.

Yet somehow Tommy and Hank have reconnected. Their friendship is different now—more mature. Maybe it's because they are both married.

I want to be married.

I want Lily to be with me forever, but after this morning, I've realized she doesn't feel the same way.

"Another round," I announce, setting down two shot glasses. My brother eyes me. I'm not typically the wild one. I drink a beer every few days, maybe two, but I don't typically let loose like this. Only tonight, I'm wound tight. I don't understand what Lily wants, but I know one thing—when she said don't kiss her, my heart stopped beating. Correction, my heart fell out of my chest, thumped on the floor, and waited to be stomped on. Then Chopper interrupted us, and there was the awkward moment when I was ready to beg her to stay, take the day off and talk. But Chopper waited. He wasn't leaving me alone with Lily. I love my kid, but I wanted to smack him upside the back of his head. He watches Lily like a hawk, protective of her to a fault. Then again, can I blame him? He loves her.

I love her.

I don't understand.

"How's Lily?" Tommy mocks.

I'd excused myself for the bathroom, tried to call her for the millionth time, and rerouted to the bar for another round of shots before returning to the table.

"Fine," I grunt, slamming back the fiery liquid in one swallow.

"That doesn't look like fine," Hank implies, eyeing my empty shot glass before his gaze meets mine, narrowing in concern.

He's right. We aren't fine. We're an emotional roller coaster. A second chance is on the amusement ride before us, but we can't seem to pick up steam. We're stuck, again. To top it off, we haven't had sex in a week. For a woman with pregnancy hormones in overdrive, the slammed brakes should have tipped me off. Things are definitely *not* fine.

"Trouble in paradise, perhaps?" Tommy jabs.

I glare back at him. "Paradise is just heavenly, thank you."

"What the fuck are you two talking about?" Hank interjects, his head swinging back and forth between the two of us. "What's going on with Lily? *Fine* is a female word. What's wrong?"

I gaze at my brother, and Tommy bursts out laughing. "A female word?"

"If Edie says to you 'I'm fine,' you know you're in trouble, right?" Hank pauses a second while Tommy stares back at him. Hank ignores Tommy and speaks to me. "Never mind. Just tell me what's happening?"

"We had a fight. Or rather, she told me off and then told me she didn't want to marry me."

"What?" Tommy and Hank exclaim in unison.

I shrug. What more is there to say?

"Is it because you asked Midge and me to be witnesses, but you two haven't gotten married yet? Are you rethinking the wedding thing?"

"What wedding *thing*?" Tommy asks.

I ignore him. "No, I said we could have a wedding later, but we need to get married now."

"You *said*?" Tommy parrots, mocking me.

Hank glares at me. "You asked her to marry you, right?"

"Yes," I hiss, narrowing my eyes at my brother.

L.B. Dunbar

"How?" Hank snaps

"Not this again. What do you mean *how*?"

"I mean, I heard the lame explanation of asking her in the tub, which doesn't sound all that romantic, unless it includes bubble bath and candles and shit. Lily didn't seem too excited to share what went down, so I'm guessing no bubbles or candlelight. So why don't you tell me how you did it?"

"What, are you the romance police all of the sudden? Got married at a courthouse yourself and now you're the judge of how others propose?" I reach for Tommy's untouched shot and slam it back.

"I already told you not to compare yourself to Midge and me. And I'm still waiting for an answer on how you asked the love of your life to be your wife. Because I'm thinking you pulled a Brut and *told her* how things would be. You told her to marry you. You told her a date. You told her we'd be witnesses."

"I didn't," I defend. But as his statements slowly sink in, my heart cowers in my chest. I wipe a hand down my face. "Fuck."

"Brut, I love you, man, but you can be so dense. And your need to control things…" Hank drifts off and shakes his head.

"Control things? You think I asked for the garage? Wanted to take charge of your life? Purposely got the wrong girl pregnant and raised a child without her?"

"You got someone else pregnant?" Tommy interjects.

"Shut up," I snap. "Lily's pregnant."

"I know, but who's the wrong girl?"

"Her…just never mind. I don't ask to be in charge, Hank. It just seems to happen."

"Because you take things upon yourself."

"Well, what else was I supposed to do? Throw Pop out? Let you hit rock bottom and die? Reject my child?" Unraveling, my voice has risen the normal noise of the pub, but I don't care. I'm at loose ends here, and I want Lily to return my goddamn phone calls.

"Brut, calm down."

"Calm down? Calm down! I want Lily to marry me. I want us together. We have a second chance, which I might add, you aided in happening, and now she's walking away."

"Brut, answer the fucking question about the proposal," Tommy demands, and it's almost as if *his* asking me pisses me off enough to admit the truth.

"I didn't ask!" The reality hits me hard. *I didn't ask her.* My romantic Lily who wants to dance in the rain and make love under the moonlight didn't get a proposal. She doesn't even have a ring or a memory or... "Fucking Christ."

My hand comes to my forehead, pressing at the wrinkled skin. Silence falls between us.

"I didn't ask her," I quietly admit, voice strained. "But she doesn't want to marry me anyway."

"How do you know? You didn't ask her." Tommy snorts, and if I didn't think he was right, I'd punch his smug face.

"Since when did you two become experts on women?" I chuckle without humor.

"When I fell in love," Tommy says.

"When I married the woman of my dreams," Hank adds.

When did we start acting like women, discussing this shit?

"You realize you two sound like chicks." I tip my beer at them and notice the bottle is empty.

"You realize you sound like a dick," Hank amends. "But I'm thinking you'd rather sound like a chick, too."

I stare at my brother a moment before bursting out in laughter. "You know how stupid that sounded?"

"Do you know how pathetic you look?" He glares back at me. For a moment, I feel like we're ten and eight again, tit-for-tat fighting that often lead to blows between us. "Man up, Brut. She's the woman you've wanted back for twenty-two years. She's here. How you gonna keep her?"

I hate when my brother's right.

I've totally fucked this up.

243

+ + +

Lily isn't home when I get there, so I decide to sleep on the couch. Isn't that what a man in the doghouse does anyway? I figure I'd give her space until she came home. But I sleep fitfully despite the drunken haze. I don't like sleeping without her, and when I wake and find our bed still untouched, I panic. After all the calls I made last night, only a text from her graces my phone in the morning.

Staying the night at the bakery.

The tone of a text can be difficult to read, so I hate to make assumptions, but this is cold. Simple. Direct. No additional information. I don't know how to respond.

I miss you.

I love you.

Come home.

I'm more confused than ever on how to make things right with Lily. I want to ask her to marry me, but if she's only going to refuse me, I don't think I can handle the rejection. On the other hand, I don't even know if she'll still live with me. We can live together, if that's what she'd want instead. I'd prefer she be my wife, but I understand she's a modern woman, and she doesn't need a legal document to prove I want to be with her. However, I also know my romantic Lily wanted marriage one day. Call me old fashioned, but I'd still like her to be legally joined to me. I want her to have my name. I want us to be a family.

We aren't playing house like Hank said yesterday morning. My house is her home.

And I'm not just having fun with her, although being with her is the best time I've ever had.

I love her.

Several weeks ago, Midge told me to stop wasting time. Hank told me to man up. Hours later, I have a plan. I force myself to stop checking my phone every five seconds and eventually leave it in my SUV as I run errands. The phone is close to dead, so when I return to the SUV, I plug it in and watch as the screen blows up with text after text. Some are from Lily's phone, but it's not her messaging me.

Brut, this is Esther. Call Lily's number.

Brut, this is kind of an emergency. It's still Esther.

Brut, don't be the dick I think you shouldn't be and call this fucking number.

Texts from Midge intermix with Esther's growing frustration.

Call me.

Call Lily.

Get to the doctor's office.

Then, there's one text from Hank. **You're fucking this up.**

Screw Hank. I call Midge.

"Thank God, Brut. You need to call Lily's doctor." My heart races at Midge's announcement echoes through the SUV.

"What happened?"

"She called me frantic. I didn't want to make any assumptions, so I told her to call the doctor. I could hear the stress in her voice, though. She was in a lot of pain. Brut, I don't think it's good. She needs you."

"Lima Bean," I whisper, but Midge hears me.

"What?"

"Never mind. Can you text me the doctor's address? I'm already driving, and I'll put it in maps."

"Got it. Call me back when you know something. I haven't heard from her, and I'm worried."

"Will do." I hang up before I've finished speaking, calling the doctor's office next.

"Brookes and Wadden OB/GYN."

I explain I'm looking for Lily Warren and how far along she is in the pregnancy.

"And who are you?"

"I'm her husband."

"I'm sorry, we don't have a husband on record. I can't offer any information to you."

I bang a hand against the steering wheel. "Damnit. Can you just tell me if she's there?"

"I'm sorry, sir—"

"Just tell me if the baby's okay, then? Just a yes or no." My knuckles pale as I grip the wheel, making an illegal turn onto the next street.

"Sir, I can't divulge any information. I suggest you contact the patient."

"So, she is a patient, and she was there today?"

"Sir." The frustration rings in her voice.

"Is she still there?"

"I'm sor—"

"Never mind." I click off the call and dial Lily's number. It rings and goes to voicemail. Immediately, I try again. And again.

"What the fuck?" The slight accent catches me off guard until I realize Esther has Lily's phone.

"Esther, please tell me she's okay."

"I think she's been better."

My fingers tighten on the steering wheel as I accelerate through a yellow light.

"Is she at the doctor's office? I'm on my way unless she's home."

"They already released her."

"What happened?"

"I think it's best if she tells you."

My chest clenches, and I grip my shirt over my heart. "The baby. Esther, tell me the baby is okay."

"Brut, you and Lily have a lot to discuss. Maybe you could start by being a man and tell her you love her."

What the fuck?

"Thanks, Esther. And how about you tell me where the fuck she is?" Tires screech and I've nearly missed a car trying to cut into my lane. *Not today, buddy.*

"She went home."

"Thanks." I end the call. Then realize I'm not certain if she's gone to our home or back to the apartment above the bakery.

I make a quick decision, hoping I'm not too late...for anything.

39

Lima Bean and Bucket Lists

[Lily]

I wake after a restless sleep. I've missed several calls from Brut and a few texts but decide I still don't know what to say to him. The day ahead at the bakery will be busy, and I'm ready to throw myself into baking to distract myself again. Esther is already setting things up, and Julia has come in early. She's come out of her shell a little bit with questions about dating and kissing, and Esther's all over her like a mother hen. I find it funny she's asking Esther for advice, but I don't judge her. I wish someone had taken me under their wings when I was her age and been open about sexual activities. Julia doesn't want information about sex, though—not yet, she says—and I smile with pride that she's willing to wait. At her age, I was so hungry for Brut I'd have done anything for a taste of him. Foolish heart.

We're in the middle of one such discussion when my back cramps. I bend forward, feeling as if I've been stabbed in the kidneys.

"Jesus," I cry out, gripping the base of my spine. The pain returns almost instantly, wrapping around to the front of me, and I cup the small bulge finally protruding from my belly. My legs tremble, and my other hand grips the stainless-steel island in the center of the kitchen.

"Lily?" Esther questions, but I can't find words to answer her. I groan out the word, "Stomach," as my knees collapse, and I lower to the floor. I'm almost twelve weeks, and the doctor has assured me I'm progressing well. I've gained a few pounds as I should, and the ultrasound I had showed a steady heartbeat. Esther folds to her knees before me, yelling at Julia to call 911.

"No," I grunt. "Call Midge."

"What about Brut?" Esther asks, her large dark eyes opening wide. She's scared, and I try to smile, but the pain rips through me again.

"He'll only worry. No. Call Midge."

247

"Midge is on the phone," Julia says, lowering my cell phone to me on the floor.

Oh God, I groan as another wave of sharp pain ripples through me. My hand clutches at my belly. Come on, Lima Bean. Be a good girl.

"We have too much testosterone in this family already," Brut proclaimed one day, declaring Lima Bean must be a girl. As if it worked like that.

"What's going on?" Midge asks on speakerphone.

"My stomach. The pain." I'm gritting my teeth.

"Lily, honey. Call the doctor."

"But is this normal?"

"Lily, call the doctor." Midge's voice rises.

"Midge, just tell me." Panic sets in. I'm way too early for Braxton Hicks. Fear grips me, and I start crying. Oh my God, am I losing Lima Bean?

Esther takes the phone and scrolls through my contacts. The doctor's next on speakerphone and suggests I come into the emergency room. Esther helps me up from the floor and escorts me to my car. She barks out an order that Julia's in charge, which doesn't make me feel better.

Esther drives like she's in the Daytona 500, and all I want to do is close my eyes to the pain. I'm clutching the door handle and my belly, keeping my eyes forward as each time I shut them, I feel dizzy.

"This is normal, right?" I mutter.

"You're going to be okay," Esther groans, determination in her tone although she seems as panicked as I am. I can't lose this baby. What if I lose the baby? Tears flow again, swimming with my fear.

I'm so sorry, Brut, I whisper in my head.

I love you, Lima Bean.

+ + +

"Thank fuck," I hear muttered after heavy boots stomp up the staircase to the loft above the bakery. I'm back in the apartment, lying on my bed. I have a clear visual of Brut as he crests the staircase. I just stare at him

Brut, the beautiful man with his golden tan, bright blue eyes, and white hair. He falls to his knees beside the bed and brushes back my hair.

"I'm sorry," he says. "I should have been here."

"It's okay," I whisper, my throat dry. "I'm okay."

He looks down at my belly, which is covered both by my knees pulled up to my chest and the light blanket over my legs.

"Lima Bean?" he whispers.

"She's fine."

Brut exhales and lowers his head to the edge of the bed, rolling it back and forth on the mattress. He stands abruptly and paces away from me, his back to me.

"I just…just give me a second." His shoulders fall forward as his hand comes to his face. His movements show he's pinching his eyes. *Is he crying?*

"Brut," I call out softly.

He responds by wiggling his head again. He gives me the back of his hand. He needs another second.

I slowly press up on my elbow, and the shift turns his attention. He's at the edge of the bed once again, gently pushing me back to the mattress.

"Just relax. Rest."

I lie back but keep my focus on his glistening eyes. "I'm sorry."

His brow pinches. "What are you sorry for?" Tender fingertips brush over my forehead. "What happened?"

"The doctor said dehydration…and stress."

"Lily pad," Brut admonishes. "You're working too hard."

I hold his eyes. "This is what I do."

"I know, but you need to let me take care of you. You need to let others help you."

"You sound like Esther."

Brut scrunches his face as he continues to stroke back my hair. "Shh, don't let her know I agree with her on something."

I smile weakly at him.

"Look, I know we have a lot to discuss, and I don't want to upset you, but I have a few things to say now. Maybe it will take the stress away." He takes a deep breath. "We don't have to get married if you don't want to."

"I do, I just—"

"Let me finish, okay? You laid a lot out on me yesterday morning, and I didn't have the chance to defend some of it."

"I'm sorry," I interrupt again, and his finger comes to my lips.

"There's no rush. In fact, if you'd prefer to live together, that's fine. I understand you're a modern, independent woman, and maybe you want different things than I do. I want you to be my wife, Lily pad. I've waited a long time, endlessly hoping I'd get a second chance with you, and I feel my prayers have been answered. But I understand you might not feel the same way, and I respect that. I want to honor whatever you think works best. I'd just like to say I think us together would be better than anything separate, but I'll do what you wish."

What I wish. How I wish you'd say you loved me? How I wish you'd ask me to marry you and mean it? Instead, I nod.

"I don't want you to make any decisions right now or even tonight, tomorrow, whenever. I'd like you to come home, though. I want you to be in my house, to make it our house. Together. But I don't want to pressure you." He sighs. He's been plucking at the blanket the entire time he's spoken, but he reaches for my hand, pulling it to his lips to linger on my knuckles. "Just don't say it's the end of us, okay? Please, Lily pad, don't leave me or tell me to leave you…"

My heart patters to a halt. I don't want him to walk away. I want him to run toward me. I want the *beyond* he promised.

"I don't plan on going anywhere," I say softly.

Brut's head shoots upward. "You'll come home then?" The hopeful strain in Brut's voice breaks my heart all over again.

"Tomorrow, yes. Today, I'm too tired to move. I just want to stay right here."

Brut lowers his lips to my fingers again. "Of course. We'll stay right here." He stands again, reaches down to unlace his boots and then climbs over me, curling around my body.

"I don't like sleeping without you," he murmurs into my neck.

"I don't like sleeping without you, either."

"I don't like fighting with you," he adds.

"I don't like fighting with you," I admit.

"Wherever you want to be is where I want to be. I just want to *be* with you. Us together."

Feeling the same way, I bring his hand up to my lips, kissing his knuckles. He kisses the back of my neck. Then his hand lowers to my belly, the expanse of his spread fingers covers most of my stomach. My hand blankets the back of his on my abdomen.

"She's okay?"

"She is."

Brut's head rolls against the back of mine. I hold my breath, expecting further ribbing from him. Instead, he says something else.

"I love her."

Tears prickle my eyes, and his fingers lightly press over my belly. *Goddammit, no more tears.*

"I'm not used to saying such things, Lily pad." He pauses as though he's trying to tell me something more.

"She loves you, too." I have no doubt Brut will be an excellent father, and any child will worship him. Chopper already does.

"If something had happened…" He blows out a breath and warm air tickles my neck. "We'd try again. And again. I'd give you anything, everything you want. I love you, Lily pad."

My heart stops, and my breath hitches. I twist in his arms to look at him over my shoulder.

"You do?" I still, afraid to break the spell of his words, afraid he'll realize what he's said.

"Of course, sugar."

"I wasn't sure." My voice lowers to no more than a whisper as my fingers tighten over his on my belly.

"What?" Hot breath hits the side of my face before he shifts and presses my shoulder to lie on my back. He peers down at me. "How could you not know?"

"You never told me."

"Lily." My name drags out with his exhale. "I loved you when you were nineteen, only I didn't know how to tell you. And at twenty-four when I saw you in a grocery store, and at thirty-six when you opened the bakery. I've never stopped loving you, sugar."

"Why didn't you ever say anything? Why didn't you come back to me?"

"And say what? Sorry I slept with your sister? Oh, and guess what, I got her pregnant and now I'm raising the son she abandoned to me. Want to date me? Want to marry me?"

"Yes." I stare at him.

He stares back. "Lily, come on. That's not an attractive offer."

"But it's one I've been waiting for." My eyes lower to the collar of his shirt.

His fingers tip up my chin. "What are you saying?"

"I was hurt, crushed even, but I loved you, then, too."

"And now, Lily pad? How do you feel about me now?"

"I love you even more than I thought possible." My voice cracks as I bare my soul to him.

"Let me kiss you," he says.

I question his asking, but then I remember I told him not to kiss me yesterday. "Every day."

The words aren't even fully out of my mouth before my lips are covered with his. He's tender, loving, telling me how he feels with the connection of our mouths. *He loves me.* He wants *me.*

The soft kisses last a few minutes before he pulls back.

"I'm so glad you're okay and the baby, too. I don't know what I'd do if I lost either of you." His fingers comb through my hair, and the earnest tone of his voice tells me the truth.

He means what he says. He really loves me.

+ + +

I wake alone, but I hear voices in the kitchen below. Brut and I slept away the remainder of the day in our clothes. We cuddled.

For once, I didn't beg him to take me. I wanted him just to hold me.

I rise and decide to head downstairs before taking a much-needed shower. The voices disappear as I come through the door Brut insisted on installing to protect the upstairs from the lower level. I search the kitchen to find it empty despite the ingredients and containers spread on the island, waiting further baking. After crossing the vacant room, I enter the bakery itself. Darkness fills the space, but the display case is lit although empty of cupcakes.

Inside the case stands a purple, plastic, kid's sand bucket. Glancing over my shoulders, I thought I heard voices, but no one is present. Turning back for the bucket, I reach for the sand toy and remove it from the larger container. A Post-it note on the side reads *Fulfill Me.*

I tip the bucket, puzzled at the meaning of the note, until I see a velvet black box inside. My fingers shake as I remove the square package. Underneath the jewelry container are seven Scrabble tiles.

M-A-R-R-Y-M-E.

A presence comes up behind me, but I don't turn. I know it's Brut as his manly, fresh scent surrounds me as does his arms. While I hold the black box in my hand, Brut plucks the letter tiles from the bottom of the bucket and arranges them again on the counter before me.

Marry me.

"I fucked up, Lily pad. My beautiful, romance-seeking Lily. My bucket list girl of dancing in the rain, and what if games, and making love under moonlight. Let me ask you properly. Let me give you the wedding you want. A dress. A party. Everything."

With my back to his chest, I shake my head. *It's too much.* It's everything…and beyond.

"You love me," I murmur, and Brut spins me to face him.

"Of course, I love you. I told you las—"

"But you really mean it." My eyes roam over his puzzled face. "You really love me. Not just because of the baby. Not because of some scare. You—"

"I…my God, Lily, is this what's been wrong?" Brut's forehead furrows before relaxing. "I love you. I love you. I love you." His mouth lowers to my forehead, my nose, my lips. Too briefly, my lips. "I loved you when I was twenty-three, and I love you even more at forty-five."

Brut stares at me, his expression shifting. "Shit, I guess I've waited long enough to tell you."

L.B. Dunbar

I laugh a little, feeling giddy at his words. Reaching up for his face, I tickle his scruff with my fingertips. "I love you, Brut."

He leans in for another too-quick kiss.

"I wanted to marry you way back when, Lily pad, but I wanted to have it all together for you. I wanted it to be perfect. I would have given you babies when you were ready. I wanted to grow old with you, not wait until I was old to have you."

"You aren't old." His white hair makes him look distinguished...and sexy.

"Tell me I'm not too late." He pauses, his eyes searching my face. "Am I too late to tell you I love you? Am I too late to ask?"

My head tilts, and I lift the closed box. Teasingly, I say, "Officially, you haven't asked anything yet."

Brut takes the box from my fingers and lowers to one knee. He opens the package, presenting me with a solitaire diamond on a white gold band. Simple. Classic. Me.

"Lily pad, love of my life, my heart, my soul, my everything. Will you marry me because I love you? Because I love us. And I want whatever lies ahead for us."

Turning for the tiles on the counter, I pick up three and hold them out to him in my palm.

Yea. There is no S in this collection of letters. No H either.

"Say it," he pleads with a laugh. "I want to hear it."

"Yes," I say. "Yes, yes, and yes."

Brut's lips twist into a sexy grin as he stands. He removes the ring from the box and slips it on my finger, kissing over it once it's settled in place.

"Accepting my proposal...that might be my favorite sound of all the sounds you've made."

"I love you," I whisper, wrapping my arms around his neck and tipping up to kiss him.

He stiffens for a second. "Nope, retraction. Hearing you say you love me is my favorite." He smiles wide and leans forward to tell me the same, then he's kissing me and the only noise I hear is the beating of my happy heart.

40

A New Game

[Brut]

Lily and I are getting married, and I couldn't be more excited. It's officially happening on New Year's Day. It's become a trend Lily tells me. *Start the new year in a positive direction.* I've waited years for her, so while I still would have rushed to a courthouse, I'm willing to wait a few weeks to begin years of being married to her. We'll be married at the beach house in Ocean Beach.

In the meantime, our new kitchen table has finally arrived in time for Thanksgiving. It's circular with four chairs, and I've decided Lily and I are going to play a game to christen this space.

"Remember the game four squares as a kid?" I ask her as she enters the kitchen after a shower.

"I'm not as old as you, so I don't," she teases.

I lunge for her, enveloping her in my arms. "Very funny, Lily pad." Wrapping my arms around her from behind, I nibble at her neck a second.

"Okay, we're going to play four chairs," I explain.

"And how does this game work?" She chuckles which vibrates up her back and forces her ass against my front. Little does she know, this is exactly how we'll play.

"First. I finger fuck you on one chair."

"Brut," she admonishes, but the additional purr in her voice tells me she approves of the rules.

"Then I'm going to eat you out on the second one."

"Oh my," she mutters, curling her back so her ass finds friction against me. I'm hard as a rock just thinking about what we'll do, and we haven't even started. I reach for the waistband of her leggings and dip my fingers deep inside.

L.B. Dunbar

"We'll move around the table where you'll then straddle me," I say, walking her to the first set and setting her on my lap before slipping a finger into her. Her legs spread wide, cradling the outside of my thighs. Open as she is, I add a second finger to the first. She grips the table before her, knuckles tense as she uses the support to rock her hips, forcing my fingers to delve deeper.

"Then," I whisper below her ear, my lips resting on her skin. "You're going to reverse cowgirl me on the last seat."

"Brut," she screams as I nip her neck at the juncture of her shoulder, and she comes instantly.

Lily's still hyped on pregnancy hormones, and I'm enjoying the side effects. Lifting her by the back of her thighs, I hoist her to the next seat. I remove her leggings and thong in one tug, and she yelps as her bare backside hits the wooden seat. Lowering to my knees, I drag her to the edge of the surface and dive in, lapping at her, savoring her like she's the feast this table will soon host.

She's extra sensitive with the pregnancy and produces more wetness than I remember. I love it. I love her being pregnant.

I love her.

She tugs at my hair as I devour her, splitting her open with my tongue. She's close, but I want to feel this one around me, so I pull back just as she reaches the edge.

"No," she whimpers while I stand and rush to lower my jeans. I sit on the opposite seat and slip my boxers and jeans from my ankles.

"Hop on Pop," I say, patting my lap.

Lily releases a snort-laugh, one of her many sounds I adore. "You did not just say that." She shakes her head, but she's heard it before from me. "You're going to ruin this for me."

I reach out for her wrist and tug her to me. "I promise to make it up to you." I promise to make up everything, and I've told her this with my actions *and my words*. We had a long talk about what happened when we were young, and I praise all things above for her understanding and forgiveness. I also kick myself for not trusting in her enough to tell her about the events that lead to my poor decision and having the faith that she'd stick around until I got my shit together.

Lily lowers over me, straddling my thighs and holding onto the back of the chair for support. She's so wet, I glide into her without any effort. The warmth. The depth. This woman is all things to me. I'm inside her body, but she's inside my soul. This is the *beyond* that I've only ever hoped for. Now, she's sharing my house, my bed, my heart.

Her eyes flick down to where we're joined. On the day I bought her engagement ring, I inked my skin similar to hers. A small cupcake on my pelvis with a mini-cupcake next to it. It isn't pink and purple like Lily's, but it matches her design in black and gray. It represents Lily and Lima Bean, whose tattoo happens to have a lima bean on top instead of a maraschino cherry.

Holding the back of the chair, Lily rocks her hips over me, holding me within as she rolls forward. I grip her hips but let Lily lead this dance. We move in a rhythmic manner. She's getting into it—her head falling back and then forward. She's going to come again, and I marvel at the miracle of her joined with me. We have a second chance at everything and I'm not wasting another precious minute.

My thumb slips down to tease her where she needs, pleasuring her until she makes another of my favorite noises.

A gasp. A hitch. "I'm coming. Again. Again." I love her noises.

She stills, milking me within her, and I'm close but not ready to finish our little game.

"One more chair," I announce, lifting her while she's still attached to me. She squeals as I shift us to the final seat.

"Brut, I can't take anymore," she whimpers, but I know she can.

"Flip," I grunt. Her rapid release of my dick almost undoes me. Our skin slides, releasing a suction sound as she slips off me. Lily does as I ask, spinning so her back faces me, and I guide her to my lap, legs dangling on either side of mine.

"I'm going to fall." She reaches for the table before us.

"Never. I'll never let you go again," I say, guiding my stiffness into her depths. Lily's practically a ragdoll, bending at my will, and I can't hold out much longer. My lower back tightens, and the orgasm builds. Increasing the pace, I lift and lower her, filling the room with grunts and groans and the sound of us coming together. "So close, Lily pad."

L.B. Dunbar

"Brut?" she questions.

The wonder in her voice catches me off guard. "What, sugar?"

"Honey, I'm...I'm gonna come again."

Holy fuck. *Yes.* I continue to move her, our skin slapping, the sexy sound echoing through the kitchen. An idea strikes, and I lift us both, bending her toward the table. Her stomach doesn't allow her to lay flat as she's definitely showing. Three full months. Six to go.

"Hold on, baby," I groan as I pummel deep, the shift in position hitting her in a new way. Her arms lie near the edge of the table, searching for purchase on the surface. "Come for me."

The command is harsh, desperate, needy. I want to feel her clench, squeezing me with her heat.

"Yes!" I cry out. The second she comes undone around me, I release inside her. The rush leaves me and enters her.

I love this feeling. I love my future wife.

"That was incredible, sugar."

Lily's breath comes heavy underneath me, and I shift to look her in the face. A grin meets me, and she struggles to find the words to answer me.

"I love you," I tell her.

"I like the sounds you make." She's teasing me because she loves these words, and then she returns them to me. "I love you, too."

Her soft smile morphs into a deep grin. She likes it when I tell her how I feel, when I say those three important words, and I've learned a big reason is because she hasn't heard them often enough in her life.

I practice every day, sometimes telling her more than once because Lily wants to hear me say them. And I like to say them, especially when she looks at me like she does.

Like I'm her everything...and beyond.

41

Restored Dreams

[Lily]

Brut and I get married. Twenty-two years, five months, and nine days from the date we separated. I'm four and a half months pregnant when it happens, and Brut says he feels like the baby inside me marks a new beginning for us. But we aren't marrying because of our little Lima Bean. We marry because he loves me, and I love him.

Standing on the edge of a breezy beach, my toes dig in the cold sand. It's only fifty degrees today, January 1st, at Ocean Beach San Diego. I'm chilly, but this is where we wanted to wed. Instead of flowers, I hold a glass jar shaped like a bucket, filled with the seashells I collected when Brut and I were first here. My dress is empire waist, allowing for the slight bump covered in layers of light material that flows down to my feet. A wreath of lilies crowns my head. Midge says I look like a modern hippie. Brut says I look beautiful, which is something he says often.

"You're practically glowing," he tells me.

I'd say it's because of the baby, but really, it's our love. The warmth of Brut's affection. The depth of his attention. He's everything to me.

Today, he stands before me wearing casual linen pants and a white T-shirt. I can't imagine him in anything else. He only owns one suit, but considering he wore it for Lauren's funeral, I didn't want him to wear it when *we* joined together permanently. He agreed and tossed the thing in the trash.

No more past.

The wind picks up, and I shiver. Brut reaches out for me, rubbing his hands up and down my bare arms.

"You're freezing," he whispers, interrupting the minister.

"I'm perfect," I tell him as his hands slip down to hold mine. The ceremony won't last long. We selected a short reading and then the

L.B. Dunbar

exchange of vows. It's a morning wedding, and afterward, the beach house will be full to bursting with our family.

Midge and Hank are our witnesses. Esther and Julia are here for me. Midge's boys are in attendance, too, as well as Chopper. I learned a little secret. When Esther took me to the doctor, all those months ago, Chopper came to aid Julia in the bakery. While he didn't know how to bake, he was a quick study and listened to Julia dictate instructions to him. I've noticed the looks he continues to slide to her. I'd dare to say he has a crush on our quiet cupcake mouse.

I smile at the love around me, around us. These are the people most important in our lives, and by summer, our little Lima Bean will join us. This is my family.

Brut and I continue to smile at one another. His grin, sexy and crooked; mine nearly cracking my face. I've never been so happy.

We say our "I dos," and then Brut kisses me, and I amend my emotions. This makes me the happiest I've ever been. His mouth on mine. His heart joined to me. Brut scoops me up after a hot kiss, and I squeal as he lifts me.

"I'm too heavy." My feet kick, and sand dusts from my toes.

"You'll never be too much for me."

My arms wrap around his neck, and I try to balance my jar of shells. Brut carries me to the deck, and we enter the house where a brunch awaits. Chopper insisted the brunch wouldn't be complete without waffles, and I agree.

Brut and I exchange a heated glance after a look at the display of cupcakes serving as our wedding treat instead of cake. This kitchen holds fond memories.

"I'm going to frost you later," Brut whispers in my ear, and I laugh, thinking he's sharing another cupcake joke. Then I see the gleam in his eyes. He's serious, and I can't wait. I love the things this man does to me. I love him, and I'm thrilled to give him everything...and beyond.

Epilogue
Fast Forward Four Years

[Brut]

"Shh, Lena, you'll spoil it for Daddy."

I already know about the party, the one that's supposed to be a surprise but no longer is because four-year-olds can't keep a secret. I play along anyway as I know Lily went through a lot of work to organize everything. It's strange turning fifty. The big 5-0. I never would have imagined this would be my life.

A beautiful wife.

A loving daughter.

And a second son.

Lily had our little Lima Bean, who we named Lena Bea, and then twenty-two months later, she gave birth to Henry. She had high blood pressure with him, along with a pre-eclampsia scare, and I didn't feel trying for more children was worth the risk of Lily's life. I had a vasectomy to put a lid on the super swimmers as Hank teased me. He claims it runs in the family. He's proud of being a father later in life, just like me, and his own daughter, Lyra, is a handful. He had the snip after her as well.

"He'll be here soon," I hear Chopper tell the crowd gathered in my backyard. Lily has added a ton of flowers over the years and strung lights over the back deck I eventually built. Somedays, I don't recognize the house as the home I grew up in—the one filled with men and attitude. Now, it holds a family stocked in laughter and love. And a lot of toys. A shit ton of toys.

I made this house as happy as I could while Chopper grew up, but I realize things are different this time around.

For one, I have Lily, who I should have had all along. She's made a world of difference to Chopper. She includes him in everything.

261

Despite his age difference, she puts in all the effort to remind him he's part of the family we have now.

Hank and I own Restored Dreams together now. He finally let me give him part of the business, or rather, he bought into it. An investment, he told me begrudgingly, but I know he loves it. We're partners as we've always been as brothers. Honestly, having him as an equal has taken some pressure off me, and I'm enjoying my family more the second time around. I did go back to school. Then I realized, I'm right where I'm meant to be. I decided to take some general business courses instead of history and completed a degree just to say I have a college education. Lily's proud of me, but I'm proud of me, too. It was a lot of work with little ones, but Lily makes everything easy.

I round the corner of the house, opening the back gate, and hear the cheers of "Surprise!"

Everyone is here. Midge and Hank, the boys, and Lyra. Tommy and Edie. Her daughter, Masie, and West, a member of the band Tommy manages. Tommy's niece, Ivy, and her husband, Gage, lead singer of Collision. Esther and her man. Julia. Some guys from the shop.

I smile, placing a hand over my heart. I'm touched, even as I pretend to be surprised. I really am blessed, and I feel it inside my chest.

"You aren't surprised," Lily whispers as she steps up to me with Henry on her hip and kisses me lightly. He reaches out for me, and I take him from Lily. Her smile shakes, but I wrap an arm around her.

"Oh, I'm surprised, Lily pad." And I am. I'm surprised where life can lead, and I'm so grateful to have my dreams restored to me.

Epilogue 2

The Letter

Dear Mati,

If you're reading this, something has happened to me. Hopefully, it wasn't something long and drawn out, but quick and peaceful. Baby, I'm also hoping it didn't take you, too, although you know I'd find you in heaven if you are here with me.

So, you've made it to cleaning out my office, which you've been asking me to do for years. I never was the neat one.

Reassure the boys I'm watching over them. I have faith that the two halves of us will find their way in the world, hopefully as fathers, as fatherhood has been one of the greater joys of my life.

The greatest joy has been your love, Mati. I know you gave it to me willingly, in sickness and in health, for richer or poorer. We know we've covered all four areas. Death does not part us, but I don't want it to stop you from living. We promised each other, young or old, whichever one of us went first, the other would continue to enjoy the gift of life. It's an adventure. Ours has certainly hit some bumps, taken curves, and ridden steep hills, but we enjoyed the ride, right? Don't stop now. You're the driver, Mati. A new road awaits.

I want you to do me a favor. Just consider it before you get mad at me. (Those vows should have included in moments of conflict and peace.) Contact Denton. He was one of our best friends. He loved you as I did, only I'm the luckier man. Despite riches and fame, I won you. I had your ear and your heart and your body. You might need someone to talk to, and he could be the ear for you. I have no doubt his heart is still open to

263

yours. As for your body, well, I'd be a selfish man, deserving hell instead of heaven, if I expected it to waste on earth without attention. We gave each other permission, in vows outside our wedding, babe. I expect you to accept them. For once, don't argue with me.

Live life.
Love from heaven,
Chris

+ + +

Next up in the sexy silver foxes collection: *Second Chance.*
Continue reading about Mati and Denton.

Want a little bit more of Brut, Lily, Chopper and Julia?
Skip ahead to *Hauling Ashe*.
Turn the page for a little nibble.

Like older characters, hot romance, and small towns?
You might also enjoy: *Silver Brewer.*

And don't miss more sexy silver fox shenanigans in my monthly
newsletter: Love Notes

+ + +

Nibble of *Hauling Ashe.*

1

PRE-TRIP

Playlist: "Unwritten" - Natasha Bedingfield

[Mae]

I'd been looking for a sign.

After stepping off the electric train affectionally known as the 'L' in downtown Chicago, I'd breathed in the fumes of the city on a warm summer day. The robotic voice of the conductor stated that the doors were closing and mixed with the chaotic sounds of people moving on the platform toward the stairs. The noise around me was different from my small hometown with its quiet afternoons of whispered breezes and chirping birds. I'd ridden the train in this dynamic city with my sister before, but never alone. And today's adventure had to be done on my own.

I'd stepped forward with the flow of people pressing toward the staircase like sugar grains filtering through a funnel and descended to the street below as the overhead train continued its loop through this city like a steel serpent, weaving in a perpetual circle around brick and mortar.

I have always loved the magnetism of this metropolis, but it wasn't home for me. My older sister Jane lived here, and it was a pit stop on the journey I was about to embark on.

My spirit trip awaited me. I was in search of renewing my soul and perhaps my heart, as mine had been shattered by Adam. My seventeen-year marriage was over. We'd been distant for some time and divorced for three years. After his first affair, I stayed with him. He made promises. He made plans. Now, I had a plan of my own. Eight states. Fourteen days. The open road. I'd hit the highlights as I went, where I pleased, when I pleased.

This was the starting point and that's why I was looking for a sign. An actual brown and white metal rectangle that signifies the beginning

L.B. Dunbar

of something special. It marks the start of Route 66, the iconic highway from Chicago to Los Angeles. Using the GPS on my phone, I had worked my way to the corner of Wabash and Adams and then headed east on Adams toward Michigan Avenue. A coffee shop on the corner had distracted me and I reminded myself I was in no rush. Ahead of me were two weeks with no timetables and wide-open highway. The Mother Road was my destination and I wanted to plant my feet at the beginning.

When I entered the coffeeshop, I'd decided on the unusual. Instead of black coffee with limited cream and sugar, I ordered something that sounded fancy and fun.

"I'll take a mochaccino." Mocha-*ccino* had rolled off my tongue in a sassy, saucy way and I sashayed my hips a bit as I ordered. I wanted to be flirty. I wanted to be fun. I wanted to remember who I was before marriage and kids and commitments. I didn't begrudge those things in my life, but I was ready for...adventure. I hadn't really ever been anywhere, and I wanted to say I'd been somewhere. If I hadn't been in a coffeeshop on a street corner in Chicago, I might have broken out in song like Belle in Disney's *Beauty and the Beast*. Somehow, I didn't think the other patrons would appreciate me swinging out my arms and spinning in a circle in the cramped space singing off key about a great wide somewhere.

Once I'd exited the café, I popped the lid off my to-go cup and took a sip. The liquid was too hot to fully enjoy the chocolate-flavored zing I anticipated, so I took a short slurp and let the sweetness rush past my tongue in hopes of not burning it. Struggling to snap the lid back in place, I crossed the street obeying the crosswalk signal. The people around me acted like cattle herded over cement and I had laughed at the image since I'd been in this town when the famous painted cow statues had been placed in various locations as decoration. A tourist mission at the time was to find all the cows.

Today's mission felt almost as daunting. Tons of signs on steel poles lined the sidewalks and as I hit the walkway opposite the coffee shop, I noticed the Art Institute on the other side of Michigan Avenue. I paused and spun in that circle like some animated peasant girl, trying to find my bearings. I pulled my phone from my oversized bag and struggled one handed to open the app where I had saved the coordinates while I stepped forward, looking at the device in my palm.

"Umph."

I slam into something hard but pliable before me. In fear of spilling my coffee, I was desperately trying not to bump into anyone on the packed city sidewalk. But the hot liquid washes over the front of me and something else. Or rather, down the impeccably tailored suit jacket stretched over the back of *someone* else.

"What the fu—" The remainder of the expletive spoken in a harsh, deep masculine tenor drones out like an echo at the end of its stream. Steel gray eyes lock on mine. For a moment I forget where I am, who I am, and what I'd been doing. Taking a moment to assess the damage, I notice the lid has popped off my cup resulting in hot liquid spilling over my wrist, splattering my once-white blouse, and dripping down my bare legs beneath the hem of my cut-off jean shorts. My sandaled feet are coated in mochaccino, and I step back from the person I've collided with.

But my foot slips off the raised sidewalk and I struggle once more with the uncovered cup in my hand. Attempting to balance the semi-full container, I'm off kilter with one foot down in the street and the other on the raised sidewalk.

"Easy there, sunshine." Long fingers catch my upper arm and yank me forward. The endearment throws me off balance even more and additional chocolate-flavored drink spurts from the cup like a sputtering fountain, sprinkling the front of his suit jacket.

"I'm so sorry." Not only is my skin hot, but I'm a hot mess, and of course, my savior and victim is a hot man. He looks like he stepped off a poster advertising professional business attire for men. His frame is a good half-foot taller than mine, with solid shoulders and long arms. His hair distracts me next as it's more salt than pepper. His cheekbones are clean-shaven cliffs but given a few days, I imagine the scruff on that firm jaw will match the coloring of the hair on his head. The potential ruggedness of ink and chrome facial hair in combination with that sharp jacket screams *sexy silver fox suit porn*. However, a sliver of leather and beads at his wrist hints there might be a rebel underneath that silk and gabardine material.

267

L.B. Dunbar

"Whatcha got in that cup?" His voice drips with insinuation. The playfulness of calling me sunshine dissipates a bit.

Sharp, silvery eyes ensnare mine and heat rushes across my cheeks because I'm caught staring. Forcing my gaze away from those eyes, I look at my cup. "Uh…nothing, anymore." He doesn't smile at my joke. "I wasn't drinking," I defend next, although I feel a little drunk just looking at him.

I'm always stupid around good-looking people, especially handsome men. I'd like to say I'm out of practice—with men, flirting and otherwise. However, I can hold my own with the best of flirty people. I'm the one with teasing comments at work or subtle remarks under my breath in public, but today I'm off my witty comebacks game.

Releasing my arm, he shakes out his, flicking droplets of coffee off the expensive-looking coat in a summer khaki color. He tips his head, attempting to glance over his shoulder, and spins in a circle like a dog chasing his tail. The sight of such a handsome man twirling around causes me to giggle like a schoolgirl. Then again, the rhythmic squeak could be the sudden anxiety rippling up my center.

I just spilled coffee on a hot man.

He abruptly stops twirling and his gaze falls to my lips. The corner of his mouth hints at a potential grin. "What's so funny?" His warm voice washes over me like the drink still soaking my thin shirt. His cadence is lyrical, like a classic rock star or maybe someone in a blues band.

Shaking my head, I apologize a second time. "Let me get your suit cleaned for you." Suddenly, I have visions of him stripping out of that suit right here on the street and my breath hitches at the possibility. *The lazy removal, slowly shrugging the jacket down his arms. The pop of buttons on his dress shirt. The quiet snick of his suit pants zipper.* Another part of me strums to life and I clench my thighs. *What is happening to me?* Is this a hot flash? I thought I wasn't due for them for another ten years.

Deciding I need his phone number, and that I can figure out the logistics of getting him out of his suit…I mean, getting his suit *from him* later, I realize I've dropped my phone and I begin my own tailspin, scanning the cement at my feet.

268

"My phone." Spotting the device in the street, I step down off the curb, and my ankle twists, throbbing as a result of my earlier slip. I wince as I bend at the waist, pitching forward at the last second to retrieve my phone. With my backside in the air, aimed at my coffee-spill victim, I pick up the device at the same time he grips my hips and tugs me back up onto the sidewalk. A taxi driver wails on his horn as the yellow vehicle zips past us.

"Sunshine, you're a real hazard to yourself." The rough sound near my ear sends shivers down my spine.

I spin to face him, forcing his hands to release me, and my face heats once more at the flirtatious endearment and sensual voice. We stand closer than two people who don't know one another should. I definitely do not look like sunshine. I'm a forty-three-year-old brunette with hints of gray; a mother of two with a belly scarred like a taxi ran over my midsection; and an exhausted business owner who has bags under her eyes packed with sorrow and stress.

"I was looking for a sign," I say to him for some reason, as if that explains knocking into him, spilling coffee, dropping my phone, and fumbling—*twice*—into the street.

He tilts his head, assessing me, perhaps wondering once more if I'd been day-drinking instead of savoring syrupy chocolate mixed with coffee.

He takes a cautious step backward. "Maybe you need some…help." His tone mocks me a bit, deepening in concern for my mental stability.

Holding my phone in my hand, I swipe the screen against my hip to wipe off the street dirt. "Let me get your number."

His chiseled face shutters to stillness. "Now you're hitting on me?" Incredulity fills his voice. His brows arch and the corner of his pale red lips twitch. The grin is more forced than flirtatious. He thinks I'm a nut.

"I wasn't… I mean, I'm not… I never… I just want to have your suit cleaned." Well, that pretty much covers it all. In my line of work, a pleasant attitude helps sales. The customer is always right, so I've learned how to master words and a wink to soothe someone who is disgruntled. Of course, a little banter never hurt anyone and some of my best customers enjoy the repartee. The innocent jesting might even be the reason they return to my garden center. But in the case of this encounter, I'm surprisingly flustered.

"It's a thousand-dollar suit. A mere dry-cleaning won't salvage this mess." He glances down at the arm of his jacket and at the once-white shirt he wore, now looking like freckles dot the material. The underscore to his statement resonates louder than the hint of his concern I was hitting on him. He's not joking about the cost and his expression tightens even more. Disgust and disappointment etch his fine cheekbones.

"Made of gold-laden thread?" I joke, hoping to lighten the moment, but in return those silver eyes pinch. His gaze becomes colder, matching the metallic posts holding up a variety of signs along this street.

"Something like that." His voice is suddenly devoid of all emotion, monotone and dry, which is everything opposite my clothing still soaked with coffee. Absentmindedly, I reach for the middle of my peasant blouse and squeeze the material, which looks like I've tried to tea-stain fabric at home. Warm liquid seeps over my fist like I've wrung out a sponge. His eyes follow the motion, and narrow when his gaze reaches my chest. I look like I've entered a wet T-shirt contest.

Without another word, he reaches into his suit coat and pulls out his own phone. My breath hitches for some reason, momentarily thinking he'll ask me for my number. Instead, he stabs the device with a forceful finger and lifts it to his ear. His eyes peer upward, locking on mine once more before he abruptly turns and walks away.

"Hope your day gets better," I holler after him, taking a mental snapshot of him walking away. He shoots me a one-handed wave over his shoulder, then closes his fingers leaving only the one in the middle upright.

Well.

My gaze falls to his backside. The slightly lifted jacket in his single arm salute gives me a clear view of firm globes in form-fitting suit pants. Those thousand dollars were well spent to accentuate him there. However, a man with a fine ass does not make him a fine man. It normally just makes him an ass.

Too bad. He was nice to look at.

On that note, I glance around me, taking in the rush of the 'L' down ᴉe block, racing over Wabash Avenue. Brakes screech and horns honk ᴤ all types of vehicles come to a stop at the red light down the street ᴉead of me. I scan the tall buildings shadowing the walkway and then I ᴣe it.

A brown and white sign marked with the iconic emblem for Route ᵼ.

Underneath the landmark rectangle is another sign with one word. BEGIN.

Read more of *Hauling Ashe*.

L.B. Dunbar

Thank you for taking the time to read this book. Please consider writing a review on major sales channels where ebooks and paperbooks are sold.

More by L.B. Dunbar

Lakeside Cottage

Four friends. Four summers. Shenanigans and love happen at the lake.

Living at 40
Loving at 40
Learning at 40
Letting Go at 40

The Silver Foxes of Blue Ridge

More sexy silver foxes in the mountain community of Blue Ridge.

Silver Brewer
Silver Player
Silver Mayor
Silver Biker

Sexy Silver Foxes

When sexy silver foxes meet the feisty vixens of their dreams.

After Care
Midlife Crisis
Restored Dreams
Second Chance
Wine&Dine

Collision novellas

A spin-off from After Care – the younger set/rock stars

Collide
Caught

Smartypants Romance (an imprint of Penny Reid)

Tales of the Winters sisters set in Green Valley.

Love in Due Time
Love in Deed
Love in a Pickle (2021)

The World of True North (an imprint of Sarina Bowen)

Welcome to Vermont! And the Busy Bean Café.

Cowboy

Studfinder

Rom-com standalone for the over 40
The Sex Education of M.E.

The Heart Collection
Small town, big hearts - stories of family and love.
Speak from the Heart
Read with your Heart
Look with your Heart
Fight from the Heart
View with your Heart

A Heart Collection Spin-off
The Heart Remembers

THE EARLY YEARS
The Legendary Rock Star Series
Rock star mayhem in the tradition of King Arthur.
A classic tale with a modern twist of romance and suspense
The Legend of Arturo King
The Story of Lansing Lotte
The Quest of Perkins Vale
The Truth of Tristan Lyons
The Trials of Guinevere DeGrance

Paradise Stories
MMA romance. Two brothers. One fight.
Abel
Cain

The Island Duet
Intrigue and suspense. The island knows what you've done.
Redemption Island
Return to the Island

Modern Descendants – writing as elda lore
Magical realism. Modern myths of Greek gods.
Hades
Solis

L.B. Dunbar

(L)ittle (B)its of Gratitude

There are always so many people to thank, but first and foremost I want to thank you, the readers, who have found a new love in the older romance – seasoned romance – we call ourselves. I knew writing a tale about men over forty (and women, for that fact) might not be for everyone, but I'm tickled silver it's been good for so many.

An extra shout out to Shannon, of course, for another wonderful cover and Jenn for impeccable edits. Also, to Karen for her extra eyes. Hugs to Mel for being an amazing cheerleader and support, and content editor extraordinaire. I'm so grateful for all of you in my life.

Additional hugs to the silver-and-ink in my life who still has mostly black hair but a sexy scruff of salt-n-pepper AND to the four children we created together. Always love you all the most.

About the Author

www.lbdunbar.com

L.B. Dunbar has an over-active imagination. To her benefit, such creativity has led to over thirty romance novels, including those offering a second chance at love over 40. Her signature works include the #sexysilverfoxes collection of mature males and feisty vixens ready for romance in their prime years. She's also written stories of small-town romance (Heart Collection), rock star mayhem (The Legendary Rock Stars Series), and a twist on intrigue and redemption (Redemption Island Duet). She's had several alter egos including elda lore, a writer of romantic magical realism through mythological retellings (Modern Descendants). In another life, she wanted to be an anthropologist and journalist. Instead, she was a middle school language arts teacher. The greatest story in her life is with the one and only, and their four grown children. Learn more about L.B. Dunbar by joining her reader group on Facebook (Loving L.B.) or subscribing to her newsletter (Love Notes).

FB: https://www.facebook.com/groups/LovingLB/
NL: http://bit.ly/LoveNotesfromLBDunbar
IG: @lbdunbarwrites

+ + +

Connect with L.B. Dunbar

Made in the USA
Monee, IL
04 January 2023

24471005R00154